# The Senator's Darkest Days

# The Senator's Darkest Days

Joan E. Histon

**TOP HAT
BOOKS**

Winchester, UK
Washington, USA

JOHN HUNT PUBLISHING

First published by Top Hat Books, 2019
Top Hat Books is an imprint of John Hunt Publishing Ltd., No. 3 East St., Alresford,
Hampshire SO24 9EE, UK
office@jhpbooks.com
www.johnhuntpublishing.com
www.tophat-books.com

For distributor details and how to order please visit the 'Ordering' section on our website.

We operate a distinctive and ethical publishing philosophy in
all areas of our business, from our global network of authors to
production and worldwide distribution.

# Contents

# Chapter One

## Syria: 40 CE

A warm breeze moved lethargically through his study, barely flickering the candle on his desk. Petronius stared at it with glazed expression until a wayward moth, attracted to the light, ventured too close and flew dizzily away. Petronius rolled his shoulders in an attempt to ease the tension in the back of his neck. The movement had no effect, the tension persisted. Picking up the stylus he let it hover over the parchment before dropping his hand and beginning to write.

'Caesar,'

He lifted his stylus, contemplating his opening sentence. It wasn't so much how he worded his sentence, he brooded, more a case of how to weather the storm when Caesar received his letter. Puffing out his cheeks Petronius blew softly through his lips before bending over the parchment again.

'*Excellency, I would beg you to reconsider…*'

His stylus scratched over the parchment, the scratching sounding unusually loud in the silence of his study. He hesitated before adding his signature and then he threw the stylus on the desk in disgust. Rising sharply to his feet he made his way over to the window where a heavy grey night sky hung like a suffocating blanket over the city.

Running his fingers through his iron grey hair he brooded over why he was bothering to communicate with Caligula at all. Caesar wasn't interested in the Jews. All this mad emperor wanted was for them to acknowledge his divinity, and that would never happen. The Jews would rather die than worship Caligula.

The knock on the door was gentle, discreet, as though its owner had no wish to disturb so late at night. Without turning Petronius called, 'Come!' He knew it was his staff centurion by the knock; a good man, a loyal man.

'I gather you wanted your letter delivered urgently, Commander?'

Petronius nodded but made no move to return to his desk. Instead he stood at the window watching clusters of white winged moths fluttering around the single lantern in the courtyard. Then with a sigh he moved resolutely over to his desk, signed his letter with a flourish, rolled the parchment and sealed it with his own personal seal.

Handing it to his Staff Centurion he ordered, 'Get that to Caesar in Rome without delay.'

The centurion who had been by his side throughout all the troubles gave him a fleeting glance that showed concern, but all he did was salute and close the door quietly behind him.

Petronius sat for a while, listening to his children thrashing about in their beds, restless with the heat. In the room above his wife hummed tunelessly as she brushed her hair. She always hummed tunelessly, usually in time to the sweeping of the hairbrush. Normally he enjoyed watching her nightly routine but he was in no mood for her company tonight.

If he was lucky, he mused trying to inject a note of positivity, Caligula might send someone to investigate what was going on, someone who would support the claims in his letter. Petronius rubbed his brow fiercely as if trying to stop the negativities from creeping in, but failed. The worst-case scenario was that the emperor would send one of his Germanic Guards with instructions to ... Petronius licked his dry lips. He could contemplate his own assassination, after all, he was a soldier. He was used to facing death. But his wife and his children?

Publius Petronius, Governor of Syria, listened uneasily to his children quietening down to allow sleep to wash over them. Even the tuneless humming of his wife faded but he made no move to join her in their bed. Instead, he sat in his chair watching the candle dwindle to an unsteady flicker before pouring himself a glass of wine. Although not a man given to late night drinking, tonight he drank. Tonight, he willed the strong Syrian wine to dull his worries over what his emperor would do when he received the letter.

# Chapter Two

## *Rome: 40 CE*

A baby?

Of course, why hadn't it dawned on him sooner? Her pale face, the sickness at breakfast, he should have known. Vivius wasn't a man given to emotional gestures so the quivers at the corners of his mouth did little to portray his excitement at the news he had received. The only hint was a quiet sigh which echoed around the empty pool of the Roman baths like a whispering breeze. The image of Aurelia's pert little chin jutting out in pride, and her twinkling grey eyes laughing up at his amazement had stayed with him as he had ridden into Rome that morning. He had held her close all night, listening to her gentle breathing, her soft brown hair tickling his chin, the smell of her bath oil drawing him into sleep.

His fingers rippled through the warm water and for a while he floated, listening to it lap against the sides of the pool, watching the colourful rainbow of early morning sun dance across the pool and bounce off the high vaulted ceilings and marble patterned walls. Another boy, he pondered, or would it be a girl this time? Yes, a girl would be nice. Aurelia would like making dresses for a girl and it would be good for Maximus and Rufus to have a sister ...

'Senator Marcianus?'

The voice, although quietly spoken, felt like an intrusion into his private world. Hearing a splash at the far end of the pool he watched the soft faced, milky white body of Praetorian Officer Cassius Chaerea wading gracefully towards him. He was an alert young man with large baby-blue eyes and light cropped hair.

'I wonder if I could have a word with you, Senator.'

Pushing the water through his hands, Vivius reluctantly brought himself into a sitting position on the steps of the pool.

'Is it important?'

'It is.' Cassius floated the last few metres and sat on the steps next to him, but for someone with an important issue on his mind the pause was a long one.

'Well?'

'I er ... I gather that as a young man you were one of the emperor's Praetorian Guards, Senator?' he began hesitantly.

Vivius raised an eyebrow. 'I'm hardly an old man now, Officer Chaerea,' he replied tersely but couldn't resist pulling in his stomach muscles and running his fingers through his peppered grey hair.

Cassius's gaze flickered over Vivius's firm body. 'Of course not. Forgive me,' he murmured.

'Would you get to the point?'

'Of course, sorry.' Cassius's voice dropped to a whisper, although there was no reason why it should. At this early hour of the morning there was only the two of them in the pool. 'I only mentioned your time in the Praetorian Guards because you have friends who are concerned about your visit to the emperor this afternoon.'

'Friends?' Vivius raised an enquiring eyebrow. He was too finer a judge of man ever to choose wrongly in friendship, and knowing the standards he set were too high for the majority of his acquaintances he was aware he had few friends. In fact, on the rare occasion he reflected on the subject, none, but it didn't bother him. 'I don't know how you found out about my visit to the emperor but go on.'

'The Emperor Caligula has been ... shall we say ... unpredictable of late. There are concerns about the assignment he has for you.'

'Assignment? And how may I ask, would you know I have an assignment?'

A rake of a man with sharp black eyes, deep and closely set together, and a beak of a nose giving him a hawk-like appearance, slid into the far end of the pool. Vivius raised his chin as the water rippled towards them.

Cassius moved closer. 'We don't, not for certain.' He ran his tongue over his even white teeth. 'I'm sorry. I'm not making myself clear, am I? Let me come straight to the point.'

'I wish you would.'

'Senior officers in the Praetorian Guards, equestrians and influential senators have been deeply concerned over Caligula's behaviour of late. You are known for being a man of integrity, Senator. Your name has come up in our discussions on more than one occasion. As a magistrate and man of the law we believe you would be of immense value to us.'

'Discussions? And what precisely have you been discussing?'

Cassius moved his lips close to Vivius's ear, 'The removal of the emperor.'

Vivius allowed a moment for the prickles on the back of his neck to settle down before saying, 'And why do you assume I would want to be part of that?'

'It hasn't gone un-noticed that he has been overruling many of your decisions in court lately.'

Vivius pursed his lips. 'Annoying, yes, but I'm not the only magistrate to have my decisions overturned by the emperor, and it hardly warrants the drastic action you are suggesting.'

Uneasy over the way this conversation was developing, Vivius pulled himself out of the pool with a force that sent a wave over Cassius. Deciding to give the warm room a miss, he wrapped a towel around his waist and moved swiftly on to the caldarium. There was a splash from behind telling him Cassius was following.

Except for the masseur, Vivius discovered the caldarium was hot, empty and smelling heavily of oil. Choosing a seat in the corner he leant back against the wall, pointedly closed his eyes, and breathing in the heavy steam from the boiler hoped to indicate this was an end to their discussion.

A moment later, Cassius sat down beside him. Ignoring the hints, he hissed, 'Caligula is mad, Senator. You must know that.'

Vivius opened his eyes reluctantly. 'Must I?'

'In the last three years he's more than trebled the taxes causing immense hardship in all quarters of the population.'

'Trebling the taxes doesn't make him mad.'

To Vivius's annoyance Cassius waved away the hovering masseur, but he let the matter pass. He could hardly relax while discussing the removal of his emperor.

'But do you know why he increased the taxes?' Cassius persisted.

'I do, but I suspect you're going to remind me.'

Undeterred by the sarcasm Cassius continued. 'It was to build a brothel in his palace, and then, if that wasn't bad enough, he wanted a carved ivory stable for his horse next to it. After that he had the audacity to hold a lavish party in the horse's honour.' Cassius's voice rose in amazement. '*A party? For a horse?* Now he's talking about making the animal a consul of Rome, would you believe.'

'So, the emperor is ... eccentric.'

'Eccentric? He's mad, Senator, totally mad! The mighty Empire of Rome is governed by a lunatic. He shows himself off in public dressed as one of the gods, Hercules, Apollo or Mercury, whichever takes his fancy at the time. Last month he asked politicians to refer to him as Jupiter, then he began signing himself as such on public documents.' Cassius shook his head. 'The physicians believe this parliamentary disease (epilepsy) has affected his mind, and I know he can't sleep. I've seen him wandering around the palace at night. That's how I know he keeps his wife and child at a distance and has an incestuous relationship with at least one of his sisters.' Cassius wiped the perspiration from his forehead with the edge of his towel. 'The Emperor Caligula is a cruel and vindictive man,' he added tersely. 'As I have discovered from firsthand experience.'

Vivius gave his companion a fleeting look. He could easily imagine the cruel jibes the emperor had directed towards Praetorian Officer Cassius Chaerea. His softly spoken effeminate manner had left him a prime target for exploitation. Yet from the little Vivius knew of him he was well respected among his colleagues, and his reputation was that of a highly intelligent officer who wasn't afraid of conflict.

'The situation is worsening, Senator. I've heard you and your fellow magistrates are being instructed what verdicts to give in court, and I can image the consequences if you disagree. Doesn't the fact that you'll face imprisonment or even death mar your judgements?' Cassius didn't wait for a reply. 'As for our industries, they are in a severe state of collapse. Don't you think action ought to be taken before he ruins Rome?' Cassius squinted at him sideway as if trying to discover whether his words were having any effect.

Vivius rubbed the nodules on the back of his neck, hoping the steam from the caldarium, or an oiling from the masseur might ease the growing tension. Nothing that Cassius had said so far was news to him, but what he did find disconcerting was hearing his own private concerns being mirrored back to him.

'He has even had two of our senior Praetorian Guards executed for no other reason than they didn't agree ...' Cassius was about to launch into another list of complaints when the door into the caldarium banged and the hawk-faced bather loomed through the steam. He glanced briefly in their direction, but then stretched out on one of the marble benches a respectable distance away. The masseur, delighted to have found a willing client, hurried to his side.

Cassius dropped his voice to a whisper. 'The rumour is, that he may have had a hand in the death of his predecessor, the Emperor Tiberius.'

'Be careful of rumours Officer Chaerea.' Vivius interrupted in a louder voice than he had intended. Dropping it again he asked, 'Supposing, just supposing, that Caligula was, shall we say, disposed of. Who do the Praetorian Guards have in mind to take his place?'

Cassius wavered. 'I know there is a growing section in the senate of who would be glad to see a return of the Republic, and yet others who question his legitimate claim as Caesar,' he said cautiously. 'But many of us in the Praetorian Guards favour Claudius, simply because there is a direct link between him and Caesar Augustus.'

Vivius pursed his lips. 'Then I think you may have a problem. Not all the senators would agree with your choice.'

'That's why there have been discussions between the Equestrian Order, Praetorian Guards and the Senate, and why we would like you to be part of those discussions.'

Vivius ran his hand down his wet face. 'Assassinate the emperor?' He raised his eyebrows. 'He is legally the head of the Roman Empire, Officer Chaerea.' But then seeing Cassius was all set to dive into another argument he waved to the masseur. 'I will, however, ponder on your comments and let you know my decision in due course,' he added before pointedly moving to another bench.

* * *

Frustrated at having to push his way through the crowds in the blistering midday sun, Vivius came to a rest under the leafy trees alongside the Temple of Jupiter. He raised his finger to his nose as he approached. The temple priests had been carrying out their official duties by slaughtering the pigs and sheep brought as sacrifices since early morning so there was a foul stench of blood coming from under the shade of the enormous columns. Perching on the edge of the fountain, he cupped his hands and drank deeply from the trickling fresh water, then wiping his wet hand around the back of his neck he watched the activities in the slave market.

Even as a boy this cosmopolitan corner of the city had fascinated him. Not that his father had ever brought him, he thought with a touch of sadness. He'd been too busy fighting for the glory of Rome, or too busy generally to see that his motherless son needed love and attention. But Phaedo, their young Greek olive grove manager would bring him when he was sent into Rome on olive grove business. Vivius had been captivated by the way the slaves of varying body shades and dress were forced to parade in front of potential buyers; the way shrewd eyed buyers prodded them to make sure they were getting a good buy. And he especially liked listening to the strangely spoken tongue of both complaining slaves and bullying traders. It was that cosmopolitan culture that had born in him the desire to travel, and he had, as a Roman soldier, expanding his knowledge of the world as he saw the countries these slaves had come from and beyond.

He sat for a while, watching the buying and selling, until he realised the activities were failing to capture his interest the way they usually did. His mind kept drifting uneasily back to his conversation with Cassius Chaerea in the baths. With a 'tut' of annoyance he stood up and straightened the creases on his white toga with its distinctive purple border. It distinguished him not only as a senator of Rome but someone who was at the top of the social structure. Forcibly dismissing the hovering negativities, he left the shade of the trees and the stench of the animals and headed towards one of the oldest parts of the city, Palatine Hill.

Still puzzling over why the emperor should want to see him when he was hardly one of his closest confidants, he barely glanced at the beautifully structured temples, the enormous public baths, triumphal arches, colourful gardens or the spacious homes of the rich and noble equestrians of Rome.

At the top of Palatine Hill, he was passed speedily through the iron gates by the guards, and arrived at the high stone columns at the entrance of the palace, sweating but barely breathless from his climb. A well-groomed Praetorian Guard in his stripped leather skirt and bronzed helmet approached. Force of habit from his days as a Praetorian Officer compelled Vivius to straighten up to receive the salute.

The Praetorian Guard spoke with deference. 'Senator Marcianus, if you would like to come with me please, sir. The Emperor Caligula is expecting you.'

Vivius followed him down a long cool corridor with wide arched windows giving a panoramic view across the city. At the end of the corridor Vivius was surprised to find a drably dressed Germanic Guard, pointedly barring their way. His muscled arms were folded, enormous feet splayed, his features coarse and square, and frizzled hair forced its way out from under a plain round helmet.

'I will take Senator Marcianus from here.'

Vivius found the accent sharp and unpleasantly guttural. He saw the Praetorian's mouth move into a hard, straight line. He was clearly annoyed at being dismissed by this foreigner, but there was little he could do about it. Having been a Praetorian Guard himself after leaving the army, Vivius could easily imagine the derogatory comments about the Germanic Guards in the barracks. With a final glare at the Germanic soldier, the Praetorian gave Vivius a courteous nod before marching swiftly back the way he had come, the clunk of his boots echoing sharply on the stone floors.

'This way, come.'

As Vivius followed the splay-footed Germanic Guard he tried to make sense of why Caligula had returned from his campaign in Germania with the intention of using these soldiers as his personal bodyguards. Admittedly, they were good fighters, he reasoned. But they were also brutal, barely spoke the Roman language, had no manners, and their drab uniform did nothing to enhance the splendour of an emperor's palace. Why forsake

11

the smart, elite Roman Praetorian Guards who had been personal bodyguards to the Caesars for years? But then he realised he knew the answer before he had finished formulating the question. It was because for the last fifteen to twenty years the Praetorians had begun to take an active role in the politics of Rome. The Senate, and especially the emperor, did not feel comfortable with the extra power this had given them. The Germanics on the other hand had no political or personal attachments with Rome, which was probably why Caligula felt safer with them.

Vivius found himself being led him through a quarter of the palace that smelled strongly of wine and garlic, and echoed loudly with the laughter and cries of a drunken orgy. A half-dressed guest with an imitation crown of leaves perched crookedly on his head staggered past slopping red wine from an over-full goblet. Vivius gave a quiet 'tut' of disgust and made a mental note to thank the gods, next time it suited him to pray, that he had spent the last three years avoiding Caligula's lavish banquets and drunken orgies. He was never at his best at social affairs anyway. In fact, his normal practice was to sink into a state of misery for days before at the prospect of being forced to attend such an occasion.

The Germanic Guard led him up a wide and elaborate marble staircase to a quieter section of the palace. Opening massive wooden doors carved with vine leaves he directed him into a room that would have looked spacious if it hadn't been so cluttered. Colourful frescoes of half-naked figures covered the walls, while busts, statues, ornaments, plants and ornate chairs and loungers claimed every available space. Vivius almost missed the figure who stood in the midst of the clutter so his bow was fractionally late. When he did raise his head, he noted the Emperor Caligula had barely changed since their last meeting. He was still a weedy figure of a man with a head shaped like an egg, the complexion of a candle and a thin fringe of artificial tight blonde curls. Vivius towered over him, but then Vivius towered over most men.

Caligula advanced towards him with a slight stoop of the shoulders, and although he glanced in Vivius's direction his unsettling fish grey eyes avoided direct contact.

'Ah! Senator Vivius Marcianus. At last! What kept you?'

Knowing he had arrived earlier than the appointed time, Vivius curbed his irritation by examining the tiny cubes of tile that made up the geometric pattern on the mosaic floor.

'I apologise, sire,' he said stiffly.

Caligula's long thin fingers waved the apology away. 'The thing is,' he said strutting across the floor and launching into his subject as though they were already in the middle of the conversation. 'The thing is you see, these Jews have this splendid temple in Jerusalem, splendid I tell you. You've been to Jerusalem, you've seen it, haven't you? Splendid, isn't it? But my argument is this; it's only built for one god and it's a god that they can't even see. I ask you, Senator, what use is having a god you can't see? A waste, a complete waste. How can you pray to a god you can't see? Take me for instance. I am a god. I am divine. The Jews can see me *and* they can hear me, but they're so *obsessed* ... 'He spat the word out sending a spray of spittle across a highly polished table. '... *obsessed* with worshipping this invisible God of theirs that it's preventing them from acknowledging *my* divine status.' A remote gaze with a hint of contempt flickered over him. 'Did you know a delegation of Jews from Alexandria had arrived in Rome pleading with me not to impose my divinity on them? I dismissed them of course, especially after they'd had the audacity to tear down an altar I'd had erected for their worship of me.' He pouted, his lower lip jutting out like that of a spoilt child. 'But then, what can you expect? They're a poor, stupid people.' His face took on an impish expression. 'So, guess what I've done?' He didn't wait for a reply. 'I've ordered a large marble statue of myself to be placed in what they call their "Holy of Holies". It's situated in their temple in Jerusalem so they will be *forced* to acknowledge my divinity, that's what I've done.'

Vivius made a point of keeping his expression neutral as he put the pieces together. So that was why he'd been called in. Jerusalem! And he could make a fairly educated guess as to what was coming next. Folding his hands behind his back he concentrated on Caligula's spindly legs braking through his purple toga as he took up his strutting again.

'You understand these Jews, Senator Marcianus. You know their culture, and their temperament. You were posted to Palestine when you were a young officer in the army. Then I'm told my uncle, the Emperor Tiberius, sent you to investigate the former Governor of Judea, Pontius Pilate.'

'Yes Caesar. But that was nearly ten years ago.'

'It was your report that had Pontius Pilate recalled from Judea if I remember.' Caligula gave a chuckle. 'He wouldn't like that. It was fortunate that my uncle died before charges were brought against him, wasn't it? I think you'll have made an enemy for yourself there, Senator.' Caligula waved a limp hand dismissively. 'Anyway, I'm sending you to Palestine because you come highly recommended.'

'Recommended?'

'By Senator Titus Venator.'

Vivius rolled the name around his head but failed to come up with a face to match it. 'Senator Titus Venator? I can't say I know him Caesar.'

'He told me you would be the ideal person for this assignment.'

'How would he know that if I've never met him?' Vivius paused a beat. 'Besides, as you know, as a senator of Rome I have my duties here to perform and cannot travel as easily as some of your equestrians.'

Caligula stopped in his tracks. 'Are you making excuses?' The unexpected screech was alarming. Vivius dropped his head and examined his sandaled feet poking out from under his toga. When he looked up again Caligula was studying him through lowered lids.

'If my Uncle Tiberius can give you special dispensation to travel, then so can I. I am your emperor, don't forget that.'

Vivius breathed in deeply. 'So, what is it you want me to do for you in Palestine, Caesar?'

'The thing is,' the emperor began regaining his former arrogance. 'I instructed the Governor of Syria, Publius Petronius, to have this marble statue carved in my image. My orders were that he was to transport it to Jerusalem and have it installed in the Jewish temple. I specifically commanded him to use two of his legions to protect it in case he met with resistance from the Jews. But what's he done?' Caligula was obviously not interested in a response as he continued with barely a pause. 'First he sends me a letter begging me to reconsider my plan. Then he tells me rumours of what I'm about to do have met with massive demonstrations from the Jews. Further demonstrations, so he claims, could mean their harvest being neglected, which could mean famine, which could lead to violence, which could ...' Caligula ran his fingers irritably through wisps of his artificial curls. 'I sent a message back telling him I wasn't interested in his problems and to get on with it. Since then, all he's done is send me back one excuse after another. Time wasting. Don't you agree?'

Vivius decided a slight inclination of the head would be sufficient for it to mean whatever the emperor wanted it to mean. 'May I ask what the Jewish king thinks of your plans, Caesar?'

'*Him*?' The edges of Caligula's thin lips dropped down at the corners. 'He is *so* ungrateful. I give him back his lands, I present him with a gold chain, and when he visits me I hold banquets in his honour. I even allow him to call himself my friend and how does he respond?' Caligula stomped across the room and back again before answering his own question. 'He tells me my idea's a bad one. He tells me the Jews will refuse to acknowledge my divinity. He tells me there'll be riots if I demand my statue be placed in their Holy Temple. When I told him I specifically wanted the statue in what they call their "holy of holies", he has the nerve to inform me that is an area exclusive to their high priest on Yom Kippur. What does he know?'

'They are his people, sire.' Vivius ventured. 'And the Jewish king is deeply passionate over his religion.'

Caligula's bony finger stabbed the air aggressively. 'Ha! And because he's my friend I listened to him. I was even generous enough to compromise my plans and come to an agreement with him.' He gave a sly grin. 'But I've changed my mind.'

'You have?'

'And do you want to know why? Because I feel he's manipulating me. He's a clever man, too clever for my liking. And secondly, because my new advisor on Jewish affairs has convinced me that these Jews have become incredibly narrow minded at having only one god. I agree. I believe they are in urgent need of another god so they can expand their knowledge and their experiences of gods in general. My Jewish advisor knows what he's talking about. He's lived among these people. He also agrees with Senator Titus Venator's choice that you should be sent to the Governor of Syria to sort this mess out.' Caligula crossed his hands behind his back while he strutted.

'I have no problem with that, Excellency, but I wonder if I can suggest you send your new Jewish advisor instead. Obviously, he's more familiar with the situation than I am.'

'Send him?' Caligula waved his hand dismissively. 'The Jews aren't likely to take any notice of *him* and the Governor of Syria certainly won't, but he will listen to one of my valued senators. Especially as you've done investigative work for the Emperor Tiberius in Palestine in the past. I want *you* to find out why Publius Petronius is taking so long in obeying my orders. He tells me it's because he's chosen the finest of sculptors to carve my statue and perfection takes time, but I suspect he's making excuses. Tell him I demand action from him before winter otherwise he won't like the consequences. Before winter, mind you.'

Caligula's strutting stopped abruptly. His lower lip trembled, and for the first time since the start of this interview, Vivius saw an expression of concern cross his face.

'There are conspiracies going on all around me, senator. I know it. I *feel* it. Is it solely in Rome or has it spread to my provinces?' He gave a shudder.

Conscious of his conversation with Officer Cassius Chaerea earlier that morning, Vivius gave the only answer left open to him.

'I shall do what you ask, Excellency.'

\* \* \*

Vivius pushed his half empty dinner plate to one side. The meal had been overcooked, bland and certainly not up to its usual standard. He stared blankly at the orange sun sinking slowly behind a row of shambolic buildings opposite the inn. He had hoped that being on the outskirts of the city and down by the river it would have been cooler, but it wasn't. Plus, he'd been forced to dine with the foul smell of the River Tiber drifting up his nostrils.

The inn-keeper, a round, placid looking man, arrived with a pitcher of wine, refilled his goblet and shuffled back inside his clean but small inn. In the stables attached, the impatient stamping of hooves reminded Vivius that his horse Warrior, so named by his two imaginative little boys, was anxious to begin their long journey back to the olive grove before dark. Vivius ignored him.

Glancing idly down the road he watched the carts and wagons lining up waiting for curfew to be lifted so they could begin the nightly delivery of goods through the narrow streets of Rome. As much as he loved the city, Vivius was relieved when his visits were over. He tried to keep them to a minimum, usually for when he was required in court, called to the Senate, or needed to visit his book-keeper.

He sipped his wine, his eye momentarily lighting on a tall skinny, red-faced youth running towards the inn. But he was a figure, that was all. Vivius was too preoccupied with the day's events and the dread of having to face a journey by sea to Palestine for the arrival of a youth to register.

Then there was Aurelia. He considered his wife briefly. He hadn't anticipated having to leave her during her pregnancy but then he mused, having babies was women's work anyway so she would simply have to get on with it. Besides, there was nothing he could do for her, other than ensure she had nothing to worry her, and that she had plenty of help while he was away.

Leaving the problem of Aurelia to one side, he aimed his deliberations towards Praetorian Cassius Chaerea. Vivius pinched between his eyes, and he wasn't simply being blinded by the setting sun. Could he in all honesty see himself being involved in a conspiracy to assassinate the emperor, he asked himself? No, he couldn't. He had always supported the Caesars; Augustus, then Tiberius and now Caligula. As he sipped his wine he came to the conclusion that if he was out of Rome on an assignment, this was one problem he could forget, for a while anyway. There'd be plenty of time to consider it when he returned.

His contemplations then wandered to the senator who had recommended sending him to Palestine. Titus ...? Vivius furrowed his brow. Titus ... yes, Senator Titus Venator. Who in the name of all the gods was Senator Titus Venator? Of course, there were hundreds of senators so it was impossible to know them all, but Vivius found it disconcerting to think that a total stranger had, for reasons of his own, recommended him to Caligula for this particular assignment. Why would he do that? What was his motive? Vivius had the distinct impression that he was being played or manipulated for some higher purpose. He didn't like that. It left him feeling uneasy. He watched the youth gasping for air as he ran into the inn.

Then there was Caligula's advisor on Jewish affairs, Vivius reflected. If this advisor was as knowledgeable about the Jewish culture as Caligula believed him to be, then he must know the risks of forcing the Jews to accept the emperor's statue in their holy temple and forcing them to acknowledge his divinity? Vivius could easily visualise the demonstrations, uprisings and bloodshed – and he'd end up being in the middle of a blood bath, he brooded.

'Excuse me, Senator Marcianus, sir.' The inn-keeper hurried out with the red-faced youth at his side. 'The lad here has come about your brother-in-law.'

Vivius's shoulders stiffened. 'Dorio? What about him?'

The youth was chewing his hard-bitten nails and only removed his fingers from his teeth long enough to say, 'My apologies, Senator, sir. I came to ask the inn-keeper here if he would send his sons to help. The Decurion's been beaten up.'

'He was drunk again, I suppose?'

'Yes, Senator.'

'Where is he?'

'The "Black Bull" in Campus Martius. We've sent for the usual physician.'

The inn-keeper wiped his hands on his red stained shift. 'I can send my sons to bring him back here and put him up overnight again, Senator?'

Vivius's stool scraped across the ground as he stood up. 'No, I'll take him home,' he said wearily and flung a handful of coins on to the table.

'Yes sir. Thank you sir.'

It took him less than twenty-five minutes to get to the 'Black Bull' on Campus Martius. To his relief curfew had been lifted. That meant his horse was able to clop steadily behind him. The youth kept close to his side as they followed the road alongside the River Tiber.

Vivius gazed proudly across the land that had, before Rome's civil war, been a floodplain for the River Tiber and a training ground for the military. But with the rise of the emperors, and each emperor seeking to glorify his own achievements, Vivius had seen the land drained, and theatres, baths and temples erected. Yet it was in the quarters of the floodplain not yet renovated that the oldest trade in the world thrived. Vivius knew it be to an area normally avoided by citizens with higher moral values than his brother-in-law, but it was here that Decurion Dorio Suranus could have the pick of any woman he wanted. They wouldn't care if he only had one arm. As long as they were paid he could do whatever he liked to them.

Vivius grimaced as he entered the dimly lit inn. There was a smell of cheap wine and bodily odours more overpowering than the stench from the river tonight. However, his grimace was not so much at the stench but at the sight of his brother-in-law lying in a pool of his own vomit. A physician was bending over his patient attempting to drag him out of it, but whenever he got too close Dorio lashed out with his one good arm.

'Lucanus?'

Hearing his name, the Greek physician swung around and judging from his expression was as relieved to see Vivius as Vivius was to see him.

'Looks like he's had a bad beating, Senator.' Lucanus was forced to raise his voice against a noisy game of dice taking place in the corner.

'What happened? Do you know?'

Vivius pulled a face at the unsightly mess and wished, not for the first time, that Dorio behaved more like the fresh-faced physician. Despite living on low wages, wearing poor quality clothes, down at the heel sandals and having a mop of unruly brown hair, the Greek physician was clean living and highly intelligent. And, as Vivius had discovered when he had been on assignment in Palestine with him, despite being useless with a sword, Lucanus had shown himself to be fiercely loyal and unexpectedly brave. He was also the only physician Dorio would allow near him after the loss of his arm.

'I've no idea what he's been up to, but I'm not taking him home with me this time, Senator.' Lucanus edged forward and dabbed at the blood on Dorio's long curls. This time there was no resistance. 'I only have one bed and I refuse to sleep on the floor again.'

'I wouldn't expect you to, Lucanus. I'll take him back to his estate. I'm heading back to my olive grove anyway.' He studied his drunken brother-in-law with disgust before snapping, 'On your feet, Decurion!' He rapped it out the way he used to do when he was in the army.

The arguments from the dice-playing drunks stopped abruptly, their attention distracted by the formidable figure in his senator's toga.

Dorio shakily lifted his head; vomit clung to his chin. 'Ah-Ha! Vivius to the rescue again.' He rolled over on to his side. 'Friends ...' he slurred waving his arm in the direction of the card-players. 'Let me introduce you to my brother-in-law, the eminent Senator Vivius Marcianus, and ...' He glowered at Lucanus, hiccupped and focussed waveringly back on Vivius. 'The gods alone know what my sister saw in you Vivius,' he growled and with that his body lurched and he vomited over Lucanus's sandals. The roars of laughter around the inn encouraged him to reward them all with a sickly grin.

Grabbing Dorio by his arm, Vivius hauled him to his feet.

'Hoy! He owes me!' The pot-bellied inn-keeper strode menacingly across the floor towards them.

Vivius dipped into his pocket and coins clinked as they dropped into the palm of the outstretched hand.

'Here, this should cover his drink and the damage.'

The inn-keeper's attitude changed quickly with the arrival of money. 'Thank you sir, extremely kind of you I'm sure, sir. He's not a bad lad, you know. Gets into trouble from time to time. It was that other fellow what set him off.'

'Really.' Vivius wasn't particularly interested who had encouraged Dorio into a fight this time. In his opinion, Dorio was old enough to take responsibility for his own actions.

'Aye, I think the Decurion lost more than he bargained for in that dice game. But if you ask me it's simply another debt to add to all the others.'

Vivius stopped. 'Debt?' he asked leaving Lucanus to drag the sorry figure out of the door.

'Aye. They keep coming in here asking for the Decurion. How'm I supposed to know where he is? But he needs to be careful. He owes some pretty nasty people a lot o' money.'

Vivius stiffened his jaw. 'What people?' He saw Lucanus struggling to sit Dorio up against the wall but he kept sliding to the side.

The inn-keeper scratched his head, and showed the palm of his other hand. 'I can't rightly say I remember their names but ...'

Vivius dropped a handful of coins into the palm. 'What people?'

'Businessmen, gamblers, horse traders.'

'You know them?'

'Aye, most of them.' The inn-keeper jerked his head in Dorio's direction. 'If you ask me there'll be further beatings unless you can keep 'im out of their way.'

'You think they'll be back?'

The inn-keeper snorted through his nose. 'They'll want paying that's for sure.'

Vivius breathed in deeply. The idea of leaving his newly pregnant wife to deal with her drunken, debt ridden brother and his violent debtors while he, Vivius, travelled to Palestine to confront ... the gods alone knew what, was not a particularly pleasing prospect.

# Chapter Three

*Caesarea*

Leaning against one of the crates on deck, Dorio silently cursed the fog that had shrouded their vessel since leaving the Port of Ostia, one of the main ports of Rome. That first part of their journey had been cold, damp and incredibly arduous. The fog's only redeeming feature was that it had hidden them from pirates which, despite claims from Rome to the contrary, still roamed the Mediterranean. They had only begun to make headway when a strengthening breeze had lifted the fog, allowing the bow-legged, weather-beaten captain to follow the Pole Star, an island or the silhouette of a mountain. But by then the sails had speeded up their journey and Dorio knew they would soon be in sight of Caesarea.

His mouth quivered at the edges at the image of Vivius scuttling below to throw up in a pail when the breeze had picked up. In fact, and Dorio wasn't ashamed to admit it, he found immense satisfaction in seeing his arrogant brother-in-law powerless with sea-sickness. Vivius might boast at having trekked an army over gruelling mountains, travelled overland under atrocious conditions and still claim to be fit enough to confront the enemy at the end of it, but to his shame, the slightest ripple on the sea had him vomiting helplessly over the side of the vessel. Vivius hated the sea, and he especially hated vessels that zigzagged between the islands to pick up timber or deliver copper, casks of wine or other merchandise, like this one.

An attractive young woman flickered a playful glance at his Decurion uniform as she sauntered by. He gave her one of his foxy grins. It usually attracted women to the fun-loving nature in him. He might even have made the effort to speak to her had his cloak not blown fiercely in the breeze uncovering the loss of his arm. He saw her smile fade and her eyelids flicker apprehensively before she moved on. Unperturbed, Dorio gazed out to sea. He was used to it.

'Caesarea!'

The cry came from the bow-legged captain at the helm. Looking up, Dorio followed his pointing finger. There were murmurs of relief from fellow passengers on deck. Others, hearing the call, began drifting up from below, staggering across the deck as the brisk wind caught their clothing.

Vivius was one of the last to emerge, white faced, unshaven and hanging on to anything that would give him stability. Dorio pointedly studied his brother-in-law's rumpled appearance before wrinkling his nose as indication of the foul smell of vomit hanging over him.

'Caesarea,' he informed him flatly. Shading his eyes, he tried to distinguish prominent features of this magnificent new Roman Port. 'I warn you, Vivius,' he said without taking his gaze off the horizon. 'I intend having a good time while I'm here. I want to see the temples, visit the baths, browse around the markets *and* I want to see what the night life of Caesarea has to offer.'

Vivius cleared his throat in an attempt to remove the crackle of phlegm. 'And I warn you, I don't want any trouble. I've no time to act as your nursemaid. Keep away from the gambling halls and whore houses.'

Dorio made no comment. He was used to the friction between them. It had been there all their lives, which meant they were relatively comfortable standing in their acrimonious silence watching vessels from all over the world manoeuvre in and out of the harbour with their import and export of goods.

As their vessel entered the harbour a call echoed across the deck for oars to be withdrawn. There was a clatter below deck, a rippling through calm waters and a moment later they shunted gently up against the wooden dock. Leaning over the edge, Dorio watched the anchor being dropped and dockers tying off the ropes and securing the gangplank.

It was no surprise to him that Vivius was first off the boat. His brother-in-law was clearly anxious to remove himself from anything that reminded him of the sea. Dorio struggled to keep up with the straight-backed figure striding towards the nearest lodging house, but decided it would be in his own best interests not to complain. Not only had Vivius paid for this trip but he'd paid off his debts and besides, it was almost evening and the sooner Vivius found a bed for the night that didn't move, the sooner he, Dorio, would be free to find out what the night life in Caesarea had to offer.

\* \* \*

'Wake up!'

Dorio grunted as a boot nudged him none too gently in the stomach. 'Go away.'

'We're leaving.'

Forcing an eyelid open, Dorio peered at the blurred figure standing over him.

'What do you mean, we're leaving? I've barely got to bed.' He licked around his furred-up mouth and grimaced. It tasted of cheap wine and garlic.

'That's your problem. I warned you not to go sampling the nightlife.'

Dorio struggled on to his elbow, wincing when he realised his head still reverberated with the steady pounding of drums that had accompanied the gyrating and highly delectable dancer of the previous night. 'You want us to leave now?'

'We had an agreement, remember?'

Dorio ran his hand down his face as he yawned. 'Yes, I remember. But I don't like being forced to jump whenever you shout.'

'And I don't like using government money to pay for a so-called assistant I don't need purely as a means of getting you out of Rome and away from your debtors. Neither do I take kindly to using *my* book-keeper and *my* money to pay off your debts.'

Dorio glowered at him. 'No need to remind me. You didn't tell Aurelia did you?'

'Of course not. What do you think I am? Your pregnant sister has enough to worry about. Now get up? The Governor's legion has been up since dawn.'

Dorio peered out of the window. 'Dawn? It's barely light out there.' He scratched his rumpled head. 'Have I time for breakfast?'

'No! And I've organised the horses, a job you should have done I hasten to add.' Vivius picked up the Decurion's uniform with a, 'Ugh! I hope you've got a change of uniform. You're travelling behind me, and as I'm travelling with the Governor of Syria I don't want you smelling like a vat of wine or the inside of a brothel.' He flung open the door. 'And for goodness sake shave. Take some pride in yourself. Remember you're still a Decurion.'

Dorio opened his mouth to retort that Vivius should have taken a look at his own dishevelled appearance after their sea journey, but by then the door had slammed and deciding he was in no condition for a confrontation at this ungodly hour of the morning, he let the matter pass.

Dragging himself out of bed he scrambled around his room for water, towel and his shaving knife. Then stretching his jaw, he ran the blade down his chin and tried to remember what Vivius had told him about his assignment. Very little, Dorio concluded, but then Vivius had never been one for long explanations. Besides, somewhere between sorting out his own debts in Rome, and Vivius's decline into sea-sickness on their journey here, there'd been little time for discussion. As far as he knew this assignment had something to do with the Governor of Syria, hence their stop-over at the Governor's summer residence in Caesarea.

Fastening his boots, Dorio tried to recollect what he knew

about the Roman Governor and the Province of Syria. Like the majority of soldiers, he'd been taught that the area was of vital importance to the Roman Empire as it guarded their frontier against invasion. He also knew the Roman Governor of Syria was assisted by lesser officials who were in charge of smaller Provinces, including the Province of Judea. He stood up. Ugh! Judea! He grabbed an apple on his way out of the door. He wasn't looking forward to going back there.

A short time later, his teeth zinging with the cold crunchy flesh of the apple, he was sitting on a sturdy dappled mare, squinting through a dazzling orange sunrise over rows of gleaming bronzed helmets. Giving a silent groan he tossed his apple core and waited for the rainbow of colours to stop flashing around in his head. They didn't. A further introduction to his dawn departure wasn't helped by the bellowed orders from centurions to march, followed by the thud, thud, thud of a cohort of boots. He winced, trying to remember where he was supposed to be. Spotting the colourful red plume of a centurion's helmet leading a straight line of immaculate troopers, Dorio managed to catch his eye. With an exasperated shake of the head the centurion indicated the Eagle of the legion leading the cohort. Embarrassed at not realising Vivius would be at the front with the Governor of Syria, Dorio dug his heels into his mare to urge her forward.

At the clattering of hooves, Publius Petronius twisted around in his saddle and to Dorio's astonishment acknowledged him with a nod of his head. Dorio noticed he was a square-jawed soldier with iron grey hair, bushy eyebrows, a pleasantly large featured face, and like all muscled men he was heavy around the waist. Assuming Vivius had informed the Governor he had a Decurion as his aide, Dorio forced his weary body to straighten up and saluted in response, but he waited until the governor was facing front again before slumping back into his saddle and settling into an easy pace behind the two men.

Once they were on the newly constructed Roman road heading south out of Caesarea, Dorio swivelled around to see what was behind them. As he had expected, travellers and traders, heavily laden donkeys, proud necked camels, and merchants with carts and wagons laden with all manner of trade were trailing behind the cohort for safety.

As the legion and their travellers moved deeper into the countryside, pleasant memories of his previous life as an active cavalry officer drifted back; the creak of the saddles, the smell of horses, their ears twitching and their breath hot and steamy in the cold morning air. Dorio breathed in slowly, relishing that deep earthy smell that he found most poignant first thing in the morning. This morning it was tinged with the scents of lime and orange groves.

As the sun rose slowly into the sky, he became aware of fields of yellow wheat whispering to them in the breeze, and red poppies waving to them from the roadside. Simply focussing his attention on the slow steady pace of farmers working their fields, women milking goats, and children playing around hamlets of mud huts was balm to his pounding head. In fact, he mused, if it hadn't been for the rhythmic thud, thud, thud of the cohort his headache would have disappeared altogether. And yet, he reflected with a touch of nostalgia, travelling with the Roman Army was what he missed most about not being on active service.

At one point he noticed that the Governor of Syria and Vivius had set a brisker pace than was necessary. He knew it wouldn't increase their chances of reaching Jerusalem any sooner. The Roman Army was trained to march at a steady rhythm of twenty miles a day, and twenty miles the legion would do until it reached Jerusalem, seventy miles away. But Dorio guessed the Governor was making space between himself and his army so that he could talk privately to Vivius. Dorio inched closer so he could hear what they were talking about.

It wasn't long before he overheard Petronius say, 'So Senator Marcianus, your note suggested there was a matter of national importance needed to be brought to my attention.'

Vivius took a fleeting look behind to make sure they weren't being overheard. His gaze flickered dismissively over Dorio. 'Yes, sir. Caligula wants to know why installing his statue in Jerusalem is taking so long.'

'Ah! The statue. I guessed correctly then.' Petronius gave a heavy sigh. 'This plan of Caligula's will strike at the heart of the Jewish religion, Senator. I've already confronted massive demonstrations on the border of Galilee. Men, women, and children throwing themselves at my feet, declaring that they would die rather than submit to the desecration of their temple.' He adjusted his reins before saying, 'A few weeks ago, I met with a high profile delegation of Jewish leaders. They made it abundantly clear that they would worship no other God but their own. There were no threats of violence – then – but I have no doubt that if Caligula persists with his plan, riots will be the next step. If that happens I shall be forced to bring in my troops to support Marullus, the Governor of Judea, and there'll be bloodshed on both sides. Does Caligula want that?'

Dorio saw Petronius give Vivius a sideways glance as if trying to ascertain whether he was safe in his next comment. He must have decided he was because he continued, 'I must confess, I was deeply moved by the Jews commitment to this God of theirs. It didn't take me long to realise further discussion was useless, which was why I lead my troops out of Judea. That was when I wrote to the emperor, entreating him to countermand his order.'

'What was his response?'

'Not good. Basically, he told me he wasn't interested in my problems. My job was to obey his orders and install his statue.'

'What's the Jewish King's stand on this?'

'Agrippa? Agrippa for all his extravagances is an intelligent and deeply religious man. He was educated at the Imperial

Court in Rome which is where he struck up his friendship with Caligula. The emperor thinks well of him, which is why he is allowed to rule under Roman jurisdiction, and up to now Agrippa is proving himself to be a capable ruler.'

A shepherd hurried his flock across the road, waving his crook in an attempt to hurry them before the Romans approached. Petronius never altered his pace.

'When Agrippa heard what Caligula was planning he was horrified. He travelled to Rome with the intention of dissuading the emperor by tempting him with diplomatic trade offers he would find hard to refuse. When the Jewish king returned to Jerusalem he was under the impression he had succeeded and that Caligula had dropped the whole idea.'

'I'm afraid to say he hasn't.'

'So I gather. In my latest letter from him he demands to know how far the construction of his statue had progressed. In my reply I told him that as we're wanting a perfect statue I'm using sculptors in Sidon, and perfection takes time. My instructions to the sculptors was to take their time.'

'What do you hope to gain by delaying tactics, Governor?'

Petronius paused and Dorio's impression was that it wasn't a throw away remark when he added, 'My sources tell me our emperor has been unwell. Who knows what benefits time can bring us.'

There was a brief silence from Vivius before he repeated, 'As you say, who knows what benefits time can bring us, but unfortunately sir, time is not on our side. The emperor's orders are that this statue must be in Jerusalem's temple before winter.'

'Impossible! It's far from being finished and the emperor knows that. What's he thinking of?'

'It's difficult to know what the emperor thinks when he has a new Jewish advisor filling his head with ideas.'

Petronius turned his head sharply. 'A Jewish advisor? Who?'

Vivius shrugged. 'I wish I knew. My first guess was Pontius

Pilate, the former Governor of Judea, but I hope not. I was sent to investigate him ten years ago.'

'You were? What happened?'

'It's a long story, but sadly, Tiberius died before charges were brought against Pilate.'

Petronius gave a short cynical laugh. 'I can imagine you've made yourself an enemy there, Senator.' He readjusted his position on the saddle and his face took on a sombre expression. 'I confess I don't like the sound of where this whole episode with the statue is heading.'

The conversation lulled and Dorio could see both men were lost in their own reflections.

'How will King Agrippa take the news that Caligula intends to go ahead with his plans?' Vivius eventually asked.

'Badly. The difficulty will be convincing him that his negotiations have failed. Agrippa is a proud man, he won't want to hear that he has had little influence on the Roman Emperor.' Petronius flung a corner of his cloak over his shoulder; the morning was rapidly warming up and he was clearly feeling the heat. 'I'll be attending one of Agrippa's banquets while I'm in Jerusalem. The king will be in a good mood so I shall take the opportunity of informing him then. I think the best way forward is asking him to intervene again. He won't like that, but at the same time he won't want an uprising of his people any more than we do.' Petronius paused. 'Having you with me at the banquet would be an added advantage, Senator. You were the last one to speak to Caligula. You could impress on the king the seriousness of the emperor's illness, and that it has made him ... shall we say, obsessional, especially over his statue.'

'As you wish, Governor.'

'I shall also introduce you to the Governor of Judea, Marullus. He's a good man. He's had a tough time clearing up the mess left by Pontius Pilate, I can tell you. These Jewish freedom fighters, the Zealots, are his main problem, especially around Galilee.

That's where it's believed they have their headquarters.'

Dorio pressed his lips firmly together. Galilee! Galilee was where he had lost his arm fighting those damned freedom fighters, and where he lost the horse he had trained since she was a foal. He glared at the straight-backed figure of his brother-in-law as he recalled Vivius's offensive comments about being over-sensitive in his grieving for his horse. The trouble with Vivius, Dorio thought angrily, is that the only person Vivius loves is himself.

Dorio's forehead gave a nervous twitch as the memories of the creature's suffering screams came to the forefront of his mind. On and on and on they'd gone during his own long hours of drifting in and out of consciousness. As they lay side by side on the ground he had wept bitterly at his inability to put the animal out of its misery, but he'd been helpless to do anything for her as his own injuries were so severe. When a Roman officer and his servant had eventually come along the officer had ended the animal's suffering swiftly, and informed Dorio that he was lucky to be alive as all his comrades were dead.

Oh, the Roman Army still had uses for him, he brooded. Hadn't his father, his grandfather and his father before him bred some of Rome's finest horses? Heavy horses for ploughing and hauling wagons, fine horses for pulling carriages, and lighter, faster horses more suited for war. Oh, the Roman Army knew how to take advantage of men with disabilities, he deliberated bitterly. They had suggested he breed and train this latter type of horse in his stables, and to use his land and his talents to the full they had sent him batches of raw auxiliaries to train with the horses. The majority of the auxiliaries came from outlying farms so they could ride anyway, but using a weapon while riding was a different tactic altogether. From that moment on it had been clear that the army had little else for a one-armed Decurion to do.

\* \* \*

## *Jerusalem*

It was around mid-morning on the fourth day when they arrived in Jerusalem.

Dorio sensed a lightness in the soldiers' spirits as they approached the Roman fort that was to be their barracks for the next few weeks. He experienced no such emotion. The sight of those thick stone walls and high overpowering towers made him sick to his stomach. Fort Antonia. He viewed the fort with loathing. It dominated the landscape. It was almost as though the Romans needed to remind the Jews of the might of the nation who now occupied their land. And, as if to stress the point further, Fort Antonia loomed even larger than the magnificent new temple next to it in which the Jews took such pride.

As Dorio rode through the wide arches of the fort behind Vivius and the Governor of Syria, he could virtually feel the walls closing in on him as they had all those years ago.

'There's better medical facilities, qualified physicians and the hospital conditions are far superior to those we have in Galilee,' his Commanding Officer had reassured him. But as far as Dorio was concerned, Fort Antonia only served as a painful reminder of where they had amputated his arm and where he had almost lost his life.

That was when Vivius had arrived in Jerusalem with Lucanus, the Greek physician. Dorio's mouth twisted into a grimace. Of course, Vivius hadn't travelled all the way from Rome solely for *him!* As far as Vivius was concerned, having a wounded brother-in-law in Fort Antonia had been a stroke of luck, a convenient smokescreen while investigating Pontius Pilate. Yes, his injuries had been convenient for Vivius, Dorio brooded. But then that's all he had ever been to Vivius. A convenience – or an inconvenience – depending on which way you looked at it.

Dorio flung his leg over the saddle and dropped to the ground as the order to dismount echoed around the parade ground. His mare clattered her hooves in discomfort as he unbuckled his luggage, tugging sharply at the straps. Slapping his mare's rump he watched the stable boys lead her and the other horses away.

As he followed Vivius into the fort they were met by a young recruit who offered to show them to their quarters, insisted on carrying all their luggage and led them along a series of gloomy stone corridors. Dorio found the sickly smell of oil lamps depressingly familiar.

'Did you know that in its day, Fort Antonia was used as a palace for the Hasmonaean princes,' the young recruit eagerly informed them. 'It's so enormous it can accommodate an entire Roman Legion *and* their auxiliaries,' he added proudly.

'Really?'

Vivius's monotone response was delivered in a manner that was clearly meant to discourage further conversation. The young recruit flushed up, embarrassed at having irritated a Roman senator. Dorio gave the young recruit a reassuring wink as he opened the door for them. One trait that Vivius could never possess, not in a hundred lifetimes, was a natural charm, he decided, as he entered his new accommodation. Then he gave a grunt.

Having expected that as a visiting senator from Rome, Vivius would be afforded one of the better quarters befitting senior ranking officers, Dorio was disappointed to find their room incredibly drab. A plain wooden table sat in the middle of the room with two plain chairs either side. There was a water jug and bowl in the corner, a colourful woven raffia mat on one wall, and a long brown sofa-come-bed behind the door. Above it were shelves for idols, books and storage. Dorio threw his bag on to the sofa, taking it for granted that would be his bed. Naturally Vivius would expect to take the bedroom.

'What now?' he asked.

'Protocol demands I introduce myself to Marullus, the

Governor of Judea, so I intend to do that this afternoon.' Vivius drop his bag onto the bedroom floor.

Dorio stared out of the open window at the rows and rows of flat rooved houses scattered across the city like tiny square blocks winding themselves down into the valley. 'So, you won't need me?' He immediately regretted his question. Since when did Vivius need anyone, least of all him?

'No.'

Dorio pursed his lips. The idea of spending the afternoon alone in the fort was too depressing a prospect to contemplate. On the other hand, finding the nearest drinking establishment and drinking with the damned Jews who were responsible for the loss of his arm was unthinkable. Pulling open the clasp of his bag he rummaged through his clothes until he found what he was looking for. He waved a roll of papyrus in the air.

'Lucanus asked me to deliver a letter to some Greek friends of his. They live in Jerusalem, so I think I'll explore the markets and then do that.' He winced. 'What?' he snapped, conscious that Vivius was pointedly looking him up and down.

'If you're going into the city I'd advise you change out of uniform.'

'Why?'

'Safer – for you.'

'You always have to be giving orders, don't you?' Dorio retorted, but he went to change anyway.

Having made enquiries in the office as to how to find the address Lucanus had given him, Dorio spent some time strolling around the market. After being on the road for three and a half days and spending the majority of that time dreading returning to a country that held so many bad memories for him, he was surprised to find how relaxing it was watching Jerusalem's craftsmen hard at work at their trade; weavers, potters, carpenters and bakers absorbed in their own creation. For a while he browsed around the colourful market stalls, enjoying time to himself, but eventually the noise of the traders vying loudly with each other, the pressure of the crowds pushing and shoving, and the stifling heat became overbearing. So, he headed through the narrow maze of dusty streets until he reached what appeared to be the predominantly Greek quarter of the city. To his relief it was considerably quieter here, although the heat bouncing off the walls of the buildings made it no cooler. He discovered the house he was looking for was square but modest with a dozen or more like it in the lane.

The door opened within seconds of his knock, and he found himself standing in front of a pleasant faced Greek with pronounced laughter lines, and a slack belly rolling over the edge of his belt.

Dorio inclined his head. Having been raised by a Greek nanny, taught to ride by his father's Greek manager, and having employed Greeks in the Suranus stables since his grandfather's day, he spoke the language fluently.

'Good afternoon. I hope I have the correct address. I was asked to call with a note from Lucanus, the Greek physician in Rome. He's a friend of mine. Do I have the pleasure of talking to Hektor?'

The introduction was greeted with a wide smile and cries of, 'Iola! Iola! News from Lucanus!'

A plump, motherly woman emerged from their living quarters and with a flapping hand drew him inside. 'Come in! Come in! A letter from Lucanus? How wonderful. He may have news of our son.'

Dorio stepped inside but soon suspected from the way they kept glancing down at the empty sleeve of his tunic and fussing over his well-being that they believed losing an arm was an illness rather than a disability.

His hosts insisted he join them for their midday meal, and it took him less than the blink of an eye for him to decide that being in the company of this affable Greek couple was definitely preferable than returning to the fort. Besides, he was hungry.

While Iola prepared their meal, Hektor drew him out to the back of the house where a small table set against a shady wall indicated this was where they normally ate. Dorio handed over Lucanus's letter and during their conversation, he discovered Hektor was a clerk to a wealthy Greek merchant who traded in cloths from around the world.

'So, you travel?' Dorio asked.

'Not me, no. My employer does all the travelling. That's one good thing I can say about the Romans. They've given us the freedom to travel anywhere in the world these days, which means access to a wider variety of cloths and silks. That's meant growth in the business.'

Dorio lifted his head in pride. 'So, life is good under Roman rule then?'

Hektor's face soured. 'I wouldn't go so far as to say that! We have our problems with them. But lately it's been the Jewish authorities who have caused us the greatest difficulties.' He sat forward, his elbows on his knees, and in a manner that suggested confidentiality added, 'I can tell you, with you being a friend to Lucanus. Iola and I, we follow the teachings of Jesus of Nazareth.'

'Jesus of Nazareth? Can't say I've heard of him.'

'You haven't? Ah! Basically, he gave us a new set of principles to live by.'

'A new religion, you mean?'

Hektor tilted his head to one side in a ponderous manner. 'Not exactly. The Jews still observe the Mosaic Law and Jewish festivals because Jesus was a Jew, but he taught us about a God of love rather than a God who binds us up with rules and regulations. We believe Jesus was the Messiah, the one God had been promising to send the Jews for generations.'

'Why do you have problems with the Jewish authorities then?'

'One reason is our growth. When the Master, Jesus, was alive, they assumed his following was a mere phase and like all phases it would die out. But after his death our numbers grew at a staggering rate. That alarmed them. That was ten years ago which proves it was no phase. The other reason is King Agrippa's zeal for Judaism. He claims our teaching is blasphemous and that we're deviating from Jewish tradition. That's why the Jewish authorities send in their guards. There have been skirmishes, arrests and even deaths.' Hektor snorted through his nose. 'Of course, they would have to find some excuse for condemning us, wouldn't they? The Jewish authorities hated Jesus' popularity when he was alive. I reckon that was one of the reasons they convinced the Romans to put him to death. Treason, they called it.'

'And the Romans? What's their view on this?'

'The Jewish authorities try to give them the impression we're a threat to Rome, like the Zealots. But we're no threat to Rome. We're not soldiers, we're grocers, fishermen, bakers, merchants and book-keepers. Our cause is peaceful but the Romans ...' Hektor snorted through his nose again. 'The Romans? Ha! What do they know? When we Greeks ruled the world the Romans were no more than barbarians.'

Dorio flared his nostrils at the unexpected insult but his host continued with barely a breath, oblivious at having offended his guest.

'The Jewish authorities keep an eye on us. Our times of worship are in different houses and at different times of the day for safety. Sometimes they leave us alone, but it's not unknown for the Jewish Guards to be tipped off, a house raided and the occupants thrown in prison.' The wisp of a cloud drifted over the blazing sun casting an uneven shadow across his craggy face. 'You'd think the threat of jail would put folk off, wouldn't you? But no, our number still grow.'

Still stinging from the slight made against the Romans, Dorio asked, 'The arrests, they're always made by the Jewish authorities?'

'Usually. Roman policy is to give this country the freedom to worship who we like, but if a crowd gets too big or there's a hint of a fracas they step in. The majority of the time they're too busy trying to control the Zealots to bother with us.' Hektor sucked in sharply through his teeth. 'I can't see the point of being a Zealot myself. It always ends in reprisals, and antagonizing the Romans makes it dangerous for us. Damned Zealots! Damned Romans!'

Dorio ran his hand uneasily down his face as it dawned on him that he had a problem. Hektor had taken him to be Greek. It was obvious how the misunderstanding had occurred. Lucanus was Greek, and he, Dorio, had claimed to be Lucanus's friend. Plus, their whole conversation had been in Greek. Dorio cursed Vivius under his breath for ordering him to change out of his Decurion uniform. He was in the process of debating how to approach the subject in a subtle manner when a clatter of dishes from inside the house, followed by the smell of warm bread told him the needs of his stomach were about to be met.

Iola had prepared a simple but plentiful meal of fresh bread, dried fish and tomatoes, and with her arrival the main topic of conversation returned to their son who had studied medicine with Lucanus in Antioch. They were obviously extremely proud of him, and when Dorio claimed to have met him and related an amusing evening he had spent with him and Lucanus, he was delighted when their meal time stretched affably into the afternoon.

It was later in the afternoon and over a second cup of apple juice, when Dorio spotted an attractive young woman sauntering down the lane towards them. A faint breeze had sprung up and was hugging a pale cream dress seductively to her slender body. As she drew closer he saw her cheekbones were high and scattered with small black freckles like punctuations, and there was the quiver of a smile on her lips. He couldn't take his eyes off her. Iola, sitting opposite him, swivelled around to see what he was looking at.

'Ah! It's our dear Sarah,' she cried happily. Rising quickly to her feet she hurried forward to greet her.

Dorio licked his lips.

'I see we have a visitor.' Sarah's voice was sweet, gentle and she grasped Iola's outstretched hands with obvious affection for the older woman.

Iola's podgy little fingers waved in Dorio's direction. 'Sarah, this is Dorio. He's delivered a letter to us from dear Lucanus which gives us news of our son.'

Dorio inclined his head, but didn't miss the way Sarah's long dark lashes flickered momentarily to the stump of his arm. He was used to that, but he was pleased to see her smile never wavered, nor did she recoil.

'Welcome Dorio.' As she squeezed on to the end of the bench strands of black hair slipped from the veil covering her head and fell in a gentle wave over her shoulder. 'If you're friendly with Lucanus you must come from Rome? What brings you to Jerusalem?' Her round honeybee eyes twinkled mischievously at him. 'Surely you didn't come all this way to deliver a letter?'

Dorio gave a half laugh and decided it would be in his own best interests to stay as close to the truth as possible. 'I'm accompanying a Roman Senator on business.'

Hektor looked at him in amazement. 'I understood you to be a physician like our son and Lucanus?'

'No, I er ... you must have misunderstood. I'm not a physician.' He cleared his throat, embarrassed at having accepted their hospitality and eaten their food under false pretences. 'I work with horses for the Roman cavalry.'

Puzzlement crossed the faces of his audience.

'Horses?'

'Your senator has business in Palestine with horses?' Hektor asked with a puzzled frown.

'Not exactly. He has another agenda for being here.' Dorio gave himself a moment to think by finishing the rest of his drink. Placing the cup unhurriedly back on the table he admitted, 'I know horses. I'm good with them. I intend to see what Palestine has to offer.' That first half at least was true, he consoled himself. And it wouldn't hurt to see what horses Palestine did have to offer.

Hektor leant forward, his elbows on his knees. 'So, what exactly is your senator's business here in Jerusalem?'

Dorio forced a laugh. 'I don't care what his business is, but I know what mine is. I intend to explore Jerusalem. I want to see the temple, browse around the markets, and I might examine those cloths you were telling me about Hektor. I have a pregnant sister who could do with a present from me. I've badly neglected her of late. I might buy her material for a new dress, toys for my nephews and a gift for the baby when it arrives.'

'Ah!' Hektor's face lit up, his ponderings distracted. 'Then you must allow us to show you around. Jerusalem has a fascinating history, and I have bales of new material you can choose from to give to your sister. Sarah can advise you?' He addressed Sarah.

'Yes of course,' she said with a smile.

And somehow the awkwardness was over. Now all he had to do, Dorio mused fixing his attention on the lovely Sarah, was listen to her talk for the rest of the afternoon. Dorio gave a silent sigh of contentment and stretched out his legs.

# Chapter Four

### Rome

'Ruth!' Aurelia tried not to call too loudly in case she woke the boys.

A moment later her tall shapeless slave with blue grey eyes the colour of gulls' eggs, and a creamy brown complexion glided gracefully into the living quarters.

'Yes mistress?' She was a softly spoken, trustworthy girl who had been with Aurelia since their early teenage years.

'Listen for the boys, will you?' Lifting her woollen shawl from the back of the chair she added, 'Rufus seems a little restless to me. I hope he's not coming down with a cold. I thought I'd take a walk through the olive grove before it gets dark.'

'Yes mistress.' Ruth's long thick plait slid over her shoulder as she acknowledged the instruction with a slight bow of the head.

Stepping outside Aurelia shivered. The evening air was cooler than she had expected. Pulling the shawl around her shoulders she hugged herself to keep warm and picking her way through her vegetable garden headed for the edge of the olive grove. There was no doubt in her mind why Vivius, and generations of the Marcianus family before him had used this long flat rock when they needed a place to contemplate. From here, the panoramic view over the hills of Rome, and the spread of the magnificent city itself, gave perspective to one's own small individual problem.

She lowered herself on to the rock with a grunt. Not that she needed to grunt, she thought with a flash of amusement. Her pregnancy wasn't far enough along to feel the weight of the child inside her, not yet. Running her hand lightly over her swollen stomach she smiled. A girl, she pondered? And for a while she allowed herself to indulge in the fantasy of having a daughter, scouring the markets for ribbons, dresses and combs, brushing long wavy hair and having a child that didn't get dirty all the time. But then glancing down at her tummy she gave it a reassuring pat.

'But if you're a boy I'll love you equally as well,' she murmured.

Pulling the copper comb out of her ring of hair she shook her head and let the thick brown waves cascade down her back. Then leaning back on her hands, she listened to the clicking of the crickets in the olive grove. They sounded loud in the stillness of the evening. Her gaze rested on the city lights casting an eerie yellow glow across the skyline, before drifting eastwards, away from the city of Rome and closer, towards the hillside and the Marcianus's gnarled old olive trees. Phaedo, the Greek manager who nursed Vivius's olive grove, was examining a cluster of olives on one of the lower branches.

'Am I right in thinking it's going to be a good crop this year, Phaedo?' she called.

Phaedo raised his head. He was a loose boned, placid looking man who had been on the Marcianus estate since Vivius was a boy. Yet despite being only a few years Vivius's senior, Phaedo had known all there was to know about growing olives from an early age. His weathered face crinkled easily into a smile at her call.

'You are mistress,' he called back. 'A few weeks and I reckon we'll be harvesting this lot. The boys should enjoy that. So will the young master if he gets back in time.'

The *young* master? Aurelia smiled affectionately at Vivius's manager even though it was dusk and he would be too far away to see it. Phaedo had called Vivius, *young* master since childhood; ever since she and her brother Dorio had lived on the neighbouring Suranus estate. Even then she had been aware of a strong bond between Vivius and his olive grove manger and she soon understood why. Vivius's father was a harsh disciplinarian at the best of times, but when he got drunk he got vicious. And he was drunk often. That was when Phaedo used to hide Vivius in the empty clay pots in the long sheds to protect him from a whipping. During the months when Vivius's father was absent, as he so often was during an army campaign, Phaedo would be there to shield the boy against the succession of neglectful and cruel house slaves who were brought in to rear the motherless child.

Aurelia lifted her head towards the gentle breeze blowing through the silvery green leaves of the olive grove and wondered if that was why Vivius rarely lifted his hand to his own sons. She smiled at the image of Maximus and Rufus waving him goodbye at the Port of Ostia. The port had been busy that morning, but before Vivius had boarded he had made a point of pointing out to his two excited boys where each vessel came from and what they were likely to be carrying. The boys had been fascinated in watching the dockers and heavy cranes loading and unloading all manner of goods from the ships; wood, stone, wine, grain to animals and slaves. Then they would load them on to the huge barges which would be hauled up the River Tiber by oxen or slaves and into the centre of Rome itself. The hustle and bustle of the docks, the shouted orders and banter between sailors and dockers, the incoming and outgoing vessels vying for a space in the harbour, and the salty smell of the sea had, for a time, taken their mind off the fact that their father would be going away. Even when they had waved at Vivius's departing vessel, and Vivius had dutifully remained at the stern waving back they had been excited. It was only when the vessel had disappeared over the horizon that their crestfallen faces had shown their disappointment at not seeing their father for some weeks.

That was when she had allowed the sense of foreboding that had hovered all day to slide over her. But it had been like an incoming tide that refused to obey the laws of nature and ebb away again. Wifely concern she had told herself as their horse and cart had laboured back up the hill towards their olive grove. Vivius hated the sea, so the idea of him spending the entire voyage huddled in the bowels of the boat throwing up was bound to trouble her. But she knew in her heart there was more to it than that.

'Pregnancy, that's all,' she firmly told herself when she had reached the villa. But the question of why she would be so troubled over this particular voyage had niggled on, and still did. Tugging a stalk of dry grass out of the earth she ran it between her teeth. She was probably concerned because this trip he had taken Dorio with him she decided. She nibbled thoughtfully on the stalk. Why would he do that? Her brother and her husband only tolerated each other for her sake, so why would Vivius take Dorio to Palestine when he knew it held nothing but bad memories for him?

Pulling the stalk out of her teeth she wondered if life would have been any different for her brother if he hadn't lost his arm. He certainly wouldn't have turned into a drinker, a womanizer, and gambler that's for sure, she decided. But Vivius knew all this, so why would he insist Dorio accompany him? He needed an aide, or so her husband had said. Aurelia snorted through her nose in a highly unladylike manner.

Turning away from the olive grove she narrowed her eyes to contemplate the place she used to call home when she was a child. It stood a distance away, the Suranus villa and stables. It had been a happy home – until they had all grown up. She gave a sigh which, to anyone who was listening, would have indicated her regret over those early turbulent years; the loss of parents; Vivius engrossed in his career rather than her; a previous marriage of deceit and debt which had left her widowed and poor. If it hadn't been for Dorio …

Her eye fell on Dorio's horses grazing lazily in his fields. The only thing Dorio cared about these days were his horses, she brooded. He'd always been passionate about his horses.

Her brow knit as she revisited her earlier question. So why was Vivius taking Dorio to Palestine? When she had asked Vivius that question he had simply given her an off-hand one shouldered shrug.

'I decided it would be good for him to get out of Rome for a while. Besides, I need an aide, and Dorio reckons there's a horse trader in Palestine that he wants to see.'

Strangely enough, Dorio had repeated those exact words when she had asked him about the trip.

Aurelia wound the long stalk of grass around her finger. 'What do they take me for, an idiot?' she muttered.

A movement in the olive grove distracted her, but it was only Phaedo climbing leisurely up the hill through the trees. She watched his long easy strides, head down, arms swinging loosely at his sides until he reached the wooden sheds at the top. Inside stood the massive stone wheels that crushed the olives, the heavy wooden presses, the winter fire which kept the olives at the correct temperature and the big clay pots for storing oil. And above one of the sheds was Phaedo's room.

Phaedo would know what was going on, she mused. Bound to, but Phaedo was unlikely to tell her. Vivius would have left him strict instructions not to have her worried in her present condition. As for the assignment, all Vivius had told her was that the Emperor Caligula wanted him to go to Palestine. He had made it sound so simple, so routine. But she was familiar enough with the workings of the Senate to know that if it had been that simple the emperor would have sent a tribune or centurion from the army, one of his Praetorian Guards, or an equestrian, someone of noble birth. Why send one of his senior senators?

Aurelia rubbed the goose bumps on her arms and brooded over the fact that trying to get anything out of Vivius was like trying to squeeze oil out of olives before they were ready for harvesting. It was frustrating having her husband and her brother placating her simply because she was pregnant.

Swivelling around on the rock she stared moodily towards her red roofed villa. From here she could see the servants lighting the clay lamps in the atrium. It showed the frescoes on the ceilings and mosaics on the walls in quite a different light, but she liked it. Despite the villa's grand exterior, she always preferred it when the lamps were lit. It gave the villa a cosy, homely feel. Not that she would even consider saying that to Vivius. He had built the villa especially for her when they were married, and he was particularly proud of the central heating system which enabled them to have their own bathing facilities.

Aurelia gave a long sigh, and deciding her mind was wandering into fretting places she didn't want it to go into, plus she was becoming chilled off, she rose to her feet and took a last look back over the city. That was when she spotted the thin film of mist gathering in the distance. She stood for a while, watching its long, gnarled fingers spreading out to follow the River Tiber upstream. It gained momentum, but gradually. The city lights flickered apprehensively at its approach, but as the mist reached the domes, palaces and temples, it thickened menacingly, snuffing out the city lights like candles and shrouding the homes and buildings in its suffocating mist. Aurelia shivered, rubbed her bare arms and made her way swiftly back to the villa. But by the time she had stepped inside the mist had completely obliterated the city and was now rolling up the hill towards the olive grove.

* * *

It was a clatter of running feet along the corridor that informed Aurelia something was amiss. She glanced up from sewing her baby clothes. 'I understood you boys were in the middle of morning lessons with your tutor?'

The garbled, 'We are but there's a scary looking man outside,' and, 'He's been staring at the house for ages,' made her to put her sewing down in alarm.

Maximus, the eldest, soon to be seven added, 'We saw him coming up the hill.' He was a studious boy with floppy dark hair that fell over his books in his relentless zeal for knowledge, and like his father, strong facial features and a serious determined manner. 'Our tutor excused us so we could come and tell you.'

'Fine, you've told me. Now you can return to your lessons.'

'Must we?' The crestfallen expression from Rufus, a year younger said all there was to say over his views on philosophy, mathematics and Greek. Unlike his brother he was a fun-loving podgy little fellow, always untidy, always up to mischief, but with an honest expression that couldn't resist dancing with glee at anything that gave him a break from learning. 'Can't we stay? You might need protecting.'

Aurelia made no attempt to hid her smile. 'And you'd protect me, would you? No, off you go, Rufus.' She saw his lip quiver but he must have decided it wasn't a strong enough reason to make a scene because he unexpectedly gave her one of his rosy cheeked smiles that never failed to melt her heart. She ruffled his unruly curls before both boys trailed back to their Greek tutor.

Ruth materialised at the door. 'There's a man at the kitchen door, mistress. He's asking to see you. The boys' tutor says he's been standing awhile watching us.'

'Watching us? A slave with a message do you think?'

'No mistress, from the looks of him he's Roman, but not the type the master would encourage to call.'

Pushing herself out of the chair, she concentrated on straightening her dress over her protruding belly to give herself time to gather her composure. 'Then I better see what he wants, hadn't I?'

Trundling through to the kitchen she discovered a thick set man with coarse features standing at the door. He had sweaty apple-red cheeks, but the apple-red that indicated an over-indulgence of wine rather than healthy living. Greasy wisps of hair from a balding head fell on to the shoulders of his grubby tunic. A labourer by the looks of him she decided.

'Can I help you?'

'I've come for the money the Decurion owes me,' the man said gruffly.

'My brother? I'm afraid you won't find him here.'

A soft footfall in the corridor behind told her their tutor was lingering. He was a studious, timid young man with a permanent ink stain on his middle finger. Although she judged he would be useless in a confrontation, his presence was nonetheless reassuring.

'He owes me.' The bulk at the door repeated.

'Owes you what?'

'Money.'

'Money? My brother owes you money?' Then realising she was repeating herself asked, 'Money for what?'

'He lost at dice. The others got paid off. It's only proper I get what's due me.'

Aurelia's gaze drifted over to Indi, their dumb, gentle giant of a slave whom the boys adored. He had sauntered into the garden and was now kneeling in her vegetable plot digging up vegetables. The muscles on his arm bulged at each plunge of the fork, the skin on his broad black shoulders shone with sweat. Vivius had picked him up cheap at the slave market seven years ago. Scarred from whippings and undernourished he was clearly no bargain. But to the household's surprise, once fed and treated kindly, he soon showed himself capable of doing the work of two men, and not because he had to but born out of gratitude. He gave the impression he was taking no notice of what was happening at the kitchen door but Aurelia knew he would be listening.

'What do you mean, "the others got paid off"?'

'The Decurion's brother-in-law, the senator, sorted it. But I never got nothing.' The man glowered at her.

Aurelia felt butterflies fluttering around her stomach and placed her hand on her belly to calm them before realising that what she was experiencing was the baby moving. It ought to have thrilled her but at that moment it didn't. 'How do I know you're telling the truth?'

He handed her a scrap of papyrus. Dorio's unmistakable scrawl confirmed that the labourer was indeed owed money. Not a lot to her but obviously a considerable amount to him. She stared at the name 'Dorio' at the bottom. 'You say the senator sorted it? If he did then why didn't you get paid off like the others?'

The man regarded her with hostility. 'The book-keeper wouldn't pay me cos there's only half a name,' he pouted. 'None of this is my fault, mistress. None of this would've happened if your brother hadn't lost one too many games of dice.'

'Dice?' She bit her lip, conscious that she was sounding like an echo every time she opened her mouth.

'Don't you know nothin' of what happened?'

'Obviously not,' Aurelia said dryly. 'You'd better tell me.'

There was silence.

'Answer the mistress.'

Phaedo's gentle voice at her side didn't startle her. She had known their Greek manager wouldn't be far away.

'I didn't come for no trouble,' the man mumbled his gaze shifting anxiously over to Indi. 'I just want what's due me.'

'And you'll get your money if you answer the question,' Aurelia said firmly.

The man shrugged and inspected his dirty feet. 'Nothin' to tell. The Decurion was in debt, he got drunk and started a fight. The inn-keeper sent for the senator. When he arrived, he paid off some of your brother's debts and arranged for the inn-keeper to send the folk the Decurion owed money to, to a book-keeper in Rome. But when I went to the book-keeper he wouldn't pay me. He reckoned there was only half a signature, but because the senator had taken the Decurion away for his own safety I wouldn't get paid till they got back.'

'Safety? My brother was in danger?'

'Reckon so.' The man dug his finger in his chest with sharp rapid movements. 'But what about the likes of me, that's what I wanna know? How'm I supposed to be paid if they're away?' A strand of wispy hair fell over his angry face.

Aurelia saw Indi deliberately stand up, one hand holding the green fern of the carrots, the other grasping his trowel. He remained perfectly still, supposedly examining the holes in the ground. Phaedo moved forward, resting his hand against the door jamb. She could feel his heavy breathing on the back of her neck.

'So, my husband paid off my brother's debts, did he?' She spoke quietly and almost to herself but the man answered anyway.

'Reckon so. All except me. Am I gonna be paid?'

Aurelia studied Dorio's I.O.U note. Taking a deep breath, she ordered, 'Phaedo, would you pay this man what he's owed please.'

'Mistress?'

'Don't worry, Phaedo, go ahead, pay him.'

Phaedo contemplated their visitor uneasily. But then Indi dropped the carrots and his trowel on the ground and folded his arms. Seeing the mistress was in good hands Phaedo moved away. It took only moments for him to return with a handful of coins which he began metering out into the labourer's open palm. The man watched the coins greedily, his head giving the slightest jerk at each clink. As the last coin fell his dirty fingers wrapped themselves tightly around them in a way that suggested not even Indi would be able to prise them away.

'Thank you mistress.' The thanks was a mumble and the bow of the head was barely perceptible before the man backed away and shuffled down the garden path. The clatter of his boots faded quickly as he disappeared towards the road.

'You knew about this, Phaedo?' Aurelia asked quietly.

'Only that there'd been trouble at the inn mistress, and the young master had taken your brother away for … to get him out of the way of his debtors.'

Aurelia breathed in fiercely through her nostrils. 'He did, did he? Hmm!' Turning to Ruth she made a conscious effort to keep calm. 'I think I'll have a lie down before lunch, Ruth.'

At the back of her mind she knew she needed time alone. She needed time to rehearse the lecture she was going to give her irresponsible brother when he returned, and time to work out how to deal with a husband who was determined to keep her cocooned from the troubled world they lived in. But first, she knew she needed time to calm herself down. However, she discovered there was nothing like sleep to dampen the venom, followed by her favourite chicken lunch to soften her spirits, and the spontaneous chatter of her sons to cheer her up.

It was later in the day, mid to late afternoon, when she came to the conclusion that the only way to stop herself fretting was to find a constructive occupation to keep her mind busy. That was what drove her into the courtyard. Kneeling down on the cold stone paving she began dead-heading a pot of red geraniums with a particularly strong fragrance. Yet despite her attempts to concentrate on the withered red petals her troubled mind couldn't stop jumping between the problem of Dorio's debts and the fact that Vivius must have considered him to be in considerable danger to have taken him away from Rome. She clipped at the dead flowers trying to make up her mind whether she was angry or afraid for the two men she loved.

It was at that point the boys raced in from their lessons.

'We have another visitor,' Rufus informed her in astonishment. 'Two in one day?'

'And he's wearing a senator's toga,' Maximus added. 'He

could have news of father?'

*News of Vivius!*

Ruth materialised at the arched entrance to the courtyard. 'There's a Senator Titus Venator in the atrium asking to see the master, my mistress.'

'What?'

'A Senator Titus Vena ...'

'Yes, yes. I heard you the first time, Ruth.' Slightly disturbed as to why a member of the Senate would journey from Rome without sending a slave to make an appointment first, Aurelia grabbed the arm of a wooden chair and pushed herself to her feet. Unless ... her heart did an involuntary summersault at the thought he could be calling with bad news. Her breath shuddered into an involuntary prayer, 'Dear god, any god, let there not be bad news.'

'Shall I bring him through to the courtyard, mistress?'

'Yes, do that Ruth.'

Rufus touched her arm. 'Can we stay? Please? He might have news of father.'

Aurelia ran her fingers abstractly through his hair. 'I shall tell you whether our visitor brings news of your father later. Now back to your lessons.'

As she waited for Ruth to show their visitor through she realised she was clasping her fingers so tightly together they were making white imprints on the back of her hands. She flexed them, took a deep breath, and prepared herself mentally for her visitor.

A rake of a man with a beak of a nose giving him a hawk-like appearance, entered the courtyard and gave a slight bow. 'Forgive me for disturbing you, mistress. My name is Senator Titus Venator and I am a friend and colleague of your husband.'

Aurelia took note of the dark cloak over the senator's toga before forcing a social smile to her lips. 'Good afternoon, Senator. I hope you don't bring us bad news?' She didn't like the way his sharp black eyes were set so closely together, nor did she like the way he sniffed with annoying regularity, as if he had a cold.

'Bad news?' The smile, which was probably meant to be reassuring was weak. 'Oh, no mistress, I can assure you I don't bring bad news. I came to see your husband, that's all.'

Aurelia grasped the back of the chair to steady her shaking legs. 'Oh! Good!' She forced a laugh, then straightening up said, 'My husband is away I'm afraid, but you must be thirsty after your long walk from the city. Won't you join me for refreshments?'

'He's away? He's left already? Er … refreshments, yes, thank you.'

Aurelia led him through the bright red potted geraniums then gestured to the marble bench under the sycamore tree. 'I confess I'm surprised by your visit Senator Venator. I had imagined my husband's assignment in Palestine would have been a topic for discussion in the Senate.' She watched Ruth place a tray with a jug and two goblets at the end of the bench.

He sniffed, rubbing the end of his nose with his forefinger. 'And why would that be?'

'Isn't it highly irregular for a senator to be sent out of Rome?'

'Of course it is, of course. I er … I knew he was going away but I had assumed he was to travel later in the year.'

Aurelia experienced a fluttering in her stomach as she poured the apple-juice. This time she knew it wasn't the baby. Wordlessly handing him a goblet, she watched his long bony fingers wrap themselves around the stem. *Later in the year*? Any *friend* or colleague of Vivius's would be aware he was prone to sea-sickness and wouldn't dream of setting sail in autumn. In fact, not even the hardiest sailors travelled in the autumn.

'It seems like you've had a wasted journey, Senator.' She deliberately injected a note of regret into her voice.

'Ah! It seems I have. I had information that might have been helpful to him, but clearly it will have to wait.'

He sat back, gazing across the garden to where Phaedo was

giving Indi instructions, and there was an awkward silence. Indi nodded his head at Phaedo before ambling towards the kitchen with long sure strides.

Catching her eye, Senator Venator gave her what he probably considered to be a charming smile, but all it did was show a row of crooked yellow teeth. He appeared ill at ease, a man not comfortable in the company of women she decided. She watched him searching for a topic of conversation.

'Senator Marcianus has a good-sized olive grove. Has it been in his family long?'

'Four generations.'

'Does it take many slaves to run an olive grove of this size?'

'It varies. We tend to hire extra slaves during harvesting or borrow them from my brother's estate which is adjacent to ours.'

A droplet appeared on the end of his nose. He wiped it away with the back of his hand. 'So, no doubt your husband will want to be home for the harvesting?'

'Probably.'

'And of course, he will want to be back for the meeting with Praetorian Officer Cassius Chaerea and his colleagues, won't he?' He paused as if waiting for a response. When there wasn't one he added, 'I was with them at the baths in Rome, the day your husband went to meet the emperor. You'll have met Officer Chaerea I take it?'

Aurelia watched a fluffy white cloud glide across a clear blue sky, and repeated the name slowly as if trying to stir her memory, but then she knit her brow. 'I'm sorry, Senator. I don't think I have.'

'Oh? I understood they occasionally met here, in your home?'

'Who?'

'Praetorian Officer Cassius Chaerea, and your husband's colleagues in the Senate.'

Aurelia smiled sweetly and as she shook her head a brown curl danced around her ear. 'We're far too far out of the city to hold meetings, Senator.'

'Then I must be mistaken. They probably meet up in Rome.'

Aurelia crossed her ankles, trying to give the impression of being relaxed but she was sure he could hear the nervous beat of her heart. 'I have no idea. Vivius didn't mentioned it.' She leant forward. 'Forgive me if I sound a little dim-witted, Senator but ... why you don't ask this Praetorian ...' She tapped her wrinkled forehead with her index finger.

'Praetorian Officer Cassius Chaerea,' Venator informed her with forced patience.

'Yes. Why don't you ask Officer Chaerea where these meeting are held? Surely that would have been easier?'

Venator's gaze wandered. 'Yes, of course. Only the situation I wanted to discuss with your husband is a delicate one.' Withdrawing a handkerchief from his belted tunic, he blew his nose.

'You live in Rome?' she asked abruptly changing the subject. 'No doubt that's where you caught your cold. The heat and the smells from the River Tiber ...' and she couldn't help but be proud of the way she was able to manoeuvre the topic away from Vivius, and whatever he was up to, and on to trivialities. But as soon as Senator Venator's goblet was empty she gave him a wide smile. 'And now sir, I must ask if you will excuse me while I speak to my boys' tutor. I need to have a word with him before he leaves for the day.'

'Yes, yes of course. I've taken up too much of your time already.' Her visitor rose swiftly to his feet as though he was only too pleased to have been given an excuse to leave. 'Thank you for the refreshments.'

'It's been my pleasure, Senator. And I shall be sure to tell my husband you called when he returns.' Although as she escorted him to the courtyard entrance it struck her that she still wasn't entirely clear as to the reason for his visit. As far as she could make out he was after information that had something to do with Praetorian Officer Cassius Chaerea and a meeting.

Indi emerged from the kitchen, his half naked body shining with the heat. He lowered his head as their guest approached. But it was the way Venator's cloak swept past him that made her think of the vicious black-eyed hawk that landed in her garden to prey on the smaller birds each morning. She shuddered.

# Chapter Five

## *Jerusalem*

The ivy-covered archway was so low that Dorio was forced to stoop to enter the courtyard. But once inside he was pleasantly surprised to find a leafy almond tree trailing over the wall and the midday air heavy with the scent of red geraniums.

Hektor beamed at him in a way that crinkled his face like a piece of crumpled papyrus. 'I'm so pleased you decided to come, Dorio. You'll probably find this different from the worship of the Greek gods you're used to, but I think you'll find it interesting.' He gestured towards a flight of steps which appeared to lead to an upper room. 'We'll find Sarah inside.'

Sarah! Dorio gave what he hoped was a nonchalant nod, but the fact was he was excited. When he had bought her a trinket from one of the market stalls yesterday, it had dawned on him that Sarah was not simply another girl passing through his life. She was different. They had spent over a week together sightseeing, shopping, walking along the Kidron Valley or simply sitting by Hektor and Iola's back door talking. But when he had handed her his gift yesterday her cheeks had flushed a gentle shade of pink; her honeybee eyes had turned liquid and her features had taken on a blurred and dreamy quality when she had thanked him. That was an image he knew would stay with him forever, and how he knew then that this relationship had the potential to be more meaningful than all the others.

The only problem now, he brooded as he climbed the stone stairs, was breaking the news to her that he was a Decurion in the Roman Army. After spending so many days with her, this was not going to be easy. He knew that and he wasn't looking forward to it.

Then there was Hektor and Iola. He had accepted their hospitality so he could be close to her but he had never found a suitable moment to put an end to the misunderstanding. It wasn't as though he had deliberately misled them, he told himself as he reached the top of the stairs, but the longer he had left it, the more awkward it had become.

Hektor opened the door and led him into a crowded room buzzing with Aramaic and Hebrew languages. Dorio set his jaw. Jews! Annoyed with himself for not giving this meeting due consideration before accepting the invitation he hung back. All he'd been concerned about was that it would give him another opportunity to see Sarah. For a split second he was tempted to walk out, but a Greek tongue behind him, and a smattering of other languages nearby was enough to assure him that not everyone here was Jewish. What did surprise him, however, was that, from the looks of them, these people came from all walks of life. From poor labourers and slaves to rich merchants and businessmen. He also noticed a Pharisee or two, distinguishable by the fringes on their garments and their head gear.

'Come; let me introduce you to a few of our friends, Dorio.'

Suspecting these friends of Hektor's might be Jews, Dorio raised his hands. 'Later Hektor. If you don't mind, I'd rather observe what's going on from the back of the room. But you and Iola go and join them, please.'

Iola gave him a look of concern as if wondering whether he was simply being polite or really did want time on his own. 'We wouldn't want to leave you alone, Dorio.'

'Please go. I insist.'

Accepting the explanation that their guest needed time without them hovering over him, they left him to his own devices. Dorio watched them wending their way through the crowded room before he sidled into a corner near the two Greeks he had heard talking earlier. He scanned the room for Sarah, but with so many women moving around with head coverings it was difficult to make her out.

He waited.

Eventually the leaders waved their hands for silence. The babble of conversation dropped to whispers as the worshippers shuffled around to find a space to sit. Dorio sat with his back to the wall. Since his conversation with Hektor on the day they first met, and his subsequent talks with Sarah, who confessed to being part of this sect, he was curious as to why this Jesus of Nazareth was so attractive to her. Why did her face light up whenever she talked about him? Why was he so special? Dorio racked his brains trying to remember a time when he had felt as enthusiastic over the ancient gods of Rome, but his memory remained infuriatingly blank. His beliefs, as far as they went, didn't seem to have done him any good over the years, he brooded. But then they hadn't really done him any harm either. Folding his arms, he leant back against the wall to see what would happen.

One of the men sang a song that sounded remarkably like a lullaby his mother used to lull him off to sleep with when he was small. It was in Aramaic so Dorio struggled to make sense of the words, but the tune was pleasant and he noticed the people had bowed their heads as if they were worshipping – or they could have been having a nap, Dorio thought with amusement.

Another man read from what Dorio assumed was the Jewish scriptures, but what he found impressive were the prayers. He discovered that, like all prayers, to whatever god you were praying to, there was always a list of requests. But what was different this time was that there were moments of silence; a sense of waiting and listening, as if these Jews expected this God of theirs to answer them, there and then. Whether He did or not, Dorio had no idea but the quietness, the relaxed sense of absorption, reminded him of the silences in the exam room, but without the frowns of concentration or the pressure of getting the answers correct as intellects frantically searched their memories.

At one point in the proceedings a tall, bony man in a long grey tunic and a neatly trimmed beard stood up to talk about their founder, Jesus of Nazareth. He explained how Jesus had been tried by the Jewish authorities then crucified by the Romans. Dorio listened intently, waiting for the condemnations he felt were sure to come against Rome, but to his surprise it never happened. In fact, Rome wasn't even mentioned, which he couldn't decide was a good thing or a bad thing, but which did leave him feeling rather unsettled.

And then it was over. The people taking part in this strange act of worship scrambled to their feet, embraced each other warmly, and the babble of conversations appeared to pick up where they had left off earlier.

Dorio stood up, rolled his shoulders in an attempt to loosen the stiffness in his back, and studied the occupants of the room curiously, trying to analyse what had drawn them together. That was when Sarah came into his line of vision. Her face was flushed and she was waving to someone at the far side of the room. For no other reason than he was pleased to see her, Dorio found a smile breaking out across his face. He raised himself up to see who she was waving at and his gaze fell on a big shouldered Jew of middling years. His features were coarse, and his speckled grey beard shaggy, but his face brightened as he lifted his hand to return the greeting. Despite his size he moved swiftly and with a certain grace towards her.

Dorio's smile faded as she drifted into his arms, and a cold shiver, like icy water, trickled down his spine. But it wasn't at seeing Sarah drift into the arms of another man. It was because he recognised the man. It was Simon; the Jew who, despite his hatred of the Romans, had smuggled him and Vivius out of Jerusalem nearly ten years ago.

A hand on his elbow startled him but it was only Hektor. 'What did you think, Dorio?'

Unable to meet his friendly and open gaze Dorio began fidgeting with his cloak, as if he was preparing to put it on. 'I ... actually Hektor I ... I need to leave.' Then conscious how rude that sounded added, 'I'm sorry. I ...' His mind stumbled around for an excuse. 'I'm afraid I need to leave,' he repeated, and was already backing away when he saw Sarah heading in his direction – followed by the Jew.

For a brief moment he clung on to a wild possibility that he might not be recognised, but even as the Jew manoeuvred his massive frame towards him he saw a spark of recognition flash across his face.

'Decurion? It is you, isn't it? I thought my eyes were deceiving me. Remember me, Simon?' His voice was deep and gruff. He turned to Sarah. 'Sarah, you've heard me talk of my meeting with Senator Vivius Marcianus? This is his brother-in-law, the Decurion who travelled with him. Decurion er ...' Simon's brow knit as he tried to remember his name.

Dorio felt his heart sink as an expression of incredulity crossed Sarah's face. Being caught out like this was the last way on earth he had wanted her to find out that he was a Roman. Realising he had been left with no option he straightened his shoulders and said, 'The name is Decurion Dorio Suranus.'

She blinked at him foggily. 'You're ... you're Roman?'

'I'm Roman,' he informed her stiffly.

'You're a Roman *Decurion*? A Roman soldier?'

'Yes. Do you have a problem with that?'

It took a while before she nodded her head. 'Yes. I do. I lost my parents and my ...' She swallowed hard. '... my brothers in a senseless massacre by Roman soldiers.' She reached out to Simon and he squeezed her fingers in a consoling manner.

'My niece lost her whole family,' he said quietly.

Dorio breathed in sharply. 'Your ... *niece*?' He stared at Sarah in astonishment. 'This Jew is your ... uncle?' He unashamedly examined the girl's features. 'You're a *Jew*?'

The pert chin lifted in pride. 'Yes. Do you have a problem with *that*?'

'I certainly do. You Jews were responsible for me losing my

arm.'

There was an awkward silence.

Dorio was aware that Hektor was staring at him. 'You're a Roman Decurion? Why didn't you say so?'

Iola's plump little hand went up to her mouth. 'You said you were Greek?'

'No, I didn't actually say I was Greek. You took me to be Greek and ...'

'Why didn't you say you were a Roman? Why lie to us?'

'I didn't lie, at least not intentionally. I admit I should have made it clear from the start who ...'

'You told us Lucanus was your friend.'

'He is, and I apologise if ...'

'I don't like being deceived,' Hektor growled.

'Neither do I,' Dorio snapped back but he was looking at Sarah when he said it. He noticed her lower lip had a quiver to it, whether of anger or hurt he couldn't tell.

Simon had been watching this angry exchange in amazement, but now he raised both hands. 'Whoa! What's all this about?'

'I've apologised, what more can I do other than ... go.' He didn't want to go. He didn't want to leave the situation like this. He didn't want to leave Sarah hating him – even if she was a ... a ... He bowed to Hektor. 'Thank you for your hospitality and for inviting me to this meeting,' he said stiffly before turning to Sarah. 'I don't know what to say other than to repeat that I'm sorry this happened.' He backed away from them and then headed quickly for the door. But as he stepped outside a large hand grasped his shoulder. It was Simon.

'The senator's here in Jerusalem?'

'Yes.' Dorio jerked his head back to where Sarah, Hektor and Iola were still glowering at his receding figure. 'I didn't deliberately set out to deceive them, you know.'

The big Jew patted his shoulder. 'Maybe not, Decurion but sadly, here in Jerusalem, tensions still run high between Roman and Jew.'

'I was led to believe Sarah was Greek. She's staying with Greeks.'

'Hektor and Iola are my friends. Having her live with them seemed the best solution after her parents died.' Simon paused before saying, 'Tell the senator ... tell him we met, will you?'

Dorio nodded but telling Vivius anything was the last thing on his mind as he took the stone steps into the courtyard two at a time.

He marched swiftly back to Fort Antonia, his sandals making little or no noise on the cobbled streets. Not that he was anxious to get back to the fort, he brooded, but at least he'd be among Romans again. He barely noticed that the street had widened and that he was passing the palaces of the rich and noble, the lavish accommodation of the High Priest, and all the places of interest he and Sarah had visited when she had shown him around Jerusalem. All he was conscious of was this wretched, depressing ache inside himself, and the astounding revelation that the woman who had made him feel so good all week had turned out to be ... a *Jewess*! His fingers clenched turning them into fists. How could he have allowed himself to fall for a ... a *Jewess* he asked himself and snorted through his nose in disgust at his own stupidity.

He had hoped Vivius would have left for the banquet at the king's palace by the time he got back as he would have preferred to have had the quarters to himself, so he was irritated to find his brother-in-law leaning back in his chair, fingers knit behind his head, and his long legs stretched out on the table. His chair wobbled precariously on two legs as it took his weight.

'You're back early.'

Dorio slammed the door behind him. 'So?'

'I had expected you to be away all day, that's all. The lady has an important engagement this afternoon, has she?'

Dorio glared at him. 'What makes you think a lady is

involved?' he snapped.

'You're up at dawn to bathe, and who else would inspire you to buy a new tunic? A woman; it has to be. Who is she?'

'Mind your own damned business.'

'Ah! I see.'

'Ah, you see what?'

Vivius's chair creaked as he untwined his fingers, dropped his feet to the floor and let the chair right itself with a thud. 'You've had an argument.'

'What makes you think that?'

'Slamming my door, glowering at me and snapping whenever I open my mouth hardly indicates a man at peace with the world, does it?'

Infuriated by the accurate insight Dorio flung his cloak on the couch. 'She didn't turn out to be the person I thought she was, that's all.'

Vivius stood up, stretched his arms above his head and gave an amused laugh. 'A Jew, was she?'

'Yes, go on, laugh.'

Vivius raised his eyebrows. 'What? That's it? The woman you've been seeing is a Jew and you didn't know?' He gave a short laugh. 'You are in Palestine, you know.'

'Shut up Vivius.' Making his way over to the window Dorio stared down into the large square courtyard of Fort Antonia, now in partial shade. Sentries were spread out at various intervals on the walls overlooking the temple. He let his gaze drift beyond the courtyard walls to the flat rooved houses scattered across the city like tiny square blocks. 'I assumed you'd be at the king's banquet?'

'I will be, later this afternoon.'

Dorio moved away from the window. 'In that case I think I'll leave you to get ready. The two of us in the same room is more than I can stand right now. I'm off to find the nearest inn.'

Vivius raised an eyebrow. 'With Jews?'

Dorio slammed the door behind him and stormed out of their quarters.

* * *

Vivius slumped back down in his chair and picking up his former position of legs on the table, knit his fingers behind his head. Whatever drinking establishment Dorio ended up in, as long as he kept out of trouble he could do what he pleased. He had enough on his mind without worrying about a lovers' tiff. The chair groaned uneasily at the uneven weight on its two rear legs but he ignored the warning. His mind had already drifted back to the previous day's disastrous meeting with the Sanhedrin.

His nostrils flared as he recalled how the chief priests, scribes and elders of the Jewish council had greeted Marullus, Governor of Judea, Publius Petronius, Governor of Syria, and himself as they had entered the council chamber. Oh, they had been polite enough, he recalled. Jews were always polite, but their stony expressions had done nothing to encourage an amicable discussion.

They had listened politely while Petronius and he had put forward their case, but when they had finished the Jews had left them in no doubt of the consequences if Caligula insisted on installing his statues in Jerusalem's holy temple, or if he forced them to worship him as a god. Tensions and voices had risen as they had had their say. What had happened to Rome's agreement to allow them to worship their own God? Had they or had they not been given jurisdiction to rule the province of Judea by the Romans? Didn't Rome realise Jewish religion was at the heart of their culture and tradition? It was their heritage. If Rome went ahead with this venture there'd be riots and military resistance, and not only from the Zealots. There'd be bloodshed – on both sides. Did Rome want that? And listening to their arguments Vivius was forced to concede that they were right. He wouldn't give up his heritage without a fight.

His chair landed with a thud as he released the strain on its two back legs. Leaning forward he rested his elbows on the table and picking up his dagger absently ran his thumb around the deep red ruby inset on the handle. The dagger had belonged to his grandfather; a gift from a Persian his grandfather had told him before embellishing a story to the young impressionable Vivius of war, rescue and honour won. How much of it was true and how much an invention on an old soldier's part Vivius had no idea, but he had loved that story because his grandfather had been the only one, other than Phaedo, to love him. Vivius rolled the dagger over in his hands and pondered on the fact that this and his olive grove were about the only possessions he deeply cared about. They were his heritage and he wouldn't want to lose either, so he could understand the Jews' passion to protect theirs.

Which meant, he mused, his chair scraping across the wooden floor as he made his way into his bedroom to get ready for the banquet, that he and Petronius had to persuade King Agrippa to travel to Rome to talk the matter over with Caligula before the onset of winter.

An hour later, dressed in his white toga with its purple edging depicting him as a Roman senator, he stepped out of the fort. He grimaced as he found himself swathed in an unpleasant hot and muggy atmosphere. Glancing up at the thickening clouds he ruefully surmised that if negotiations with the Jews progressed the way they were, Jerusalem was in for more than one storm.

With two Roman legionaries as escorts he strode briskly towards the King's Palace. So, he reflected ignoring Jerusalem's magnificent temple and its surroundings. When he spoke to the king it might be a good idea to mention his own heritage. The Marcianus family olive grove had been built up over four generations making him a wealthy man, and from what he'd heard, Agrippa set great store on heritage and wealth. Knowing that should convince Agrippa that he, Senator Marcianus, wasn't simply Caligula's messenger boy but that he was a man of some standing. And that, Vivius reflected with a swell of pride, it had nothing to do with his heritage but came solely from his own ambitious drive. He had moved swiftly through the ranks of the Roman Army, been promoted to one of the emperor's elite Praetorian Guards, and it had been his own superior intellect and business acumen that had raised him to the dizzying heights of a senator and magistrate. Agrippa needed to know that.

His ponderings continued as he walked swiftly through the hot streets of Jerusalem, so he was startled when his Roman escorts stopped abruptly and he found himself outside King Agrippa's thick turreted walled palace. He had been so engrossed in his ponderings that he had arrived at his destination without being aware of how he got there.

Dismissing his Roman escorts, he gave his name to the Jewish sentries at the gates before stepping inside the palace grounds. As he was led towards the banquet he examined the palace structure with interest. It was made up of two massive buildings resting on a series of retaining walls. But he was even more impressed with the portico where the banquet was held. It was impressively decorated with coloured frescos, a stucco ceiling, and a fusion of green plants trailing towards a sunken garden. In fact, he found it hard to make out where the portico ended and the garden began.

Guests had already arrived and were standing around politely conversing. Vivius took a deep breath, preparing to put on what he called, 'his social face'. A servant materialized at his side with a tray of drinks. He took one before examining the other guests. Judging from their language and mode of dress he guessed them to be of Roman, Greek or Jewish origin; probably businessmen, diplomats and officials. Elegant women wearing vividly colourful dresses, hair coiffured and adorned with ribbons and pearls, hovered with silver goblets in their hands. He took them to be wives or ... maybe not. He knew from experience that at an event like this it didn't pay to delve too deeply into relationships.

That was when his eye lighted on Governor Publius Petronius. In his leather uniform, bronzed clasp and all the trimmings of a general, the Governor of Syria stood out as being one of the more important guests. He was listening intently to the conversation of a fellow Roman, but when he caught Vivius's eye he raised his silver goblet in greeting.

'You like my palace?'

Vivius spun around, surprised to find that the man who had addressed him in flawless Latin was a Jew. So, this was King Agrippa. Vivius bowed his head. Agrippa was tall, easily as tall as him, and elegantly dressed in rich purples and blues. There were jewels on his belt, scabbard and crown, but the exaggerated way he flashed the enormous rings on his fingers told Vivius that here was a man who wanted to show off his wealth. The king was transmitting a heavily scented rose oil which Vivius suspected had been combed into his neatly trimmed black beard or artificially curled black hair – or both.

'I do, sire.' Vivius forced his social smile into place. 'I've travelled widely but have never seen such splendour.'

Agrippa looked pleased. 'Yes, it is splendid, isn't it?' His half-lowered lids regarded Vivius curiously. 'But you should see my other palaces,' he unashamedly bragged. 'Come, let me introduce you to my guests. We rarely entertain a senator from Rome so they will be interested to talk to you.'

Agrippa led him along a narrow winding canal with leafy bushes and deep ponds filled with white and pink water lilies. Occasionally he would stop by a splashing fountain to introduce him to one of his guests, but the majority of the time Vivius found himself having to listen to a detailed explanation of the Jewish king's vast new building ventures. The canal then wound them back to the portico where he found Petronius in conversation with Marullus, the Judean governor. Stopping by a bed of bright red flowers with heavy perfumes, their polished host left him with his fellow countrymen and moved swiftly on to his other guests.

Petronius came forward to greet him. 'Any opportunity to ...?'

Vivius shook his head.

'I have a problem, Senator,' he murmured soberly.

'A problem?'

'I've been speaking to a ...' His expression changed swiftly to an open-mouthed smile as a Roman businessman approached. 'Ah! Accius! Let me introduce you to Senator Vivius Marcianus.'

Vivius had always considered himself too intelligent a man to indulge in trivial conversations, but as the afternoon wore on into evening he had the feeling that the gods must have been against him, for that was all there was for him to do. Bored and restless he waited for an opportunity to speak to Petronius alone, but was frustrated to find he wasn't the only guest clamouring for his attention. So, he focussed his sights on Agrippa. But it seemed that he too had his own fawning guests to deal with. They clung to him like leeches, competing as to who could laugh the longest and the loudest at his jokes. Deciding he had no chance of breaking through this constant flow of trivia, at least for the foreseeable future, he helped himself to wine, and tried to stay focussed on a tiresome oversized Greek diplomat who seemed convinced he had a lot in common with a senator from Rome.

Vivius's boredom was only partially broken when slaves bearing trays of food made a grand entrance accompanied by drums, flutes and tambourines. There were cheers and applauses from the steady stream of guests following the food.

Vivius moved into the portico with them to find a seat close to Petronius, but the overbearing fat Greek diplomat caught his elbow with a firmness bordering on rudeness.

'This way, Senator Marcianus, this way. We shall be able to hear what the king has to say from here. He is an extremely entertaining man, don't you agree?'

And Vivius, unable to detach himself without seeming discourteous, found himself being manoeuvred on to a long low couch where, to his annoyance, he was forced to wade through the first course of his meal listening to an alcoholically infused explanation on Greek policies. The second course was no better, although by this time Vivius had overheard Agrippa's subject matter changing from his building projects to the deviations from Judaism by some new Jewish sect.

Vivius stifled a yawn.

As it grew dark servants emerged to light the oil lamps sending eerie yellow shadows against the walls. Moths fluttered excitedly around the lights, and entertainers in the form of storytellers, musicians or flame throwers came in.

They were between courses three and four, or it could have been four and five, Vivius had lost count at this point, when a dark-skinned dancer with long naked legs, bare feet, and pink feathers barely covering the interesting parts of her body, glided gracefully across the floor towards them. There were rumbles of approval as her voluptuous figure swayed seductively in time to the music. Conversations faded, the fat Greek diplomat's eyes bulged with desire, and Greek policies forgotten he left his seat and moved closer to the dancing. Vivius breathed a sigh of relief as Petronius, seeing the vacant seat, sidled over to him.

'I've received some rather disturbing news,' Petronius informed him without preamble. He glanced around to make sure they had privacy, but he needn't have worried. The guests, lulled by wine and the hypnotic music were fixated on the gyrating movements of the dancer. 'Caligula has ordered the suicide of the Governor of Pannonia and his whole family.'

'What?' Vivius breathed in sharply. He knew the man and had admired his work for some time. 'Why?'

'A slight disagreement between them, I gather.' Petronius paused. 'Caligula was also overheard to say, and in a manner he knew would be reported back to me, that if his statue isn't installed by winter, me and my family ...' he stared straight ahead of him. 'We will meet the same fate, Senator.'

Picking up his towel, Vivius wipe his greasy fingers. It gave him time to think, but primarily over the fact that if he were to put his support behind Petronius, he could easily find himself – *and his family* – facing the same fate as the Pannonia and Syrian Governors. Unexpectedly, he found Cassius's plans for an assassination not as unwelcome as when he had first heard them. He allowed them to churn around his head for a while before reaching for his goblet to wet his unexpectedly dry mouth.

Leaning towards Petronius he said, 'You are the Governor of Syria. You hold one of the highest posts in the Roman Empire. Why would Caligula order the suicide of an influential and popular official like yourself?'

'And the Governor of Pannonia and his family? They have the advantage – or disadvantage – of being relatives of Caligula, yet he still orders their suicide.' Petronius said quietly. 'We need to find an opportunity to speak to Agrippa. We urgently need his help.'

'He's been surrounded by guests all evening.'

There was a clash of symbols as the dancer, her body shining with sweat, flung herself on the floor in submission before the King. Agrippa threw back his head and laughed with delight. His guests applauded. Agrippa raised his goblet to the dancer and with a graceful bow she floated out of the room.

Petronius murmured. 'We need to speak to him before he gets too drunk. Perhaps ...'

It was then Vivius caught Agrippa watching them from under semi-lowered lids. The king put his fingers to his mouth, belched, and then rose to his feet and swayed in their direction.

'Serious conversation over dinner is not good, gentlemen,'

he greeted them flinging himself down in the space between them. They moved swiftly apart to make room. 'I was watching you. Weren't you enamoured with my new dancer?' He raised a quizzical eyebrow.

'Forgive us, sire,' Vivius said. 'But we have a serious problem.'

Agrippa waved his jewelled fingers dismissively. 'What serious problem could you possibly have so many miles from Rome?'

'As you know, sire, the Emperor Caligula's influence stretches the sphere of the entire world.'

Agrippa's eyes narrowed. 'Caligula is your problem?'

'I am afraid the assignment he's given me is,' Vivius informed him.

Agrippa's bulging eyelids flickered. 'Caligula has given you an assignment in *my* country, in Palestine?'

'Yes sire. He has sent me to hasten the installation of his statue in your temple.' Vivius paused to give his words time to sink in before adding, 'The emperor is passionate about declaring his divinity in Jerusalem but ...' He made a play of shaking his head. 'But having listened to your views on Judaism earlier, I can easily understand how his plans could be in conflict with your religion and your culture.'

Vivius could sense a dark cloud of rage descending on the couch.

'This matter has been dealt with!' Agrippa bellowed. Guests glanced up, alarmed by the sudden outburst. 'I spoke to Caligula myself. We came to an agreement! He assured me he would drop this absurd idea.'

Vivius waited for the king to calm down and the conversations around them to pick up again, although he was aware that the majority of ears were now tuned in their direction. 'I can understand why you assumed it had been dealt with, sire,' he said calmly. 'Nothing has happened for some months but that was due to the emperor's ill health. While he suffers from these er ... attacks he isn't focussed on matters of state, but now he's better he's putting pressure on Governor Petronius to finish the statue and have it brought to Jerusalem.'

Agrippa's nostrils flared. 'Is he now?'

'It occurred to me that if you could come to Rome before winter and speak to him ...'

'Before winter? No! No! No! Impossible!'

Vivius left a lengthy pause before saying, 'I shall be returning to Rome in a few days, sire. I am a senator of some standing so if you want me to take a message ...'

'No! I shall speak to him in the springtime.'

Vivius bit his lip, wondering how far he dare press the king on this point. 'Unfortunately, the matter is an urgent one, sire. If the emperor goes ahead with his plans I have no doubt there will be riots on your streets. If that happens, Governor Petronius will be forced to bring in his legions to support the Governor of Judea, and that would cause the unnecessary bloodshed of both Roman and Jew. Not to mention it being a waste of time, money and man-power for Rome and Palestine.' He paused a beat. 'But I gather, from what you were saying earlier, that such moves would cause delays in your building programme.' Vivius glanced pointedly across at Petronius.

The governor rested his hands on his thick knees. 'As I see it, sire, as our emperor's closest and wisest friend he would listen to you. But time is of ...'

Agrippa raised his hand for silence and a contemplative expression crossed his face. They waited.

'Despite what you say,' Agrippa continued. 'I doubt Caligula will take action before the bad weather sets in. Besides, I have pressing issues to deal with in Jerusalem. My building projects for one. So, this problem with Caligula will have to wait. However,' he paused, tapping his lower lip with his forefinger.

While Agrippa had been talking, Vivius's gaze had momentarily drifted across the room to where a Roman legionary with long skinny legs and unusually blonde hair was being escorted by Jewish Guards to Marullus, the Judean Governor. The blonde legionary whispered into his ear before, to Vivius's concern, both men looked in his direction. Vivius set his jaw. His first thought was Dorio. But then he gave a silent tut of dismissal wondering why he should think it had anything to do with Dorio.

'However,' the king continued. 'When you return to Rome, Senator, would you tell the emperor that I have been assured by the Syrian Governor that his statue is magnificent. Tell him I am impressed by its size but need time to confer with the Sanhedrin as to where would be the best place for it.' He studied Petronius's concerned expression. 'Another delaying tactic, I know Governor. I certainly have no intention of having it in my temple, but it gives me time to settle my affairs, and it gives the emperor time to change his mind.'

Vivius bowed his head. 'Yes, sire. I shall return to Rome with that message immediately.' His gaze drifted over to Marullus. The Governor of Judea gave a slight jerk of his head, indicating he wanted to speak to him but Vivius stayed where he was, etiquette demanding he remain in the king's presence until he was dismissed. Nothing was as important than this conversation with Agrippa. If Dorio was in trouble, he would have to wait.

# Chapter Six

## *Jerusalem*

'Inns are the same the world over, don't you … think so?' Red wine slopped on to the counter as he hiccupped. He frowned. He didn't like the way the rosy cheeked inn-keeper was looking at him as he wiped up the mess.

'If you say so, sir.'

Dorio recognised the placating attitude. 'I do say so,' he informed him irritably. 'And I should know, believe me, I should know. I have frequented more inns and (*hic*) and houses of public entertainment than you could possibly imagine.' He sniggered. 'And been thrown out of them.'

'I believe you, sir.'

'And you should. I don't lie. I'm a (*hic*) a Roman Decurion. Did you know that? No, I suppose you wouldn't, would you, I'm not in uniform.' He peered across the dingy inn at a table of decrepit old Jews who, like himself, were drowning in their tankards, then wagged his finger at the inn-keeper to get his attention. 'So where do the off-duty Romans go for entertainment?'

'Not here, sir.'

Dorio gave a snort of disgust. 'Don't blame them! Typical of my luck to end up in the worst drinking establishment in Jerusalem.' He pushed his tankard across the counter. 'Another one of these.'

He watched the inn-keeper fill his tankard, with some reluctance in seemed. He knew he wasn't drunk enough to be thrown out – not yet – but another couple of these might do the trick, he reckoned. In fact, another couple of these and the image of Sarah's liquid honeybee eyes might disappear altogether. He stared despondently into his tankard, swilling the dark liquid around and around like a whirlpool. It wasn't so much the *image* of her that disturbed him, he brooded. It was … it was … He furrowed his brow, trying to clarify the muddle in his head. It was … yes … It was the way she had looked at him the day he had bought her that trinket from the market. As though … as though she hadn't seen a one-armed, redundant from active service Decurion but … *him!* He let out a throaty chuckle, pleased with himself for having such profound insight when he was drunk. She was seeing *him* rather than his disability. He liked that. He took a long slow swig. The wine was cheap, bitter and warm.

His deliberations sobered. She ought to be told she was playing a dangerous game, messing with a Roman, he brooded. He slammed the tankard down on the counter and wiped his mouth with the back of his hand.

'You don't mess with a Roman Decurion,' he informed the inn-keeper.

'No sir.'

'She'd be punished if they discovered she'd been messing with a (*hic*) Roman.' He was unsure who he meant by 'they' but somehow it didn't seem important. 'She ought to be told.' He belched.

He wasn't sure when the idea came to him that he ought to be the one to tell her. It may have been somewhere between knocking his drink over and the inn-keeper suggesting that if he wanted Romans for company he might find them at the inn by the market place, or in the predominately Greek quarter of the city. But it was certainly the blast of cool evening air that was the deciding factor. Yes, he would see her, one last time, to tell her … whatever.

Leaning heavily on the inn doorpost he stood watching servants lighting lanterns to direct customers to the nearest inns, and pondering how to get to the predominately Greek quarter of the city. What he needed, he decided, was the decent company of Romans to drink with. Running his hand down his face in an attempt to clear his blurred vision he scanned the horizon to get his bearings.

'Who's moved the fort?' he muttered trying to stop himself from swaying.

An old Jew leaning heavily on a stick watched him warily but passed on by.

By screwing up his eyes, Dorio discovered that he could follow the horizon until the four thick square towers of the fort came into view. So, he reasoned, if the Roman garrison is over there, then he should be heading ... His finger wavered in the air. Where was he going again? Ah! Yes! To tell Sarah ... something – or was it to drink with Romans from the fort? He couldn't remember. Making sure he headed in the right direction, he followed the line of his finger which wobbled from the fortress to King Agrippa's palace then in the general direction of the Greek quarter of the city where Hektor and Iola lived. That way, he decided.

Staggering in what he considered to be a reasonably straight line towards the lower part of Jerusalem, it wasn't long before he found himself in a maze of narrow alleys and half empty streets. Confused, he stopped at the crossroads and scratched his head. He had always prided himself on having a good sense of direction, but he had the distinct impression that tonight Jerusalem was setting itself out to prove him wrong. Nothing was in the right place. On top of which the moonless sky was making it difficult to distinguish the turrets of the fort from the Judean hills. He tottered in the middle of the road, undecided, until the faint strum of a lyre caught his ear. He tilted his head. Was that Greek music? Greeks, he didn't mind, he told himself. Greeks, he liked he decided furiously nodding his head. It was the damned Jews that ... He swayed, slightly nauseated from the nodding activity he had forced on his head, and trying to decide whether he was going to throw up. But after a while the nausea passed away. Re-tuning his ears to the music, he staggered in that general direction.

A few minutes later he was surprised to find he had stumbled into a lively little square where, judging from the scattering of flowers on the ground, he'd chanced upon a Greek wedding celebration. Lanterns hung off doorways, and a trio of musicians played a lively melody for the bride and groom and their guests. Dorio felt his spirits lifting. Ah! This was more like it.

His eye lighted on a group of Romans lounging outside an inn in the corner watching the celebrations. He recognised the situation. Off-duty legionnaires bored with the fort, chancing a night out. There were enough of them to make it safe. They'd keep away, enjoy the entertainment, and even let it go beyond curfew if there was no trouble.

Crossing the square in what he hoped was a reasonably straight line, he pushed his way through the Romans hanging around the door, and finding a vacant stool slumped down and ordered a drink.

'Anything,' he told the inn-keeper. 'It doesn't matter.'

After several hours of drowning in alcoholic beverages, he came to the conclusion that whether it was a local brew or a local wine, they all tasted the same after a while. As the inn-keeper poured his drink Dorio examined the legionaries. They were drinking, talking, laughing and barely glanced in his direction, but then he didn't expect them to. He wasn't in uniform. He wasn't one of them anyway. He was no longer on the front line. Wrapping his fingers around the tankard, he lifted it to his lips and lost himself in an alcoholic haze.

Time passed; how much time he had no idea. But at some point, he grasped the fact that the tone of the music had changed. The chords on the lyre were softer, slower and accompanied by the reedy notes of the pipes, and the dulcet tones of a woman singing.

Dorio raised his head out of his tankard as the tune became familiar. Knitting his brow, he tried to figure out where he'd heard it before. Grappling around his sodden memory it occurred to him that it sounded like the music he'd heard when he'd accompanied Hektor and Iola to the Jewish house to worship that God of theirs.

Curiosity drove him unsteadily to his feet. Edging his way through the drinking legionaries he made his way to the entrance where two Roman officers, tankards in hands, were propping up the inn door. Forcing his way between them he peered outside. A lantern hanging on a nearby doorway had bathed the singer in a soft yellow light.

*Sarah!*

Dorio ran his fingers through his hair, waiting for his brain to clarify what he was seeing. Sarah? What was she doing here? Maybe she was with the Greek wedding party? And ... by Jupiter! Wasn't that Hektor and Iola and Sarah's uncle, Simon the Jew?

'Good, isn't she?'

'And pretty.'

Dorio realised the Roman officers had been listening to her singing. He had a sudden impulse to tell them that he knew her. He wanted to feel their glow of admiration that he, a one-armed Decurion might not be on the front line of battle any longer but he had spent time with a beautiful creature like that. But then the singing faded and the pipes drew the music to a gentle close. There was a moment of silence before a rapturous applause broke out from the wedding party. Sarah smiled shyly and stepped back.

Hektor stepped under the lantern. 'Brothers and sisters, you have been listening to a Jewish psalm telling us that our God is a God of love. But I would like to tell you about God's son, the long-awaited Messiah who expressed his Father's love in a way that stirred me deeply. I remember the day ...'

Dorio screwed up his bleary eyes, aware that Hektor's personal recollections had begun to catch the attention of the Greek wedding party, passing Jews and Roman legionaries. Everyone likes a good story – well almost everyone. His gaze lighted on a handful of Greek youths.

'This is a night for celebration, music and dancing, not story-telling,' one young man shouted.

Unperturbed, Hektor continued.

Dorio was slow to register the conversation of the two Roman officers beside him until one of them said, 'What do you think? They could be from that sect the Jewish Guards have been ordered to keep an eye on?'

'Which sect is that then?'

'You know, the ones the Jewish authorities are so set against.'

There was a sigh from his companion. 'I hope not. I'm in no mood to support the Jewish Guards if they make an arrest, not tonight.'

'Those are the orders.' He paused a beat. 'It is them, it must be.'

The first Roman officer shrugged. 'They're not doing any harm. They're peaceful enough. Besides, we're off duty. Let the Jews handle their own religious problems.'

'Looks like they are.' The Roman Officer's hand brushed Dorio's shoulder as he pointed to the shadows in the far corner of the square. 'Look!'

Dorio followed the pointing figure. Five Jewish guards were murmuring amongst themselves, as if they were unsure of their next move. They were taking note of all the activities in the square; Hektor and his group, the wedding party, and the Roman legionaries in the inn. But when the Jewish officer, a stumpy little man but with an air of authority about him, gave the order, Dorio registered a stab of alarm. There was a stamp of boots as the Guards snapped to attention.

'Huh! Looks like they're not going to let this one go,' one of the Roman officers said.

It took a while for the remark to sink into Dorio's befuddled brain, but it was the steady rhythm of the Guards' boots on the cobbled square that confirmed his worst fears. Arrest? Sarah was going to be arrested? No! No, that mustn't happen. He was about to lurch forward when a restraining hand landed firmly on his shoulder.

'Hey friend,' the officer said. 'Let the Jewish Guards handle this one.'

Dorio tried to shrug the hand away. 'Get off!'

The pressure increased. 'Don't interfere. We don't want trouble.'

The youths in the wedding party, seeing the approaching Guards, quietened down and backed away. The legionaries, drawn by the marching boots crowded around the inn door to see what was going on.

The stumpy Jewish officer drew his sword from its scabbard.

Dorio watched Hektor step back in alarm. Simon, and the other men in their party, made a protective wall around him. Sarah and Iola grasped each other's hands fearfully.

Something inside Dorio snapped. Shaking off the Roman officer's restraining hand he lurched forward with a cry of warning. 'Sarah! Run!'

In his head he was hurdling across the square on a rescue mission. In reality he was stumbling over Romans legionaries and spilling the contents of their tankards. There were annoyed bellows of, 'Hoy, watch it!' and chuckles of, 'One too many drinks, eh?' but he ignored them. All he could see was the Jewish Guards advancing towards Sarah, and in his befuddled brain he knew he had to stop them.

Half-way across the square he vaguely registered that he was unarmed, but a mere triviality like that didn't stop him from flinging himself at the stumpy Jewish officer. The officer staggered back, taken off guard by the unexpected onslaught from the direction of the Romans. His second-in-command drew his sword in defence of his superior and lunged forward. Dorio stepped back, but not fast enough. His movements were sluggish. He felt the blade pierce into the flesh on his side. He knew instinctively it wasn't a deep wound, nevertheless, he grunted in pain. The second-in-command was about to thrust again with his sword, but before the weapon had time to find its mark an unarmed figure hurled himself at the attacker. Both men landed in a heap of arms and legs.

Dorio clutched his side, watching the red stain spread across his tunic. He knew he should be suffering more pain that he was, but then he realised it was probably being dulled by the amount of alcohol in his system. Good! That meant he wasn't finished yet.

With his one good arm Dorio formed his hand into a fist and lashed out at the nearest Guard. The soldier reeled back. And then Dorio heard the welcome 'call to arms' from the direction of the inn and caught a glimpse of legionaries running in his direction. One of the Roman officers had drawn his sword but to Dorio's surprise he was shouting, 'Support the Guards!'

*Support the Guards*? Dorio staggered back, confused.

A young and clearly inexperienced Jewish Guard, either not hearing or not understanding Latin, and believing he was under attack from the Romans spun around to confront them. His stumpy officer yelled 'No! Withdraw! Withdraw!' But inexperience made the young guard falter, unsure of his enemy.

But then, Dorio saw a handful of Greek youths from the wedding party bearing down on them. Two of them had knives. Through the fog in his head, he wondered why they were getting involved. Was it because Greeks were being arrested by Jewish Guards? There wasn't time to work it out. There wasn't time to distinguish friend from foe. To be on the safe side Dorio kicked the knife out of the advancing Greek's hand. The youth blinked rapidly. Taking advantage of his hesitation, Dorio swung at him, placing all his weight behind the swing. He missed. His clenched fist landed on a Roman officer's jaw.

'Get out of here, Decurion! Get out!'

Someone was bellowing in his ear, pushing him away from the fighting. He didn't want to be pushed away. He was here to rescue Sarah; wasn't he? Twirling round he swung his fist at whoever had shouted. There was a crunch of bone, a grunt, and a thud as a hefty figure sprawled across the ground. That was when he saw another Greek approaching. Dizzy from swinging his fist he reached for his sword, only to remember that he wasn't carrying one. By now he was totally confused who he was fighting. But then a heavy blow to the back of the head brought a dark and total oblivion to his one-man rescue mission.

* * *

'He's what?' Vivius realised, too late, his response had been overly loud. Heads turned curiously in his direction.

The legionary that had brought the message leant forward and repeated quietly, 'Decurion Suranus is in jail, Senator. I'm afraid the officers at the fort didn't realise he was a Roman. He was drunk, out of uniform and they assumed he was from the Greek wedding party.'

A swift glance across the room told Vivius that Petronius was still in a deep conversation with the King. Relieved that a least one of them was getting somewhere with the Jewish king, he made a point of keeping his voice down this time when he asked, 'What did the Decurion do to warrant being thrown in jail?'

'He attacked a Jewish guard.'

'He attacked a Jewish Guard? Why would he attack a Jewish Guard?'

'Five of them to be precise. One of them wounded the Decurion, but not seriously.'

Vivius ran his fingers through his hair disrupting the neat combing he had given it earlier. 'Better get him a physician.'

'No need, sir. There was a physician in the Greek wedding party. He was arrested along with the others.' The legionary's mouth twitched at the corners.

Vivius glared at his misplaced amusement. 'Others? What

others?'

'A Jew by the name of Simon.' The legionary hesitated. 'I wouldn't have mentioned him, except he was insistent he knew you.'

Vivius rubbed his jaw. 'Simon? Yes, I know him. Is that it?'

'No Senator. There were four members of a religious sect, three Greek youths from the wedding party and a Jewish guard also arrested.'

'What?'

'Although I understand the Jewish Guard is to be released. He was a recruit, inexperienced and his superiors have convinced us it was simply a matter of being overzealous on his first day.'

'Why, what did he do?'

'He drew his sword on a Roman sir.'

'And the Greek youths?'

'I gather they went to rescue their countrymen.'

'And what was the Decurion's part in this ... *fiasco*?' Vivius spat the word out.

'I gather from the Roman officers present that he started the whole thing, sir.'

The heavy breath going through Vivius's nostrils whistled faintly and it wasn't totally with anger. It was at the sight of a frowning King Agrippa moving purposefully across the room in his direction.

'Unfortunately, there's not a lot I can do about this now,' Vivius murmured.

The legionary bowed and made a hasty retreat.

'Ah! Senator! I swear you have quite ruined my banquet by bringing up this problem of the statue.' Agrippa's greeting had a touch of irritation about it. 'And now I find you've walked off and left me and the Governor of Syria to solve it.'

Vivius bowed his head. 'I apologise your Excellency. I assure you I would not have allowed myself be drawn away if it had not been a matter of some urgency.'

'Another matter of urgency? And what was the urgency this time, Senator?'

Vivius was uncomfortably aware that Agrippa's entourage were listening curiously, waiting for his reply.

Agrippa, sensing the possibility of an entertaining story, lost some of his irritation, tilted his head to one side and beckoned teasingly with a heavily ringed finger. 'Tell! Tell!'

'A triviality, nothing more I assure you.'

'You're avoiding my question, senator.'

'I was informed that my brother-in-law, Decurion Suranus, was arrested, sire,' he said uneasily.

'A Roman arrested? What for?'

'I gather he er … he was fighting.'

Agrippa raised a questioning eyebrow. 'Who with?'

'Greeks.'

'Greeks? Is he hurt?'

'He's wounded.'

'Where is he now?'

'In a … a Roman jail, sire.'

Agrippa chucked. His entourage tittered. 'A Roman Decurion has been arrested and thrown in his own jail? My goodness, what next? He's wounded you say? Then I suggest you get him a physician.'

The overbearing fat Greek diplomat who had commandeered Vivius's attention early gave a half laugh. 'There's no need, Excellency. I overhead the Roman messenger say a Greek physician was arrested in the same incident.'

Vivius didn't like the amused chuckles from Agrippa's entourage.

'How convenient. So, the Greek physician who wounded the Decurion is now tending him in jail. Anyone else arrested? A cook to feed them perhaps?'

There were sniggers from around the room. Vivius could feel his cheeks reddening.

The Greek diplomat spoke up. 'I believe there was a Jewish Guard, three Greeks from a wedding party and a member of some religious sect ...'

'Goodness! My dear Senator, what an interesting life you lead.'

Vivius bowed his head, gritted his teeth and fumed full vengeance on Dorio, when he caught up with him.

# Chapter Seven

## *Jerusalem*

It was dawn before Vivius was able to leave the banquet. He chose his moment carefully, making sure the most important guests were either too drunk to notice, or sprawled out on couches exhausted by exotic food, lively conversation and non-stop entertainment.

If the situation had been different he would have enjoyed the cool morning air drifting down from the hills, feeling it rumple his hair as it wound its way through the empty streets of Jerusalem. The gently rising sun bathing the Judean hills in a dark purple, and the solitary hawk soaring high above him in the pale blue sky would have calmed his fractured nerves left by the event at the banquet. The solitude, the peace and the respite from people, who drained him at the best of times, would have eased his pounding head. But that didn't happen, not this morning. Jaw set, head down, hands clasped behind his back, he strode towards the fort, oblivious of his sandals splashing through the puddles.

In his usual logical manner, he turned to the most important issue first; his return to Rome, and having to relay Agrippa's message to Caligula. He pursed his lips, trying to imagine how the emperor was likely to take the news that the Jewish king needed time to confer with his Sanhedrin as to the best place for the statue. But then he found he was answering his own question before he'd had a chance to formulate it. It was impossible to predict what Caligula would do. If he saw it as yet another delaying tactic, which it obviously was, it would certainly not bode well for either Petronius or for himself. But what was really concerning he brooded as he approached the fort, was hearing that the emperor had ordered the suicide of the Governor of Pannonia and his family. If the emperor could do that to one of his own relatives, and threaten an influential man like the Governor of Syria, it was difficult to ignore the danger to himself and his family if he should fail in his assignment.

Realising that what he needed was to sit down and formulate a diplomatic way of putting Agrippa's message over to his emperor, he shelved his current problem for the time being and reluctantly turned his attention to Dorio. His feet began to stomp angrily across the cobbles as he contemplated what he was going to do to his reckless brother-in-law for subjecting him to undue embarrassment and humiliation at the palace. The sentries at the gates of Fort Antonia, seeing the foul mood of their visiting senator, let him pass without the usual challenge.

Deciding to sort the Dorio situation out first, Vivius headed for the dungeons. He found the entrance to be a cold and dingy chamber. Narrow slits in the stonework told him he was on a level with the courtyard but the little daylight that did slide through offered no sun. A bleary-eyed prison guard, wearing his uniform in a manner that suggested he'd given no consideration to his appearance, sat bored at his desk. Shaken at receiving a visiting senator at such an early hour of the morning, he leapt to his feet and gave a sloppy salute.

'I have a release note from Marullus, Governor of Judea for one of your prisoners,' Vivius barked but winced as his voice jangled in his head like the peal of heavy bells.

The guard regarded him curiously. 'Yes Senator. Which prisoner would that be, sir?'

Vivius threw the note on the desk. 'His name's Simon, he's a Jew. He was brought in last night.'

'There were four Jews brought in last night, Senator.'

Vivius indicated the staircase leading down to the dungeons. 'Show me.'

The guard's jaw dropped. 'You mean you want to go down there, Senator?'

'Yes,'

The guard shrugged in a manner that suggested he was washing his hands of all responsibility, and then proceeded to take an intolerably long time finding the correct bunch of keys from a long row of nails hanging by the dungeon door. They rattled with annoying persistence until he found the correct bunch and took them off the hook. Lighting the lantern on his desk he said, 'If you'll follow me, Senator.'

Vivius shuddered at the blast of cold air that engulfed him when the guard opened the dungeon doors. Cursing himself for not bringing his cloak, he cautiously followed the flickering lantern down a steep flight of stone stairs. The guard's boots echoed with a repetitive 'clunk' as they descended. Vivius had a vague recollection of being told that Fort Antonia was built over the subterranean springs of Gihon, and he could easily believe it. The deeper they descended the colder and damper it became, until he found his fingers were touching thick green slime.

The guard led him along a corridor on one of the lower levels where prisoners, hearing footsteps, grasped the bars of their cell and hammered on their doors, their chains rattling loudly as iron clashed against iron. Frantic arms reached out through the bars, shouting for food, desperate for freedom. Some cried loudly and pitifully of their innocence, their voices echoing through the cavernous dungeons. Vivius covered his mouth with the edge of his toga as an overpowering stench of urine and faeces drifted up his nostrils.

'You also brought in a Roman last night?' Vivius asked.

'Yes Senator. He was drunk and barely conscious. We took him to be Greek, that's why we threw him in jail. He's still sleeping it off in the cells above this.'

Vivius couldn't resist a stab of pleasure at the thought of his irresponsible brother-in-law locked up in a cell. 'Keep him there till he's sobered up.'

The lantern wavered sending their shadows flickering across the walls. 'You want me to keep the Roman ...? Er ... yes Senator.

If you say so, sir.' He came to an abrupt halt and his keys rattled with an annoying persistence. 'The Jew, Simon, he's in this cell, senator.' A heavy wooden door groaned as it swung open.

Vivius stepped inside, squinting in the unexpected darkness. But as the guard followed him in with the lantern he saw a huddle of shadowy figures in the corner.

'Which one of you is Simon?' the guard barked.

At first there was no answer. But then a bulky figure rose unhurriedly to his feet. 'Who's asking?'

Vivius stepped forward. 'Simon?'

There was silence.

'Yes Senator.' The voice was gruff, the accent thick, and even though it had been years since their last meeting Vivius recognised him the moment he stepped into the light of the lantern.

'That's him.'

Simon's cell mates, sensing freedom rose hopefully to their feet.

The guard waved his sword at them. 'I'd advise you to keep back, Senator. If anything should happen to you it'll be me what gets strung up.'

'What about ...?' Simon jerked his head towards his cell mates.

Vivius shook his head and gestured they step into the corridor. The guard slammed the prison door after them with such force the vibrations shuddered through Vivius's head like the onset of an earthquake. He swore under his breath and waited for the tremors to settle before following the guard back up the stairs. However, this time, he noted they made a detour. The corridor he led them down emerged into a gloomy alley outside, somewhere between the walls of the Temple Mount and the side of Fort Antonia. The guard clanged the gates shut behind them.

His ears ringing with echoes, rattles and clangs, Vivius leant against the wall of the fort and rubbed the heels of his hands into the sockets of his eyes. Then running his hand down his face, he examined the former Zealot who had helped them escape from Jerusalem.

They were worlds apart, he knew that. Not only culturally but in their beliefs, and in their standing in society. Their only point of interest was that they had both been soldiers, albeit on opposing sides, and they both believed in justice. But Simon had never made a secret of the fact that he hated the Romans. He was a big, rough Jew with coarse features which looked even worse after a night in the dungeons. His hair and beard were mattered, his clothes dirty and he smelled like a sewer. Otherwise he had changed little. He was rubbing his bruised wrists while blinking up at the bright morning sunshine. Vivius watched him roll his massive shoulders, stretch and breathe in deeply before dropping his arms. He regarded his liberator warily.

'You got me out then.' He said brusquely and made it a statement rather than a question. 'I wondered if you'd bother.'

Vivius shrugged. 'I owe you. Besides, I was told it was the Decurion's fault you got arrested in the first place.'

'That's true,' he said grimly. 'And it wasn't only me. There's members of our Brethren, Greeks from a wedding party *and* a Jewish Guard.' He tenderly rubbed his jaw. 'He's got a heck of a punch for a one-armed Decurion.'

'He hit you?'

'Aye, and every Jew, Greek and Roman within reach.'

Vivius ran his thumb ponderously around the ruby inset in his dagger and averting his gaze surveyed the fort. All of a sudden, his cramped quarters, the incessant stomping of boots on the parade ground, and having Marullus hunting him down for a post-mortem on his conversation with Agrippa held little appeal. He pointed to the stone steps at the end of the alley that would lead them down to the main gates of the fort. They ambled towards them and despite the steps being wet both men sat down.

'How'd you get me out?' Simon asked.

Vivius rested his elbows on his knees. 'It wasn't easy. Legally, I have no jurisdiction in Palestine so I had to rely on the goodwill of the Governor of Judea. I simply told him that Rome had good reason to be grateful to you.'

'What?' Simon glanced uncomfortably around, although, other than the odd early morning worker hurrying to his place of business they were alone. 'You didn't tell him I used to be with the Zealots, did you?' he asked in a hushed whisper.

'No. You haven't gone back to them, have you?'

Simon shook his head. 'Those days are over for me senator. I could get myself arrested for consorting with Zealots.' There was a brief pause before he gave a coarse laugh. 'But what the heck! I was arrested wasn't I, and that wasn't on account of no Zealots I can tell you.'

You're part of this new sect Agrippa was talking about?

'The Brethren? I am. We follow the teachings of Jesus of Nazareth.' He paused. 'The Jewish authorities are getting fanatical when it comes to us preaching about the Nazarene. There have been more arrests this last year than I care to count. Sometimes they let us go with a beating, other times …' he shrugged. 'King Agrippa's behind their reasoning. He, reckons we don't conform to the teachings laid down by Moses. But we do. We follow the Mosaic Law, and we're no threat to Rome. The arrest by the Jewish Guards last night was merely a taste of what we have had to put up with. The Romans only got involved last night because the Decurion turned it into a drunken brawl.' He shook his head. 'It was a shambles, absolute shambles. I only hope Sarah's safe.'

'Sarah?'

Simon looked at him sideways and raised an eyebrow. 'Don't tell me the Decurion hasn't told you about Sarah? Huh! Imagine that! She never stopped talking about him. Sarah's my niece, senator. I sent her to live with my Greek friends, Hektor and Iola, after her parents were massacred by Rome.' He examined his grazed knuckles. 'I guess that's why the Decurion took her to be Greek. But then, with the Decurion being out of uniform and bearing letters from a Greek physician, Sarah naturally assumed him to be Greek.' He gave a chuckle. 'The sparks flew when the truth came out, I can tell you.'

'She was with you when the arrests took place?'

'Hektor was preaching in the square. Sarah was singing. We told the women to run as soon as we saw the Jewish Guards approach. I'm only hoping she made it back home.' Leaning forward Simon rested his arms on his knees. 'My worst fear is for Hektor. Hopefully all they'll do is beat him up and send him home. That's what they usually do.' Simon examined his liberator ponderously and there was a long pause before he said, 'Any chance you can get him out, senator? I assure you he's no threat to Rome.'

Vivius hesitated, unwilling to commit himself to further humiliation by asking yet another favour of Marullus. 'I'll see what I can do, but I can't guarantee anything.'

'That's good enough for me. When do you return to Rome?'

'Probably tomorrow.'

'Tomorrow, eh?' Simon contemplated the row of steps leading into the city and Vivius could almost hear the cogs of his brain ticking over. 'It's Sarah I'm worried about,' he continued. 'After last night the Guards will be keeping an eye on Hektor's house.' He wavered. 'Sarah, she has relatives on her mother's side in Rome. They're followers of the Nazarene, like us. But with Rome having so many gods I hear they're free to worship as they please.' He regarded Vivius cautiously. 'I'd be a lot happier knowing she's safe.'

Vivius's heart sank as he realised he was being landed with yet another problem. 'So, you want me to take her to Rome?'

Simon nodded his head.

* * *

Dorio lay stretched out on the couch in their quarters listening to his stomach rumbling with hunger but too embarrassed to suggest going for a meal. Gingerly pressing the wound in his side, he sucked in sharply through his teeth. It was painful but not as bad as he had imagined. It was his head that was causing him the most problems, he decided. It was pounding like the heavy beat of a drum and he knew it wasn't with an over-indulgence of alcohol, or even the blow to his head. He glared up at the culprit. Vivius had been pacing the floor of their quarters hurling streams of accusations and profanities at him for ... it felt like hours. If there'd been any choice in the matter, Dorio thought sullenly, he would have stormed out. The trouble was, he had nowhere to go.

'Do you know what it cost me to get you out of there?'

Dorio raised a swollen eyebrow. 'You had to pay?'

'Oh yes, I had to pay alright,' Vivius stormed. Spreading his fingers he began ticking them off. 'Firstly, I had to pay the jailor to get you out. Secondly, I had to pay the official fine, and thirdly I had to pay to get Simon out.'

'I'll pay you back as soon as we get home.'

'Pay me back? What with? You're already drowning in debt. Besides, it's not all about money Dorio.' He waggled another finger. Fourthly, I had to pay by losing the goodwill of Governor Marullus and it's vital I keep a good relationship with him, especially at the moment. And finally, the greatest cost was to my reputation as a Roman senator and magistrate. To be embarrassed by your escapades in front of King Agrippa and his guests was humiliating to say the least, but more importantly, I lost valuable talking time with King Agrippa. My discussion with him was of vital importance. Lives depended on it. Need I go on or will that suffice?' He didn't wait for an answer but storming over to the window stood with his hands clasped behind his back, his thumbs twirling around each other.

'Yes ... so ... I apologise,' Dorio said grudgingly.

'Apologise? And you think that'll do it, do you? A newly recruited Jewish Guard has been severely disciplined by his superiors. Simon, who put his life in danger by getting us out of Jerusalem was thrown in jail. Those Greeks er ...' Vivius wafted his fingers in the air.

'Hektor and Iola?' Dorio offered.

'Yes them. Hektor will be going to trial because of you, and the gods alone know what will happen to him.'

Dorio sat bolt upright in bed, cringing as the sudden movement sent a stabbing pain through his side. 'What do you mean? I was under the impression you had bailed us all out.'

'No. Hektor has been turned over to the Jewish courts where he'll be tried for blasphemy and inciting public disorder.'

'But ... but he didn't.'

'You might know that, but try telling the Jewish authorities that.'

'Can't you stop it? Can't you appeal to Agrippa or Marullus or ...'

'Or what? What influence do you think I have here, Dorio? Marullus is governor of this Province, not me. I can't act without his approval. It took me all my powers of persuasion to get you and Simon released.' He turned back to the window in such a manner that left Dorio with no doubt that the view outside was better than the sight of his unkempt brother-in-law sprawled on his couch.

'But ... but to arrest Hektor for public disorder and *blasphemy*! The Jewish authorities can ask the Romans to crucify him for that, can't they?' Dorio began to feel physically sick. 'I didn't mean to bring trouble on the Greek. I didn't think ...'

'You never do,' Vivius snapped. 'And when you do it's usually through an over-indulgence of wine. You know Dorio, I had you down as a drunk, a gambler and a womaniser but that would be simplifying matters. You're a ... a self-centred, useless piece of ... Ah!' Vivius wafted his hand in his direction as if he was throwing away a piece of rubbish. 'You're not worth wasting my breath on.'

An angry silence hovered between them until Vivius said, 'We're leaving tomorrow. Will you be fit enough to travel?'

'I think so.'

There was a long silence.

'I suppose the fighting started because of Sarah?'

'How do you know about her?'

'Simon told me.'

'All I did was step in to stop the Jewish Guards from arresting her. Damned Jews!'

'Hmm! But if it hadn't been for one of those damned Jews you'd be dead by now.'

'What?'

'One of those "damned Jews" as you call them, brought down the guard who was about to thrust his sword into you. That's how Simon ended up in jail. Now, thanks to you, he's a marked man. A stretch in jail won't do the reputation of the Nazarene's followers any good either. They've got enough problems with King Agrippa trying to stamp them out.'

'I ... I didn't realise ...'

'No, you don't realise anything until it's too late, do you?'

Dorio let out a breath of relief as a timely knock on the door interrupted them.

'Come!' Vivius barked.

A messenger cautiously opened the door. 'Sorry to bother you, Senator but I have a message from the Governor of Syria, sir.' He thrust a parchment into Vivius's hand before rapidly backing out of the door.

Vivius unrolled the parchment.

*Senator Marcianus,*

*As King Agrippa continues to insists on spending the winter in Jerusalem, all I can do is continue with my delaying tactics. I pray the gods be with you in your dealings with Caligula on your return to*

*Rome.*

*Publius Petronius. Governor of Syria.*

Vivius dropped the letter on the table. Next step – Caligula! And Vivius didn't like the way his thoughts strayed uninvited towards Praetorian Officer Cassius Chaerea and his plans for assassination.

# Chapter Eight

## *The journey home*

Dorio clung on to the rail of the cargo vessel as it dipped and rose and high waves thundered up against the side, tossing it like a play thing. Aware that his knuckles were stiffening with the effort, he waited until the vessel was on an even keel before stretching his fingers. They were cold and white and cracked when he flexed them. At least they were making good headway to Rome, he reflected trying to inject a note of optimism into the despondent mood that had dogged him for days. He ran his tongue around his wet lips. They tasted salty from the stiff sea breeze that had accompanied them since leaving the Port of Caesarea.

He turned his face to the wind. Not even the fact that Vivius had been sent scuttling below deck to empty his stomach into a pail, and was now having to contend with other retching passengers, the smell of vomit and the airless conditions below deck was enough to lift his spirits.

Letting go of the rail he stepped smartly back as a high wave rolled threateningly towards them. Grabbing the ropes around a bale of cargo he narrowly missed its spray. It washed over the slippery deck where a sailor, slithering past, pointedly weighed up his passenger's missing arm and then the heavy seas. The indication was clear enough. Having a one-armed man washed overboard would be a considerable drawback – to the vessel and to the one-armed man.

Inching forward Dorio grasped the rail again and squinted up at the swollen rain clouds tumbling towards them. If the rain kept away, and this wind kept up there was a fair chance they would make the mouth of the River Tiber by midday tomorrow, he mused. He chewed his lip as he tried to decide whether he was pleased about that or not. On the plus side, he'd be back in Rome, and with the only person who really cared about him – Aurelia. But on the down side, he'd have to find a way of repaying Vivius for baling him out of his debts. Then he'd have to brazen it out with the people he still owed money to and – and he'd have to leave Sarah.

Leaning on the rail Dorio gave vent to his depression, willing it to sink into the waves that parted to make way for their vessel. Sarah had barely said two words to him since they began their journey. Neither, come to that, had Vivius, he brooded. They had behaved as though he had leprosy. Oh, they had conversed affably enough with each other; too affably for his liking. In fact, he'd been disturbed by the way Vivius had brought out the rarely used charming side of his nature when Sarah had been telling him about her life in Jerusalem.

Loosening his grip on the rail for a split second to run his fingers through his damp hair, he wondered why having Sarah had been such a confusing mixture of pleasure and pain. Her constant presence had left him more disturbed than he could have imagined. Although that wasn't quite true, he reflected. When they had boarded the vessel at Caesarea she had initially spent her time in the hold tending to Vivius, but having discovered what a foul mood he could get into when he was sea sick, she had tactfully withdrawn and spent the rest of her time on deck.

Peering over the crates of cargo he discovered she was standing alone, holding tightly to one of the ropes on the other side of the vessel. He noticed she had removed her pale blue veil and was allowing gusts of wind to play gleefully with her thick dark hair. She wore an expression of sadness as she watched an affluent Syrian merchant spill his breakfast over the side of the boat. But Dorio suspected the sadness wasn't with compassion for the Syrian. He watched her surreptitiously for a while. The wind was tugging at her grey dress forcing it to hug the delectable curves of her body. Dorio couldn't stand it. Forcing himself to turn back to the sea he wallowed in his misery. He knew she wouldn't join him, or even attempt to be friendly, but then he didn't expect her to.

'Aahh!'

He swung around at her cry of alarm. A vindictive gust had snatched the veil from her hand and was carrying it up the rigging. It wafted furiously in the wind, trying to get free. Letting go of the cargo ropes she lurched towards it, trying to catch the offending object, but the wind, enjoying its game, blew it out of her reach.

'I'll get it!' Dorio shouted above the crash of the waves but whether she heard him or not he couldn't say. Slithering across the wet deck he reached her side but the wind, seeing help was on the way, tired of its game. Snatching its prize from the rigging, it presented it to the sea with a flourish. The losers watched the veil float away.

'I'm sorry,' Dorio said, and even in his own mind he was unsure whether he meant he was sorry she had lost her veil or sorry for what had happened in Jerusalem. Then because this was the first time they had been alone since the start of the journey, he took a deep breath and injecting a note of contrition in his voice repeated, 'I'm extremely sorry for what happened in Jerusalem you know.'

She faced him coolly, but he couldn't meet her eye. 'And you think an apology will put it right, do you?'

'For goodness sake, don't you start?' he snapped, but then bit his lower lip. Common sense told him he deserved her recriminations, but having had them non-stop from Vivius for days he was wearying of hearing how useless and irresponsible he was. 'I was under the impression that you people were supposed to forgive?'

Her chin jutted out defensively. 'By "you people" I suppose you mean us Jews?'

'No, I mean you followers of the Nazarene.'

'Oh!' She dropped her head. 'Yes, we are but sometimes

it's not that easy, especially when it's someone else's stupidity that has thrown one man in jail and forced another to leave her home and all the people she loves because of … of one drunken Roman.' She gave him a quizzical frown. 'Anyway, how do you know we're supposed to forgive?'

'Because that's what the speaker at the Brethren's Meeting preached. He told us we should forgive those who have wronged us, because God forgave us when we wronged Him.'

'You were listening?'

'Of course.' He paused and with an unexpected burst of courage added, 'The rest of the time I was preoccupied with a lovely young lady who had presented herself to me as Greek.'

She tottered as the boat rolled. With his feet placed firmly apart Dorio reached out to steady her. Her arm was pleasurably cool to the touch and he noticed she didn't pull away.

'Firstly,' she informed him when the boat had settled on to an even keel again, 'I didn't present myself as Greek. That was an assumption on your part.' She spoke calmly, and in a matter of fact way but there was an awkward pause before she added, 'This hatred between Roman and Jew; it goes deeper for you though, doesn't it? You blame all Jews for the loss of your arm. But may I remind you that it was only the Jewish freedom fighters who were responsible for that, and all they were doing was reclaiming land that was rightfully theirs. You happened to get in the way.'

'And I suppose you don't blame all Romans?'

She didn't speak for a while, and when she did he got the impression he was listening to her deepest pain. 'My … loss … was different. It wasn't a limb. It was my … my family,' she said quietly. 'My father, mother, my brothers; they were all massacred by Romans. It was a senseless killing. They weren't soldiers, or Zealots, they were decent law-abiding Jews. I was angry for a long time. I hated *all* Romans for what they've done.' She turned her head as a fine spray washed over them. When she spoke again he noticed her voice had softened. 'Do you know what Iola told me?'

'No. What?'

'She said, if I continued hating the Romans I would turn into a bitter and twisted old woman. I would lose the beauty inside me. People would see it; I would make myself unapproachable. It could even make me ill.' Sarah stared out to sea, and Dorio wondered if she was regretting having confided so deeply. Obviously, she hadn't because after a moment's pause she continued, 'Iola said there was no way I could tell other people about God's love and His forgiveness if I hadn't experienced the pains and struggles of learning to forgive for myself?' She tucked a wayward strand of hair behind her ear. 'Since then, I've prayed daily for God to help me to forgive the people who did this awful thing to my family. It's been difficult, but ... I'm getting there.'

Moving across to the cargo she grasped hold of one of the ropes and he noticed her voice had a hard edge to it when she added, 'I do, however, find it hard to forgive one Roman in particular for disrupting my life by an uncontrollable bout of drunkenness. You weren't fighting a war Dorio, you were being irresponsible and stupid.' She glowered at him accusingly. 'And if I gave you any suggestion of ... of friendship it was because I understood you to be Greek.'

'That was an assumption on your part,' he snapped.

'Not exactly. You didn't deny it when Hektor and Iola introduced you.'

Dorio grimaced as a huge wave thundered up against the boat delivering a heavy spray over them. He staggered away from the rail, although it was no dryer there. They stood apart, holding on to the ropes securing the cargo. Dorio wiped his face with the back of his hand, hurting and angry but wanting desperately to break through this wall of antagonism that had arisen between them. Part of him rebelled at the idea that he should have to apologise – again– and especially to a Jew. But with Hektor's fate still gnawing at him, and guilty over the upheaval he alone had been responsible for in Jerusalem, it pained him to accept it but apologising was the only way forward. He struggled for the correct words.

'I shouldn't have hidden the fact that I was a Roman. I was stupid. I deeply regret it.' He spoke quickly, wanting it over and done with. 'Every night since it happened I've regretted charging across that square and causing trouble.'

The silence was an awkward one.

'You do?'

'Yes, I do,' he said vehemently and was surprised at how sincerely he meant that. Turning away he moved back to the rail and stared out to sea. 'You're right, Sarah. I've hated the Jews ever since … since this happened.' He jerked his head in the general direction of his missing arm. 'And look at where hating has got me.' He hadn't intended saying that and now that he had he was embarrassed. He heard her footsteps slithering across the deck towards him and then she leant on the rail beside him. He could smell her fragrance and wondered how anyone could smell so good on a cramped and dirty cargo vessel.

'I wish I wasn't angry with you Dorio, but I am. I'm worried about Hektor. It's your fault he's in the dungeons. I know you're sorry but whenever I think of …' Her voice choked.

He waited.

'I will accept your apology,' she said shakily. 'But …' she bit her lip. 'Whenever I see you Dorio, you remind me of how you were responsible for me losing the people I loved most in the world. I can't deal with that, not yet. I may do one day but …' Taking a deep breath she added, 'Still, we'll soon be in Rome and we can get on with our separate lives, can't we? That'll help us forgive and forget.' Standing back from the rail she added, 'I think I'll go below and see how Vivius is.'

Dorio threw back his head to catch the fine spray and decided he had never felt so miserable in his whole life.

\* \* \*

Dorio was disappointed to find that his earlier forecast of making good headway had been a bit presumptuous. The reality was, that with the unpredictable sea-faring weather of autumn, it was after midnight the following day before their vessel limped into the Port of Ostia.

He staggered down the gangplank after Vivius, Sarah and the other passengers, but by the time his feet had reached solid ground he was aware of the fine, cold drizzle soaking through his clothing. He shivered, hunched his shoulders and swore vehemently when he saw that the last barge up river to Rome had left. He glanced at Vivius. Under the dim lighting of the dock he looked white and gaunt after his constant bouts of sea-sickness, and in no condition to make decisions. Nevertheless, all Dorio could think of to say was, 'What now?'

Vivius cleared his throat which still clung on to a crackle of phlegm. 'It's too late to hand Sarah over to her relatives tonight. Besides, I doubt we'll find transport into Rome,' he said, and as his hands were filled with luggage he used his head to indicate the lantern above the door of an inn. 'I think we should stay there till morning.'

It seems they weren't the only ones with that idea. Dorio noticed the affluent Syrian and a Roman Centurian were following them. Vivius banged on the door of the inn, but it took a while before they were greeted by a scowling inn-keeper who, disgruntled at being dragged out of his bed, offered them conditions not much better than those on the vessel. Dorio consoled himself with the likelihood that he was so tired he would probably sleep through anything. Unfortunately, after a greasy, lukewarm meal he found it was indigestion that initially kept him awake. Then he discovered his lumpy mattress had bed bugs so he spent the majority of the night scratching. When he did eventually fall asleep it was the thudding of a vessel docking against the wooden docks that disturbed him. He drifted into the first light of a watery dawn with a head that pounded as though an entire legion were marching through it, and skin that crawled. Judging from the exhausted look of his travelling companions at breakfast, he guessed their night hadn't fared much better.

As for breakfast, Dorio curled his lip at the sight of the hard strong-smelling cheese and bruised fruit, so by mutual consent they decided to forgo breakfast and take the first barge into Rome. Vivius paid the disgruntled inn-keeper reluctantly.

The sky was still grey and overcast and the pavements wet when they left the inn, but the dockers and sailors were already hard at work unloading cargo from the last vessel docked and transporting it to the warehouses. To his relief, Dorio saw the slaves being assembled by the ropes in readiness to pull the first barge up river to Rome. He judged from the pace Vivius was setting and his marked lack of communication over breakfast that all he wanted to do now was get Sarah to her relatives so that he could return home to Aurelia, his boys and his olive grove. But as they approached the first barge Vivius released a stream of blasphemies under his breath. The barge was carrying horses for the circus. Dorio pushed roughly past him with a snigger. Having been in the cavalry he had no objection to the smell of horses. In fact, in his opinion, they smelled considerably sweeter than his outraged brother-in-law after days at sea, although he wisely declined from saying so.

Relieved to be back in Rome and proud of his heritage, Dorio wondered what Sarah's impression would be at being in the heart of the most powerful empire in the world. He watched her reaction carefully as they were hauled up the River Tiber by barge, but was disappointed to find that far from being over-awed by the experience, she barely noticed the tall columns, triumphal arches, impressive temples, amphitheatres, baths and other buildings that made up this magnificent city. Her mind was elsewhere, and he had a good idea where.

'I hope Uncle Abram and Aunt Judith will remember me?' She had murmured on a number of occasions on their journey. And that was when Dorio had understood that questions like, 'Will they take me in?' 'Will there be space for me in their house?' 'What will happen to me if they're no longer there,' would be churning around her head, as those same thoughts had occurred to him.

They disembarked in the centre of Rome as the city was stirring and an overcast sky was reluctantly giving way to a determined yellow sun. The address Simon had given Vivius was a short distance from Rome's largest forum where, at this early hour of the morning, traders were setting up their stalls with goods brought in by the overnight vessels and travelling wagons. Making their way through the forum they turned into a narrow street of shops. Half-way down the street, Vivius stopped at a simple two-storey house. It was part of a block of old, badly built but carefully maintained houses with a central courtyard through a narrow archway. Judging from the bales of material, tailors dummy and ready-made clothes behind the partially open blinds, Sarah's uncle was a tailor. Dorio guessed the living quarters were at the rear and upstairs. After the splendour of Rome's public buildings this was a sharp reminder that the poorer classes still existed within her walls.

Vivius dropped his bag and rapped impatiently on the door; too impatiently for Dorio's liking. There was almost a rudeness to it. As they waited he glanced sideways at Sarah. She was nervously chewing the inside of her cheek. The door opened and a tall, grey bearded Jew with kindly brown eyes and a pleasant face one automatically trusted, greeted them.

'Good morning to you, sirs.' The voice was equally pleasant and his Latin perfect, but he wore the sort of puzzled frown which asked why two dishevelled Romans, and a Jewess laden with luggage should stop at his humble abode at this early hour of the morning.

Vivius gave a polite nod of the head. 'Good morning, sir. My name is Senator Vivius Marcianus. I have ...'

'Uncle Abram?' There was a tremor to Sarah's voice. Dorio noticed her face was pale and she was gripping the handles of her bag. His gut instinct was to move to her side to give her moral support, but he reckoned she wouldn't thank him for that so he stayed where he was.

The Jew studied her, momentarily puzzled, but then his expression changed to one of amazement. 'Sarah? Oh, my dear Sarah. Judith! Judith! Come and see who's here.' Throwing his arms wide he stepped outside and embraced his niece warmly.

'Come in, come in all of you,' he beckoned.

Dorio sensed Vivius's hesitancy so he took the initiative and followed Sarah inside leaving Vivius with no option but to follow. The tailor's shop was small and tidy and the living accommodation at the back was larger than he had imagined.

A small round woman with wisps of grey hair protruding through a blue headscarf bustled in at the sound of voices. When she recognised her niece she threw her podgy hands up in the air and squealed. 'Oh my goodness! It's our Sarah all the way from Palestine. Oh my dear it's been so long since we've seen you, but ... where are my manners. If you've travelled from Palestine, you must all be hungry.'

It hadn't dawned on Dorio that he was until she made that comment, so it was a pleasant surprise when warm biscuits and fresh milk materialized on the table almost without effort. That was when formal introductions were made. Like Vivius, Dorio sat quietly on a cushioned chair while Sarah gave them news of Hektor and Iola, Simon, and the Nazarene's followers in Jerusalem. As the conversation was now taking place in rapid Hebrew, Dorio had difficulty following it, but as far as he could make out, the episode of his own drunken behaviour was not mentioned. Although no doubt he guessed it would be when he was out of earshot.

They stayed for half an hour before Vivius, politely begging fatigue and the need to return to his wife and children, made their goodbyes. They paused on the doorstep but Dorio noticed it was Vivius Sarah smiled at, not him.

'Thank you for bringing me to Rome, Senator,' she said softly.

And Vivius was plainly not too tired to throw her one of his charming smiles, the ones he saved for social occasions or beautiful women. 'It has been my pleasure,' he said warmly.

Dorio simply inclined his head but he didn't think she noticed.

* * *

'Father! Father!'

Aurelia gave a wide smile as the excitable cries of her children echoed around the house. They were followed by a clatter of feet and slamming of doors. Struggling out of her chair she made her way over to the window as fast as her pregnant condition would allow. Seeing Maximus and Rufus racing down the road towards a weary but familiar figure, she let out a sigh of relief. Pulling off her pinafore she straitened her dress over her pregnancy bump and hurrying through the atrium called, 'Ruth! The Master's home! Get cook to prepare food!'

There had really been no need for her to rush as she saw Vivius had stopped to watch his sons racing down the track to greet him. Pulling her shawl around her shoulders against the cool October wind she waited at the front door. Even at this distance he looked tired, she thought, but then he always did when he returned from a sea voyage. Shielding her eyes with her hand, her gaze drifted momentarily over to the Suranus Stables in the distance. Taking a deep breath, she blew softly through her lips, relieved to see Dorio's horses galloping across the field to greet her brother.

Turning her attention back to Vivius, she noticed he had dropped his bag and opened his arms wide to his sons. Maximus reached him first but then, being the eldest, he had the longest legs. He let out a squeal of delight as Vivius swung him high in the air before unashamedly planting a kiss on the boy's forehead. Aurelia smiled with pleasure to see the warmth in their relationship.

Folding her arms on top of her bump she watched Rufus's chubby legs splashing through the puddles towards his father. He was squealing in anticipation at being hurled into the air like his brother. He wasn't disappointed. But once in the air he stuck out his legs for Vivius to carry him on his shoulders. His father obliged, and as the men in her life walked up the road towards her she rubbed her swollen tummy, excited but unexpectedly apprehensive. It occurred to her then, that when Vivius had left in the summer she had been slim and had carried her clothes with elegance. But during the weeks he had been away her stomach had ballooned, her ankles had swollen and she had begun walking with a waddle. He drew closer, and as his eyes met and held hers she felt her apprehension drain away. He swung Rufus off his shoulders and the boys ran towards the olive grove to tell Phaedo that their father was home.

Aurelia examined the stubbles on Vivius's chin as he approached, then scrutinized his stained clothes with mock severity. 'I gather it was a bad journey?'

'How did you guess?' he murmured and as his hand caressed her swollen tummy his face lit up with pleasure. 'A girl, do you think?'

She wrapped her arms around his neck. 'A few weeks my love and we shall find out. But first ...?'

'Ah yes. But first you want me to bathe?'

'Yes. Then I shall have a simple meal made for you. Nothing too rich,' she murmured and kissed his ear.

'Hmm!' His sigh of contentment warmed her. He held her

close. 'And later ...?'

'Ah yes, later ...' She kissed him. He smelled of vomit and tasted of salt but she didn't mind. 'So much news to catch up on,' she said and that was when she decided she wouldn't tell him about that unsavoury debtor of Dorio's she'd had to pay off. It would only make him cross with her brother and she didn't want that. And it might also be wise to keep quiet about the visit from Senator Titus Venator, she mused. After all, it possibly wasn't that important, not compared to the worries he must have had over Caligula's statues. No, these were not issues for today. Vivius was home and tonight was theirs and theirs alone.

# Chapter Nine

### Rome

Ruth gave a discreet cough at Vivius's study door. 'Excuse me, Master, but Senator Felix Seneca is here to see you. He says you're expecting him?'

Vivius raised his head from studying his parchment. 'I am. No doubt he will be dining with us. Tell my wife, tell the cook, and show our guest in here, Ruth. Oh, and bring refreshments.'

'Yes Master.'

Vivius sat back in his chair, stroked his chin, and as he listened for Felix's approaching footsteps puzzled over the urgency of his message. Their lives had overlapped for many years. They had first met as young men working their way through the ranks of the Roman Army together. They had fought in the same battles, been promoted into the Praetorian Guards together, and now they were both senators. Vivius had no doubt as to Felix's integrity. As far as Vivius was concerned, Felix had proved himself a trustworthy comrade on more than one occasion. Yet despite their involved history, Vivius had never considered him a close friend. Possibly because they shared too much history. Aurelia for one.

The door opened, and Felix, immaculate in his senator's toga, stood on the threshold. Vivius rose to his feet to greet him, carefully studying the man who had once, and probably still was, in love with his wife. Felix had the bearings of a former officer of the legion and Praetorian Guard. He was a handsome man with high cheek bones, a classic nose and thick brown hair peaking over an intelligent forehead giving indication his lineage came from the aristocracy of Rome. He was a sociable man with a warm smile that could break easily into laughter given desirable company and situation. But Vivius noticed that this morning the smile of greeting was watery and he wore a look of concern.

'Welcome Felix.' Vivius indicated the chair nearest the iron brazier where he could warm himself after his cold journey into the hills. 'I hope you will stay for lunch.'

'I will. Thank you.' As Felix sank down into the chair his gaze wandered outside to the bare olive trees that Vivius, Phaedo, Indi and their hired slaves had harvested at the end of November. 'It's pleasant up here. I don't blame you for keeping your distance from Rome.'

Vivius watched Ruth slide a tray with steaming cups of apple juice on to the desk. 'Not by choice I can assure you,' he said. He waited until she had served the drinks and left before adding, 'Caligula simply hasn't responded to my report. I've heard nothing for weeks. I'm rapidly coming to the conclusion that he must have forgotten he sent me to Palestine.' He sat down, and wrapping his hands around his cup said, 'Your note sounded urgent.'

'Yes,' Felix said slowly. 'There have been incidents.'

'Incidents?'

'They happened while you were in Palestine.'

'Oh?'

'Firstly, Caligula demanded we bestow honours and medals on him for his victories in battle. We were to celebrate his bravery by having an elaborate event.'

Vivius frowned. 'Victories? What victories? What battles? I wasn't away that long.'

'Exactly! They were all imaginary, and cowards that we were the Senate agreed because we were too terrified to do anything else.' Felix sipped the hot apple juice before running his tongue around his lips. 'I can't believe I allowed myself to be part of the fiasco. The only good that's come out of it is that it's made me face the truth. Our role as senators has become meaningless, Vivius. We're nothing more than puppets dancing to the tune of a madman. I ask you, is this how the mighty Empire of Rome will fall? Our emperor living in Egypt, being worshipped as a god while Jupiter alone knows who will have power in Rome.'

'What? Living in Egypt? When did this come about?'

'He's been playing with the idea for weeks. He believes he's more likely to be worshiped as a god in Egypt than he is here in Rome, so he's informed the Senate he plans to move there permanently.' Felix shook his head. 'The prospect of Rome losing its emperor, and its political power being transferred to Egypt has been the final straw for the Senate. Where does that leave them, and where does it leave the Praetorian Guards?' Felix leant forward in a manner that suggested confidentiality. 'Which brings me to the reason for my visit. I understand you were approached by Praetorian Officer Cassius Chaerea before you left for Palestine?'

Vivius studied him uneasily. 'You know about this?'

'I do. What's your opinion?'

'About the assassination?' Vivius cleared his throat, annoyed with himself for being indecisive. Indecision was not in his nature. 'They're going ahead with it then?'

'They are. When, only those directly involved will decide for security reasons. There have already been three foiled attempts on Caligula's life. If this one fails heads will roll. Senators' heads *and* Praetorian heads.'

'There's support from the Senate?'

Felix pondered a while before answering, 'Partial support. Caligula still has a good number of supporters. My guess is they either believe in his divinity, or they're afraid of repercussions if the assassination attempt fails. Meanwhile, Officer Chaerea and his fellow officers are trying to assess who is with us and who isn't. Having furtive discussions and closeted meetings has already raised Caligula's suspicions, and if action isn't taken soon there'll be further arrests and executions.'

'So why the delay?'

'That's down to the Senate. We've asked the Praetorian Guards to bide their time until we can agree on a replacement for Caligula.'

'Cassius Chaerea told me the Praetorian Guards have proposed Claudius.'

Felix's eyes flashed with annoyance. 'They have. Although why they think they have the authority to do that is beyond me. It's not their job to choose a successor. That's the job of the Senate and I can't see the senators agreeing to Claudius.'

'Any reason why not? He might not be a natural heir to Caligula but he has links to the Emperor Tiberius and to Augustus, so this does give him a lineage edge on his rivals.'

'True, but do we want someone who has been known as the runt in the family to be our emperor? He's hardly imperial material, is he?' Felix laid his cup on the desk. 'The other reason we need a speedy decision is that Caligula has plans for a second Germanic campaign along the Rhine. My guess is he suspects an attempt is to be made on his life so he wants to increase his Germanic bodyguards. The Praetorians are worried that if they, and the Senate, don't agree on a successor soon, Caligula will surround himself with so many bodyguards none of us will be able to get near him.' Felix rubbed his chin with his thumb and forefinger and his expression soured as if his next sentence contained an even more unpleasant issue. 'The other bad news,' he continued regarding Vivius steadily, 'Is that Caligula announced yesterday, in front of a wide gathering, that he intends to appoint a new Governor of Syria.'

'What?'

'He claims Publius Petronius has failed to obey his orders despite having been warned what would happen if the statue wasn't in Jerusalem by winter. When I left Rome this morning the emperor was in the process of drafting a letter to him. Petronius will be told to ...' Felix dropped his gaze. 'Petronius will be told to take not only his own life but the lives of his wife and his children.' He waited for his news to sink in before adding, 'You know what this means, don't you?'

Vivius stood up and making his way to the window stared across at his harvested olive grove. All of a sudden the scenery didn't look so peaceful. If Caligula believed Publius Petronius had failed him, then Vivius was in no doubt Caligula would view him in the same light. After all, his assignment had been to make sure Petronius installed the statue by winter, but he hadn't. All he had done was use the same delaying tactics as Petronius, waiting for spring, hoping that when the Jewish King visited Rome he could persuade Caligula away from his present course of action. Vivius found his hand was trembling. With fear? Yes. He was afraid, he admitted quietly to himself. But not for himself – for his family.

'Aurelia's due to have your child soon, isn't she?' Felix spoke quietly so they couldn't be overheard.

Vivius gave a nod. He couldn't trust himself to speak.

'I was thinking … I have a villa in the north. It's a two-day journey, longer with Aurelia's condition. You and your family will be safe there until Caligula is … disposed of.'

'Then his assassination is imminent?'

Felix shrugged. 'As I say, only Praetorian Chaerea and his closest associates are privy to that information, but the way things are going I would imagine so.'

Vivius ran his tongue around his mouth. It was dry. Terribly dry. 'Thank you for the offer, Felix but travelling north in winter with a heavily pregnant wife and two small boys is too dangerous. After the difficult delivery of our youngest boy, Aurelia needs to stay close to home. If we could hold out here until the child is born …'

'I doubt you've that long.'

It was at that moment Vivius experienced the calm that always descended on him on the eve of battle. The time when you finally understand you have no other option but to confront unpleasantness. It lingered over him like a persistent rain cloud, and he knew that in all good conscience there was only one course of action he could take.

'Felix; if anything should happen to me ...'

Felix raised a reassuring hand. 'You know I'll take care of Aurelia and your boys,' he assured him. 'Why? What are you going to do?'

Vivius's nose whistled faintly as he breathed in. 'I can't in all good conscience ignore the threat to the Governor of Syria. The letter Caligula has drafted hasn't left yet?'

'No, not yet. The emperor is probably so wrapped up with the festival and games he'll forget he has it until they're over.'

'So, if I can convince Caligula that the Governor of Syria intends to ... I don't know, I'll think of something. I'll find some excuse to stall him until Cassius Chaerea's plan has been executed.

Felix looked uncertain. 'Don't underestimate his mood swings. He's unpredictable.'

'I have to try.'

'And are you with us in the assassination attempt?'

'I didn't say that. My first priority is making sure my family, and the family of the Governor of Syria are safe.' He smiled grimly. 'And for that I must try to reason with a madman.'

\* \* \*

Vivius miserably regarded the heavy grey sky which had hung over the seven hills of Rome for the last week and rapidly came to the conclusion that winter was his least favourite time of the year. The days were short, it rained continually, and if it didn't rain it was foggy.

Hunching his shoulders against the persistent fine cold drizzle that had seeped through his heavy cloak on his journey, he wondered whether he should have kept Aurelia informed as to what was going on before leaving the olive grove. But he quickly dismissed the idea. His explanation that as a senator he was obliged to attend at least a few of the numerous festivals on the Roman calendar should suffice, he decided. No sense in alarming her so close to the arrival of their baby.

As he manoeuvred his horse into Palatine Hill he was relieved to see that, despite the atrocious weather, the citizens of Rome had gathered in their droves for the event. That would please the emperor, he mused. He would see that as a sign of his popularity and hopefully put him in a good mood. Not that these games were as spectacular as those performed in the amphitheatre, but then the sheer splendour of the palace grounds were attraction enough for the plebs.

Relieved that curfew on horses had been lifted for the day, he steered his horse through the palace gates and saw that the usual events were taking place; children being encouraged to poke sticks through a cage at a bear, a small crowd surrounding two young men engaged in a sword fight, a wrestling match, acrobats, races, dancing and feasting. His eye fell on a scattering of sightseers loitering around the wooden theatre waiting for the next play or entertainment to begin.

He took the track leading to the stables, away from the main field of entertainment. The animal tossed his head in anticipation as the smell of warm hay and feed reached his nostrils. Vivius laid a settling hand on his neck ruefully reflecting that if the emperor cared as deeply for his people as he did for his horses he might even make a reasonable Caesar.

Dismounting in the stable courtyard he waited for his horse to be led away by one of the stable hands before making his way to the palace entrance to ask for a private audience with the emperor. The Praetorian Guard on sentry duty led him into a spacious but bitterly cold hallway with too many marble columns, marble walls and pillars, and too few plants and pictures to take away the starkness.

'If you would care to wait here, Senator Marcianus, I'll see if the emperor has time to speak to you.' The sentry's boots echoed as he made his way down one of the three corridors.

Vivius blew on his frozen fingers and wondered how long it would be before Caligula's progressive plans for underfloor heating reached this old quarter of the palace. The whole place smelled dank and musty. He unhooked his cloak. It was heavy with rain and the fur collar was wet and flat. He shook the garment sending a fine spray across the floor. Glancing around for somewhere to leave it, he saw two plain wooden chairs behind the door. Knowing there was little likelihood of it drying in these temperatures, yet unwilling to have an audience with the emperor in a saturated cloak, he draped it over one of the chairs and rubbed his arms. Even his clothes felt damp to the touch. Making his way over to the open window he viewed the dismally grey city of Rome shrouded in mist. Although how much of it was mist and how much smoking braziers he found it difficult to tell at this time of year.

He didn't stand there long. It was cold by the window. He wandered back to the corridor to see if there was any sign of the sentry; the clunk of his boots echoed across the marble floor. There was no sign of him, but there was a sweet smell from a smoking brazier burning olive branches which told him that at least somewhere in the palace was warm.

He waited, straining his ears to make sense of the noises in the palace; muffled voices, laughter, a shout, a clatter. And then he heard something rolling towards him. It sounded uncannily loud in the spacious hallway. Glancing down he saw a small red marble had come to rest at his feet. Looking in the direction from which it had come, Vivius caught a glimpse of a small creature with twinkling eyes, a mop of brown curls and an impish grin watching him from behind one of the columns.

Resting on his haunches he picked up the marble and held it out in the palm of his hand. A little girl, he judged her to be about three, ran out from her hiding place, her hand stretched out for her toy, her feet tripping over her pale blue dress. Vivius deposited it in her podgy palm with a smile.

'Mine,' the child proudly informed him.

'And what is your name?' Even though he spoke quietly he was conscious that his voice echoed around the hallway.

'Julia Drusilla.' The child stumbled over her name giving it too many 'shushes'.

She then toddled a few feet away, and squatting on her haunches like Vivius, rolled the red marble towards him. He caught it and rolled it back. Julia Drusilla let out a squeal of delight as it rolled past her. Leaping to her feet she chased it, tripping over her dress in the process. Vivius's amused smile faded as it occurred to him what a lonely existence this child must lead if her only playmates were visitors to the palace. The red marble rolled in his direction. He caught it and rolled it back. He was beginning to wonder how to bring this game to an end when the pleasantly husky voice of a woman interrupted it.

'Ah! There you are Julia Drusilla. I hope she isn't disturbing you, Senator.'

Vivius raised his head as Caesonia, Caligula's third wife, glided elegantly towards him in a striking combination of mauve and purple. Although, he was forced to admit, it wasn't the colours that attracted him but the way her thick dark hair spiralled over her shoulders coming to rest in the curves of her ample bosom. He rose effortlessly to his feet and bowed.

'No Empress, not at all. She is a delightful child,' he said with a wide smile. 'My wife is expecting our third child any day now and I would be overjoyed to have a little girl as beautiful as yours.'

Caesonia's face lit up at the unexpected compliment. But then, Vivius guessed, being married to Caligula there probably weren't too many of those around, either for her or her daughter.

'Thank you, Senator.'

Small fingers crept into his hand. Glancing down he found Julia Drusilla's bright little face twinkling up at him.

'Play?'

'No my darling child,' Caesonia intervened. 'The senator is here on business.' She moved gracefully towards him, and as she bent down to take the small hand from his, her musky perfume floated up to him. 'Thank you for entertaining my daughter, Senator.' As she straightened up her grey eyes flickered approvingly over him. 'Unfortunately, the wet morning has meant she was deprived of her usual romp in the gardens and its difficult confining her to the nursery.'

'It has been my pleasure, Empress. Although I believe it has been she who has been entertaining me.'

A rich smile lifted the corners of Caesonia's mouth. 'I hope you don't have to wait too long for an audience with the emperor.' The smile stayed as she looked down at her daughter. 'Now Julia Drusilla, let's go back to the nursery. It's time for your dinner. Oh! Senator,' she added as she turned to leave. 'I wish your wife a safe delivery of your child.'

'Thank you.'

He watched mother and daughter making their way back to the nursery. The little girl's chattering fading down one corridor as the rhythmic march of an approaching sentry echoed up the other.

'Senator Marcianus?'

Vivius bristled at the arrival of a Germanic Guard. This one was square, heavily set, heavily armed and his accent on the Latin was sharp and guttural.

'The emperor, he will see you. Follow me.'

As Vivius followed the Germanic Guard a welcome flow of warm air drifted towards him from the underfloor heating system. Running his fingers through his hair in a vague attempt to dry it, he realised this was the first time he had felt even vaguely warm since leaving his olive grove that morning.

At the end of the corridor the Germanic Guard flung open thick wooden doors and indicated he enter. Vivius stepped into a large square room cluttered with busts, statues, murals and paintings, all of Caligula. They dominated every shelf, wall, table and floor space. But what drew his attention was a massive table in the centre of the room. That was laden with all manner of highly exotic, colourful and beautifully decorated foods. Dragging his attention away from the food, he noticed that at each corner of the room stood a Germanic bodyguard, at ease but watchful of the small gathering of senators, businessmen and members of the equestrian order attending the festival of games.

As he hadn't been announced and no one appeared to have noticed his arrival, Vivius took his time assessing the other guests. Servants, in a strange uniform that resembled something that might be worn in Egypt, were bustling around making sure each goblet was full. It was, if the raucous laughter and high spirits were anything to go by. Vivius cringed inwardly at the idea of having to spend any length of time in this company. But being well practised at having to attend social functions he forced his lips back into a smile, and was about to join the nearest group when the sight of a familiar, but unwelcome figure brought him up sharply.

Pontius Pilate!

Vivius stepped sharply behind a pillar, curious as to why the former Governor of Judea was here. He was the last person he had expected to see, and he didn't relish having him around listening to his forth-coming conversation with Caligula. Peering surreptitiously around the pillar he was shocked to see how much weight Pilate had gained since their last encounter – and how much hair he had lost. His bulging frog-like eyes were glued on his companion, and Vivius guessed, from his sombre expression and the animated way he was waving his hands in the air, that the conversation did not please him. Vivius studied Pilate's companion, a thin, sharp featured senator with dark hair that peeked in the centre of his forehead, like that of a hawk.

Vivius rubbed his chin, trying to recall where he had seen him before. Unfortunately, his attempts at observing unobtrusively were interrupted by a high-pitched screech.

'Aahh! Senator Marcianus. You've decided to grace us with your presence I see.'

Swivelling around, he saw Caligula bearing down on him like an eagle on its prey. Out of the corner of his eye he saw Pontius Pilate's head jerk in his direction.

Vivius bowed his head towards his approaching emperor. 'Sire,' he said stiffly. Trying to ignore the ridiculous posture of Caligula's fingers flopping in the air like a bunch of bananas hanging from a tree waiting to be plucked, he concentrated on the emperor's spindly legs.

'The thing is you see,' Caligula began in his high-pitched voice. 'I usually have lunch midday but I was late leaving the theatre because I've had this troublesome stomach after yesterday's banquet. I swear it has quite upset me.' He fondly patted his stomach. 'But this morning's entertainment at the games Senator Marcianus was simply wonderful, wonderful! The races, the jugglers and as for the sacrifice of the flamingo, that was magnificent. Did you see it? And did you see the people as you rode in? They loved it. They love coming to see me. Hmm. And of course, I'm sailing for Alexandria tomorrow. Unfortunately, I shall be forced to stop at all the ports because of this dreadful weather. Have you heard I'm planning to move there permanently? Yes, I am, beautiful place. I shall set myself up as their god.' Caligula tapped his blue lips with his long bony finger. 'But I didn't call you here to talk about that, what was it? … Oh yes. I didn't call you at all, did I? You've come for the games. No matter. Or was there something else you wanted to see me about?'

'Yes Sire. Your statue.'

'Ah! Yes. My statue,' Caligula said slowly but Vivius didn't like the strange blue glint that materialised in his eyes. 'Firstly though, I should show you a copy of the letter I've sent to the Governor of Syria only this morning.' The emperor waved his floppy hand in the direction of the garden. 'Except that, on the way I want to find out what my performers have to offer me for this afternoon's entertainment. I always like to look forward to pleasant activities after I've had to deal with er … *unpleasant* matters. Come! Come! Come!' The bunched banana fingers wagged rapidly at him to follow.

Vivius wavered, slightly unnerved by the 'unpleasant matters' comment. Caligula stopped and was looking back at him through lowered lids, an unpleasant smirk across his thin white lips as though he was taking pleasure at having alarmed one of his senators. Taking a deep breath, Vivius was about to follow the emperor when he noticed the Germanic bodyguards, and the guests, including Pontius Pilate and his hawk-faced companion were joining them.

Caligula took one horrified look at his entourage and his cheeks turned a deep shade of red. 'No! No! No!' he screamed. 'Not all of you. This is a private conversation between me and one of my senators. You can follow me if you like but keep your distance.' He shooed them away like a flock of geese, until satisfied they were out of earshot he grabbed Vivius's arm and pushed him towards the door as if he was a small boy in trouble. The entourage, wary of upsetting their volatile emperor, dutifully followed at a distance.

Caligula led the way down a flight of stone stairs to a tunnel shaped corridor. A blast of cold air swept around Vivius's ankles. From what he remembered of the layout of the palace, this was a route that would bring them out into the garden, beside the wooden theatre.

'In your report you say my statue is magnificent,' the emperor stated.

Vivius was relieved he had come straight to the point but he had to resist the temptation to reply, 'So you did read my report then?' But recognising the folly of such a remark he kept his voice casual when he replied. 'It is Caesar. The Governor of Syria insisted on perfection so ordered the sculptors to take their time over it. The finished result will, I am sure, take your breath away.'

He didn't like the way Caligula said, 'Hmm,' in the manner that showed marked disbelief. 'And there was no opposition from Agrippa?'

Vivius's gaze flickered over the line of crude paintings drawn by Caligula and stretching the full length of the tunnel. 'There was some opposition, Caesar. But nothing that can't be resolved.'

'I understood that was why I sent you to Palestine, Senator, to resolve them.'

Vivius clasped his hands behind his back. 'You did, Caesar, and I have. All that needs to be decided now is where in the temple you want your statue.'

'I've told him where I want it! I've told him! It's to be installed in what the Jews call their "Holy of Holies".'

'The thing is sire, King Agrippa has his own outstanding ideas of where it should be placed which he would like to discuss with you first.'

'Outstanding ideas?'

'Yes Caesar.'

'Name one.'

Vivius took a fleeting look behind as the pounding of boots told him the entourage of guests and bodyguards were now in the tunnel and following at a discreet distance. 'I'm afraid I can't do that, Caesar. The King wanted to surprise you so he refused to share them, with either me or the Governor of Syria. As I mentioned in my report, King Agrippa would like to discuss this fully with you when he comes to Rome in the spring. But meanwhile, the Governor of Syria is working out strategies to transport the statue. He has suggested having celebrations at various points on the way ...'

'Not ... good ... enough, Senator Marcianus.' Caligula's voice cut through Vivius's speech like a sword before dropping to an angry whisper. 'Petronius has failed me. He has wasted my time. He has been unable to get the Jews to accept my divinity. Whatever grand plans the Governor of Syria or King Agrippa may have, the truth is, my statue is still not in Jerusalem.'

Vivius swallowed hard. 'It was difficult to convince King Agrippa, Caesar. Neither Petronius nor I wanted to upset him. As you say, he is your closest friend, which is why he wishes to discuss this matter further with you in the spring.'

'Delays, and even more delays.' Caligula snapped. 'Do I have to do everything myself? Huh? It seems like I do otherwise nothing gets done. I sent you to Palestine to sort this problem out. I had expected it to be resolved by winter, and is it? Is it? No!'

Vivius found his palms were sweating. 'It's been difficult ...'

'Excuses and more excuses. You sound like Petronius.'

Vivius listened to the pounding of boots in the tunnel behind him with a sense of trepidation. 'I do apologise, Caesar,' he murmured, and even though apologising didn't come easily to him, he managed to inject intense emotion into this one.

'Apologies are no use to me,' Caligula's anger seemed to bounce off the wall as his voice grew louder. 'It's action I'm after. Action!'

Vivius decided silence might be the better option.

'So,' Caligula dropped his voice. 'I've taken control of the situation myself.'

Vivius remained silent.

'I plan to escort the statue to Jerusalem in person. Once Agrippa sees I'm determined to have my way there'll be no more resistance. Who conquered his land anyway? Has he forgotten that?' He paused briefly. 'And if there is resistance ...' He gave a nonchalant shrug of his shoulders.

Vivius breathed in heavily as the awful truth he had been

trying to ignore was spread out before him. Caligula was not simply mad, he was not simply sick, *he was evil*. He couldn't care less how many Jews would be massacred in the protection of their holy temple, or how many Romans would be killed in their effort to retain control of Palestine. He was oblivious to the well-being of the Roman Empire or its loyal people. Caligula only cared about one thing – Caligula.

'And the Governor of Syria, Publius Petronius?' Vivius asked warily.

Caligula's chin jutted out. 'For these unforgivable delays, I've commanded that he and his entire family end their lives immediately. I have no wish to hear from them or set sight on them ever again.' Caligula stopped abruptly and to Vivius's disgust his angry face unexpectedly lit up. 'Look! My performers! Come and meet my performers. See what they'll amuse us with this afternoon.'

Caligula skipped forward like a small boy, excited by the sight of the colourful and exotically dressed actors who had emerged through the doors at the end of the tunnel. Vivius glared at his back with a loathing he had never expected to feel for his emperor. It was obvious that in that split second, Petronius and his family had been forgotten. Their lives of little or no consequence compared to Caligula's afternoon's enjoyment with his performers.

As Caligula reached his performers he swivelled around and there was a glint in his eye when he addressed Vivius. 'You should enjoy the entertainment while you can, Senator. I doubt you'll feel in the mood later.'

Vivius cleared his throat. Although why he should do that he had no idea. He had no intention of responding. What could he say? He was being toyed with, taunted, he knew it. It infuriated him, made him fearful, for himself and his family, but there wasn't a thing he could do about it – except clear his throat.

'Come! Come!' Caligula urged beckoning him forward.

Leaving him with no option but to obey, Vivius stood a few steps behind the emperor while he jigged from foot to foot with excitement as he questioned each actor. 'Tell me where you're from? Yes, yes; Asia? And you? Where are you from? Ah! Greece. And what should we expect for your next performance? Tell! Tell!'

Vivius looked fleetingly back down the tunnel. The entourage, anxious not to approach without their emperor's bidding, had also stopped and were huddled in groups murmuring quietly among themselves. Vivius wondered how much of the conversation they had overheard, and it gave him no pleasure to think that if Pontius Pilate had been close enough to hear he would be rubbing his hands with glee.

All of a sudden Felix's offer of his villa, despite being a three-day journey into the hills in the middle of winter with a heavily pregnant wife and two small boys, sounded extremely appealing. He ran his sweating palms down his toga knowing there was nothing he could do to help Petronius now. In fact, he brooded, getting himself safely out of the palace was going to be difficult enough. He studied the thick double doors leading to the outside theatre. He wasn't stupid enough to think he could make a run for it but ...

The doors swung open and a cold draught blew up the tunnel as three immaculately dressed Praetorian Officers, their bronzed helmets shining with raindrops marched through.

The steady beat of Vivius's heart moved up a tempo as he recognised the leading officer. It was the soft-faced Cassius Chaerea, although, not looking so soft faced now. His expression was grim, his hand steady on the hilt of his sword and his stare fixed intently on the emperor. Behind him, at a set distance, marched two other officers. Vivius recognised the strategy immediately. He sensed the tension that they brought into the tunnel with them. All concerns for himself dissipated. He found his mind unexpectedly clear, alert. It was always that way for him before battle. He glanced towards Caligula. The emperor was still talking to his performers, incessantly talking, talking.

Cassius Chaerea's gaze flickered momentarily in Vivius's direction as if weighing up whether he would be an opposition. Vivius stared back, then deliberately took a step back to indicate he would not stand in the way. But his fingers surreptitiously moved through his toga, briefly touching the dagger under his senatorial robes. He braced himself. Caligula looked over at Vivius. 'Are you listening to what ...?'

There was a scraping of steel as Cassius Chaerea unsheathed his sword. His steady march broke into a run, as did that of the two Praetorian Guards behind him. Caligula swung around at the unexpected clatter of boots across the stone floor. His expression changed to one of alarm when he saw the unsheathed swords. His mouth opened as if he was about to scream, but no sound came out. If it had, his Germanic bodyguards might have reacted sooner. It was the running boots that alerted them. A Germanic Guard shouted a warning in his own tongue; there was the sound of swords being withdrawn, and then all four Germanics were charging towards their emperor. The performers, seeing what was about to take place, screamed in panic and fled.

Vivius stayed perfectly still.

Cassius was only yards from the terrified emperor when a heavily set Germanic bodyguard stormed forward. Vivius caught a flash of alarm in Cassius's face when he realised the Germanic Guard was going to reach the emperor first. Vivius didn't hesitate. As the Germanic Guard charged past in an attempt to protect his emperor, Vivius flung his whole body-weight in front of him. There was a thud as the thick set foreigner crashed into him. Vivius grunted as they both landed heavily on the stone floor. It left the way open for Cassius. The Praetorian Guard never faltered. Leaping over Vivius and his assailant he plunged his sword into Caligula. This time the emperor found his voice. With a high-pitched scream he clutched at his stomach, staring in disbelief at the red stain spreading over his purple robe. His legs gave way beneath him and he fell to his knees.

There were three Germanic bodyguards upon Cassius now, but Cassius had his supporting Praetorians. The first Praetorian stabbed Caligula with his dagger, ensuring his death. The second protected both his comrades by slicing a sword out of the nearest Germanic Guard's hand. It clattered to the ground and slid in Vivius's direction. Grabbing it he rolled over and thrust it into the Germanic Guard he had brought down.

Staggering to his feet he saw four Germanic Guards pounding towards him from the direction of the palace. There was a clatter as a handful of Praetorians burst through the thick wooden doors leading outside. Vivius looked both ways, alarmed to see he stood in the middle of the battlefield. He gripped his sword in readiness.

The first to reach him was the heavily armed Germanic Guard who had escorted him into the palace. Vivius recognised an experienced soldier when he saw one. He gritted his teeth. At the first clash of steel he was alarmed to feel his muscles jangle. He swore under his breath as he realised how out of shape he was. Out of the corner of his eye he saw one of Cassius's younger officers striding across to help him. His wounded pride cut in; he could manage, he told himself. He didn't need some youngster fifteen years his junior coming to his aid. Nonetheless, he was relieved when his years of experience on the battlefield cut in and he was able to bring a satisfactory conclusion to his swordplay. As the Germanic Guard lay wounded at his feet, Vivius took a quick look around for another opponent. To his relief the Praetorians give the impression they were gaining the upper hand.

He lowered his sword, and that was when he spotted Pontius Pilate. He was pressed up against the wall, staring in disbelief at the blood of his fallen emperor spreading across the stone floor.

Cassius Chaerea raised his sword, his expression wild, his

shout aggressive. 'The emperor is dead! Death to the tyrant Caligula and his descendants!'

Vivius examined the still and silent form of the Emperor Caligula. His open eyes stared lifelessly in his direction, his face wore an expression of incredulity. Having spent the last few weeks pondering on the rights and wrongs of the assassination, Vivius found his initial reaction was one of overwhelming relief that the Marcianus family would not be threatened with the same fate as Petronius and his family.

*Petronius!*

Vivius breathed in sharply as he realised he needed to send a fast rider to the Governor of Syria immediately.

The chant of, 'Death to Caligula and his descendants!' was now echoing down the corridor as armed senators, equestrians and Praetorians Guards regrouped. Vivius pushed his way through to Cassius with the intention of asking him to send one of his men with all speed to stop the messenger to the Governor of Syria. That was when it dawned on him what they were chanting. He grabbed Cassius by the arm. 'The Empress? Her daughter? You want them dead? Why?'

'We have to Senator.' Cassius had to shout about the chanting. 'We can't leave anyone in Caligula's family alive to claim succession.' Pulling abruptly away he raced up the tunnel after his companions. Vivius was about to chase after him when he found his path blocked by Pontius Pilate.

'Leave it!' he snapped.

Vivius pushed him roughly to one side but Pilate grasped his arm. He didn't say a word, but it was the look of pure hatred that was so unnerving. Vivius tried to shake himself free but the grip tightened. Unsheathing his jewelled dagger from beneath his robe Vivius dug it threateningly into Pilate's throat. 'Out ... of ... my ... way.'

Pilate's expression wavered, his arms raised in submission before he reluctantly backed away. It was only as Vivius raced up the tunnel after Cassius that he found himself questioning what Pilate's motive was in all this, but only briefly. Right now, he knew his main objective was to stop further bloodshed

Vivius wasn't overly familiar with the layout of the palace, but he discovered he didn't need to be. The clashing of swords, screaming of women, the odd wounded Guard, Praetorian and Germanic, lying on the ground were enough to direct him towards the Empress Caesonia's quarters.

When he reached the lofty hall leading into her apartments he saw two Praetorians already engaged in combat with Germanian Guards, and terrified screams coming from inside her quarters. Sword raised he charged in to find Cassius fully engaged in fighting off a flaxen haired Germanic Guard. One glance told Vivius the Germanic not only had stature on his side but he was an adept swordsman.

The terrified empress was cowering behind the sofa. When she saw Vivius she screamed, 'My daughter! My daughter!' and thrust out her arm towards the nursery as if attempting to snatch her child from impending danger.

Side-stepping Cassius and his opponent Vivius sprinted into the nursery, then stopped abruptly. He believed he had seen all there was to see in battle; the severed limbs, the blood, the torture, and every gruesome death imaginable. But the sight of the tiny lifeless body of the innocent child, a *Roman* child, who had played marbles with him less than an hour ago, sickened him to the pit of his stomach. The Praetorians has obviously picked her up by her feet and smashed her skull against the wall. He stared in horror at the mangled bloody mess of tissue and curly brown locks running down a mural of childish animals. The rest of her tiny body lay in a twisted heap on the mosaic tiled floor, indistinguishable, except for the pale blue dress, and the fact that one podgy hand was still clutching a small red marble.

Fragments of pale blue material and brown curls still clung to the bloodied swords of the two Praetorian Guards. One of the

Praetorians was smiling and had begun wiping his weapon on the small lifeless body of Julia Drusilla, carelessly rucking her dress, as though he was defiling her.

It was fury that sent Vivius storming towards them.

Confusion registered on the Praetorian's faces. Vivius could almost hear the unasked question of whether this aggressive senator was with them in the assassination – or not? They stepped back, unsure.

'Whoa! Senator!' The first Praetorian reacted by showing the palm of his hand, but he kept his sword raised. Fortunately, both men were saved from having to make a decision by a bellowed cry for support from the hall. They backed cautiously away.

Vivius blew furiously through his lips to cool his fury. That was when he heard the heart-rending scream from the empress.

Darting back into the apartment his eyes lit not on the empress but on Cassius. To his concern, the Praetorian had lost his battle against the flaxen haired Germanic and was on his knees, his left arm hanging bloody and useless, a deep and bloody gash across his forehead, and another in his chest. The flaxen haired bodyguard was standing over him, arms raised, both hands gripping the handle of his sword, ready for the kill.

Vivius didn't hesitate. He flung his jewelled dagger. It landed into the back of the Germanic Guard. The guard gasped, his knees buckled but he clung on to his sword. Vivius lunged across the room to catch the Germanic before he fell and before the sword penetrated the body of Cassius Chaerea. But he was too late. As he flung himself at the Germanic the sword penetrated Cassius's groin. Vivius landed on Cassius's body with a grunt. That was when he glimpsed the four Praetorians. They had caught the empress by her throat and one of them was plunging his sword through her heart. He heard her gasp; he heard the breath go out of her body, and as she slumped to the ground, her final whisper was, 'Ju ... Julia?'

'Traitor! Arrest him!'

To Vivius's alarm, Pontius Pilate was standing in the doorway with the hawkish senator by his side, and he was pointing an accusing finger in his direction. The Praetorian who had killed the empress was staring at Vivius in disbelief.

'Arrest him? What for?'

'You saw him! He killed Officer Chaerea,' the hawkish senator bellowed.

Realising how the situation was looking, Vivius staggered to his feet, his sword raised. But four Praetorian Guards were too many.

He had been wounded many times, but the sword that penetrated his side this time went deep, so he knew instinctively this wound was bad. He made a vague attempt to fight back but the unexpected blow to the back of his head blurred his vision. The walls wavered in front of him. He felt the strength leave his body, his legs buckled, and as he fell over the body of the soft-faced Praetorian Officer, Cassius Chaerea, his world turned black.

# Chapter Ten

Dorio pushed his empty tankard across the table. 'Fill it up.'

The bleary eyed inn-keeper with hair like straw and a grubby tunic shuffled over with a large jug and poured without a word.

Dorio flung his coin on the table. The wine was cheap and strong, and the air was stale as the shutters were partially closed to keep out the rain, but he liked the rough, dingy atmosphere with its smoking brazier. At least it kept the winter chills at bay.

Wrapping his fingers around the lukewarm tankard he agonised over the latest horse he'd been forced to sell to pay Vivius back. His debt might be considerably less but it still wasn't paid off, he thought gloomily. There was a horse dealer he owed money to, but at least he knew this debtor wasn't likely to hire thugs to beat him up. As a regular at the 'Black Bull' in Campus Martius, he might even get a good deal for one of his horses.

Dorio stared miserably into the deep red liquid in his tankard and wondered why he had talked himself out of going back to the 'Black Bull'. He missed the old crowd, he missed their friendly banter, and even if half of them were crooks at least they had helped take his mind off his misfortunes. The trouble was, he brooded, if he did return to his old haunts he was bound to get caught up with his old gambling companions so it was inevitable he would slide back into his old ways. And if he did that he would be in danger of losing everything; his horses, his stables, the estate, everything. *Everything!* He couldn't stand that; not after losing the one thing that had become most dear to him.

He rubbed his forefinger fiercely over his forehead as if trying to erase the vision of the lovely Jewess who dominated his thoughts through the day and his dreams at night. But he found it difficult to shake away her attractive shyness when he had bought her a present at the market in Jerusalem, or that memorable occasion on the boat when, for a few beautiful moments, they had leant on the rail and talked. He could still smell her perfume, feel the flesh of her arm as it rubbed against his and see her gentle expression as she had listened to his apology.

No one ever listened to him, he brooded. He had been hurting for years but no one had ever considered asking him how he was mentally coping with the loss of his arm, the loss of his career, or the humiliation of being seen as less than capable because he had a disability.

He cringed inwardly at the lame excuse he had made that morning when he had called to see her. Stupidly, he had said Vivius had sent him to see if she was settling in with Abram and Judith. It was obvious from her expression that she hadn't believed him. She had greeted him coolly, looking him up and down as he had arrived at the tailor's shop in his smart Decurion uniform. He had wanted to look his best. He had wanted to show her who he was, no lies this time. But their conversation had been stilted and impersonal.

It was reasonable for her to hate him, he conceded. She had been forced to leave her country, her home, her friends, family and all she held dear. It was *his* fault she had been sent to Rome. His *fault*! Why he had imagined he would feel better for seeing her he had no idea. He had felt worse, especially when seeing her had been a sharp reminder of Hektor rotting away in a Roman jail in Jerusalem – all because of him. He dropped his head in his hand as guilt wagged its ugly finger in his direction.

'Wine?'

Dorio found the inn-keeper standing over him with a full jug of wine. Dorio was used to thrusting his tankard out, but it was thinking of Hektor that made him hesitate. He wafted him away, alarmed at how difficult it was to refuse, yet conscious of the fact that it was his drunkenness that had brought trouble on the

Greek in the first place.

The inn-keeper shuffled away leaving Dorio to his reflections. He felt sick whenever he thought of Hektor. Was he dead? Had he been crucified? Could he still be in jail? No one had told him, and he didn't dare ask Vivius for fear of another lecture. The Jews were bound to have asked the Romans for the death penalty, bound to have done, he reasoned. Wouldn't they? And what about Iola? What had happened to her? He had hoped Abram, Judith or Sarah would have given him news of the couple during his visit but no one had uttered a word and he had been too fearful of hearing the answer to ask.

He dropped his head in his hand and pulled fiercely on his thick dark curls as if pain would rid him of the awful guilt inside. It was one thing killing an enemy in battle, he could justify that. But it was quite another matter being responsible for the death of a man because you were drunk. Stupid! Stupid!

Vivius was right. Dorio found the idea that Vivius might be right extremely disturbing. At one time he had been an honourable Decurion serving Rome, he brooded. Now he was nothing more than a drunkard and a lousy gambler with no sense of responsibility whatsoever; not for his sister, his nephews, his horses, his stables, his slaves, servants or his heritage. It should have been him on trial, not Hektor. He was nothing more than a worthless piece of ...

'Wine!' he shouted. Might as well, he thought miserably. That's all he was fit to be, a drunkard.

* * *

It was the agonising pain in his side that brought Vivius back into the world of consciousness again; that, and the penetrating cold. He lay perfectly still and for a while he couldn't think where he was. In fact, he couldn't think at all. His mind was a blanket of fog, his head pounded like a legion of troops on the march and he had a vague sense that if he moved the pain would worsen.

The sense of smell came to him first, a foul bodily smell. He opened his eyes, only to find the world around him black. He blinked rapidly but it stayed black.

He knitted his brow, trying to find a way through the confusion in his head. His frozen fingers flexed, cautiously exploring the space either side of him. A stone floor and ... straw? He was lying on straw?

The penetrating cold pressed in on him. He lay for a while, trying to control his shivering, forcing himself to regulate his breathing, focussing on bringing his senses together rather than trying to work out what had happened. Gradually he found his eyes growing accustomed to the darkness. Sluggishly, cautiously, he moved his pounding head, sucking in sharply through his teeth as the movement sent him dizzy. He waited for the dizziness to settle. When it did, he realised he was looking at a long slit high in the wall. It gave enough light for him to see he was in a small, square cell – alone. So, he was ... in prison? *Prison?*

He lay quietly for a while, trying not to work his way through the fog but to listen, but the only deduction he felt capable of making was that if the light was from outside then he ought to be able to hear the sound of carts, the clop of horses' hooves, voices. He strained his ears, but there was only silence.

Gingerly moving his fingers, he lightly touched between his stomach and his hip, flinching with pain as he felt the wet sticky blood. A stab wound he decided, and if pain was any indicator, a severe one. He wiggled his toes. He could move them but they were stiff with cold. He flexed his fingers and his wrists; they too were cold, icy cold. If fact his whole body felt rigid from the penetrating cold. He ran his hands over his clothes; they felt damp to the touch. Damp? Why were they damp? Cautiously raising his arm, he touched the back of his head. That too was wet and sticky with blood. He knew instinctively that left too long in this state his body would soon begin to shut down. He flared his nostrils as he fought against the sudden rise of panic. At least you're alive so there's always something you can do, he told himself.

Deciding that if he moved his hands and feet he could stimulate the flow of blood to warm himself up, he decided to try bringing his knees up gradually, one at a time.

'Aahh!'

Sweat broke out on his forehead as an excruciating pain shot through his body. He could feel the darkness washing over him again. Straightening his legs, he lay perfectly still, clinging on to consciousness, waiting for the pain to ease.

So, he deduced, as he regained control of his senses again. He was in a bad way. Possibly a bone or a vital organ had been punctured. He decided not to try to work out how but to concentrate on his bodily needs. That was the most urgent. He licked his lips and wondered if there was any water. Stretching out his cold stiff fingers his arms covered a wider sphere either side of him but all he could feel was the stone floor and straw.

'Guard!'

He was startled at how weak his voice sounded. He waited. No one came. Being careful not to jar his wound he pulled the straw around him. It offered little warmth and smelled disgusting but at least it would stop him from shivering.

That was when it came to him why his clothes were damp. The rain! It had been raining on his journey from the olive grove to the emperor's palace. Was it still raining? He listened, it was impossible to tell.

'Guard!'

His call was louder this time, but the extra effort only brought on a fit of coughing. He clutched at his warm sticky wound and waited for the pain to subside. No one came. He twisted his face, trying to join the fragmented pieces of his memory together.

The palace. That's where he had been when ... when ... a

picture of a little girl's bloody and mutilated body, clutching a red marble in her podgy hand, drifted into his memory. He groaned as other random images flashed before him. Caligula dead in the tunnel; Officer Chaerea's cry of victory; the death of the empress; throwing his dagger at a Germanic Guard; falling on Cassius's body; Pontius Pilate's cry of ... 'Traitor!'

Vivius held his breath. *Traitor*? No! Surely not? But ... if he'd been labelled as traitor then ... then it was likely he was in Mamertine Prison, and that was reserved for prisoners of state or traitors prior to their execution.

'*Traitor*!'

No! No! He was no traitor! But if he'd been labelled as a traitor then ... *His family!*

'Guard!'

The shout was more urgent this time and made him cough again, a deep rasping cough. He writhed on the straw bed as the effort sent his body into a spasm. He waited for it to pass, trying not to dwell on what happened to the families of traitors. Trying not to dwell on the fact that there wasn't a thing he could do to stop it. He clenched his teeth, hating not being in control. He was always in control. Always! He forced himself to keep calm knowing that the only way he could save Aurelia and his children now was to think clearly and logically.

Felix! If he could bribe a guard and get word to Felix to take his family ... He paused a beat. Of course, if anything should happen to him that would leave the way open for Felix and Aurelia ... No! Felix wouldn't ...? Would he? Felix was a man of integrity. Vivius clenched his jaw realising the first thing he needed to do was get a guard to answer his call.

Of course, there was Phaedo! He trusted his Greek manager implicitly. Phaedo had been with him since he was a child. He would protect Aurelia and his children but ... but Phaedo was no swordsman. There'd be nothing he could do to protect them against troopers sent to deal with the family of a traitor. As for

Indi, he may be strong but one man against ... There was no one else, except ... Dorio. His drunken brother-in-law flashed through his mind, but that's all it was – a flash.

Wiping his forehead with the back of his hand he realised he was sweating profusely. He also suspected he was becoming delirious. And he was cold, so cold. He could feel his body shutting down. He needed a doctor. He needed one urgently.

Strange how the mind picks out what it should think about in a crisis, he mused uneasily. Why was he thinking of the day Felix had left his house? He could distinctly remember standing at the front of their villa with Aurelia watching Felix mount his horse for his journey back to Rome. Aurelia's fingers had been nervously playing with the long blue ribbon stitched to the bodice of her dress. Her body had been bulky and warm as she nestled up against him.

'You were listening?' he had accused her with mock severity.

She had chuckled. 'Not all the time, but I would never find out what's going on if I didn't listen behind closed doors, Vivius. You're not terribly forthcoming, you know.'

'I know.' He had held her close. 'You don't have to worry about a thing, my love. I shall take care of you.'

*'But who will take care of you, Vivius?'*

That's what she'd said. He remembered it clearly now. But he had laughed, mainly to reassure her.

'I'm quite capable of taking care of myself.' He had responded. 'Have I ever let you down?'

'That's not the point,' she had retorted. 'People need each other, Vivius, but you, you're too proud to rely on anyone – even me – and that's a dangerous attitude to have.'

Well, she was right about one thing, he brooded. He needed help now, but more importantly, so did his family.

\* \* \*

Dorio raised his head as the door opened and smoke from the iron brazier drifted lazily around the scattering of occupants in the inn. The customer who had entered was an inch or two under six feet, but having only one leg and leaning heavily on a crutch made him look smaller. He was a ruggedly pleasant-faced man, his uniform that of a Roman legionary, but it was shabby, torn and hung on him like it would a scarecrow.

'Summit's happening up Palatine Hill,' he announced addressing his comment to the gathering in general. The door slammed behind him. 'Anybody heard anything?' Hobbling across the floor he leant forward on his crutch to warm his hands over the brazier.

'What sort o' thing?' The inn-keeper poured him a drink without waiting for the order which led Dorio to believe he was a regular in this establishment.

'Beats me, but there's smoke belching out from the palace grounds and folk are scuttling away like rabbits. I passed a troop o' legionaries headed up there at the trot.' He glanced at Dorio's Decurion uniform. 'You heard anything?'

Dorio shook his head. It always rankled when he was asked about the cavalry as it only emphasised how remote from their activities he really was. An icy blast blew around his legs as the inn-keeper came from behind the counter and opened the door out of curiosity.

'Ay,' he said folding his arms over his grubby tunic and looking towards Palatine Hill. 'There's trouble brewing up there all right.' There was a pause. 'Hoy!' he called to a passer-by. 'What's going on?'

The voice that replied was breathless, and that of a younger man. 'They say the emperor's been murdered. Dunno how true it is mind you. I didn't hang around to find out, but I did see fighting between the Germanics and the Praetorian Guards.'

Dorio chewed the inside of his cheek, recalling how worried Aurelia had been when she had told him Vivius had left earlier that morning to attend the palace games. She'd been holding on to her enormous belly and had her swollen ankles up on the stool. She said she'd had this uneasy feeling, but all he did was tease her, tell her it was her pregnancy, patted her hand and reassured her that Vivius was more than capable of taking care of himself.

Reluctantly scraping his stool across the wooden floor, Dorio made his way to the door and joining the inn-keeper peered in the direction of Palatine Hill. It was still drizzling outside, a fine misty drizzle. The sort that would creep into your bones if you were stupid enough to go out there. But he saw the legionary was right. Smoke was belching out from the direction of the emperor's palace and the crowd who had attended the games were scuttling down Palatine Hill; men glancing nervously behind them, terrified women dragging crying children behind them. Dorio watched as the streets of Rome became alive with traders, business men, shoppers and workers. They lingered in their doorways, straining their necks towards the palace to see what was going on.

Wandering back into the inn he sat down at his bench and would have downed the rest of his drink in three long swigs if a persistent niggle hadn't told him he ought to keep a clear head. Running his finger around the rim of the tankard he wondered what he should do, but didn't like the way his reasoning told him that if he didn't at least make a token effort to check on Vivius, and something awful had happened to him, he'd never be able to look his sister or his nephews in the face again.

Pursing his lips, he brooded over the fact that he had certainly chosen the wrong place to drink today. 'Damn you Vivius,' he muttered. Scraping his stool across the floor again, he threw a handful of coins on to the table.

'You going up there?' the one-legged legionary asked.

'I ought to. My brother-in-law was supposed to be at the games.'

'Need any help?'

Dorio noted his eagerness but knowing that a one-legged legionary was more likely to be a hindrance than help wavered, conscious of the times it had been assumed he was incapable because of the loss of his arm.

'I'm only going as far as the gates.'

'Fine! Any objection if I come with you?' He gave a lopsided grin as if he had read Dorio's mind. 'I won't hold you up.'

'That would be good. I'd appreciate the company,' Dorio said.

Throwing his cloak over his shoulders, Dorio and his companion made their way unhurriedly up Palatine Hill through the drizzle. Unhurriedly, not because of his companion's disability, for he was, as Dorio discovered, extremely agile for a one-legged man negotiating a crutch. But progress was slow because the day-trippers were still running down the hill from the palace, while legionaries and Vigiles were trotting uphill to the palace.

Dorio's companion nudged him with his crutch. 'Look! I've never seen Vigiles do anything but fight fires and police the streets. Never seen them guard the palace gates before. Summit's definitely going on.' He whistled softly through his lips. 'Hey! Look at that.' This time he pointed to where flames from a wooden theatre inside the palace grounds soared high into the grey leaden sky. Vigiles were attempting to contain it by hurling buckets of water over the flames, but all that did was to belch thick black smoke across the lawns and over the steady stream of Praetorians and senators leaving the palace. They were coughing and spluttering as they staggered across the lawns. One of the Praetorians waved his arm angrily at the Vigiles and bellowed some indistinguishable order that Dorio was too far away to hear. The only sorry sight, and Dorio noticed them only because of their colourful costumes, was the theatre company. They were huddled closely together watching their livelihood burning.

Dorio's companion took his weight off his crutch and pointed towards the figures sprawled over the wet ground near the caged animals. 'Prisoners?'

Dorio squinted through the drizzle. 'Wounded I think. Those look like Army Medics attending them.' Dorio indicated the side of the palace where a line of Germanic Guards was being tied up. 'They're the prisoners.'

'It's chaos in there. How will you find your brother-in-law?'

Dorio shrugged. 'Being a senator, he could be anywhere.'

The one-legged legionary addressed a bystander. 'What have you heard?'

The young man he spoke to was a scrappy little fellow with a cloak barely long enough to keep off the rain. He jerked his head. 'This old man claims Caligula's been assassinated.'

The bent old man, sensing an audience jiggled his head fiercely up and down. 'Ay, that's what I heard.' He was toothless and his lips flapped when he talked. 'That's what I heard,' he repeated.

Dorio had never had a love for the Caesars, so was not unduly moved by the news but he was curious. He moved up to the gates.

'Don't get too close,' the old man advised. 'The Vigiles are jumpy. They're getting orders from senators, Praetorians as well as their own chain of command so they're confused.'

'This Decurion's brother-in-law is a senator. He was at the games,' Dorio's companion explained.

The young man with the short cloak sucked in sharply through his teeth. 'That's not so good, is it? He could be among the dead, the wounded or been arrested.' But then he added, 'But you never know, he might have got out. He might even be on his way home.'

'I expect you're right,' Dorio agreed. Which is why he ought to return home, he reasoned. No sense standing in the freezing rain wondering. At least he could say he'd made an effort to find him.

'On the other hand, the young man could have a point. He could be among the wounded,' his legionary companion intervened. 'You should check, eh?'

'And how am I supposed to do that?' Dorio asked. 'As you pointed out, the Vigiles are edgy. They're not letting anyone in, and they're certainly not likely to let in an unarmed Decurion without his horse.'

The four of them stood in silence contemplating the problem. At least Dorio assumed his three companions were contemplating the problem. He had no doubt what he was going to do. He would give it two minutes so he could say he'd tried and then he'd find an excuse to leave.

His one-legged companion gave him a nudge in the ribs. 'Your lot might be able to help. What do you think?'

Dorio wasn't as enthusiastic as his companion to see eight cavalrymen riding up Palatine Hill towards them. 'I'm ... I'm not so sure. As I said, I'm unarmed, and like you I've been out of action for ...'

'Once a soldier, always a soldier, that's what I say,' his one-legged companion informed him with an affirmative stamp of his crutch on the ground.

'I'll stop them, shall I?' the young man asked eagerly, too eagerly for Dorio's liking.

'Aye, worth a try,' the old man agreed.

'I don't think ...' Dorio began but the young man was already moving into the middle of the road waving his arms. Dorio clenched his teeth realising that he could hardly back down now. He watched the cavalry approach, hoping that they would shove the young man to one side. Dorio's one-legged companion had obviously had the same idea because he shuffled forward, and with surprising speed flicked back the edge of Dorio's cloak to reveal his status as a Decurion officer.

The Decurion in charge of the unit reined in his horse,

narrowly missing the young man with his outstretched arms. 'What do you lot want?' he snapped. But then his eye fell on Dorio, and recognising a fellow Decurion his attitude changed dramatically. 'What can I do for you, Decurion?' His tone became respectful, friendly, as that of one Decurion to another.

Dorio had forgotten how good that camaraderie could feel, the sense of self-worth in knowing you had been accepted into an organisation that was highly valued. Forgetting his earlier apprehensions, and with a touch of the confidence he used to possess when on active service, he reached out and grabbed the officer's rein. The animal nuzzled him as though sensing a man who loved horses.

'My name is Decurion Dorio Suranus. My brother-in-law, Senator Vivius Marcianus, is somewhere in the palace. I need to find out if he's been wounded.' He jerked his head towards the Vigiles policing the gates. 'But I doubt they'll let a cavalry officer in, especially one without a horse. My animal is er ... in the stables.'

The Decurion hesitated and Dorio didn't blame him. He could get into serious trouble for accompanying him into the palace grounds when the obvious intention was to get everyone out. After all, there was nothing to prove Dorio was who he claimed to be. But then one of the cavalry men who had been listening to the conversation steered his horse forward.

'Sir,' he addressed his officer. 'I've seen Decurion Suranus at the fort. His stables provide the cavalry with their mounts.'

'Do they? Ah!' The officer glanced up at the palace then down at the unarmed Dorio, his gaze sliding to Dorio's missing arm as though asking himself what harm an unarmed, one-armed Decurion could do?

'I doubt one extra man in my unit will make a difference,' the Decurion said uneasily. 'But once inside, you make your own way. You're not with us, understand?' Addressing the cavalry man who had come forward he said, 'You, double up. If

Decurion Suranus can ride …' another glance at Dorio's missing arm made the meaning clear enough. But as the cavalry man dismounted, Dorio grabbed the reins and leapt easily into the saddle, resisting the, 'I told you so' glare which he usually saved for such occasions.

The Decurion made no comment but urged his mount forward. Dorio followed at his side, acutely aware that events had veered way beyond what he had intended. Yet he couldn't resist winking at the beaming young man with the short cloak, or the old man with the flapping gums who was waving his fist in the air, delighted at having been of service in this venture. The one-legged legionary wobbled when he stood to attention to salute but he gave a wide grin when Dorio returned the salute. And then the Decurion officer was having a word with the Vigiles, a Praetorian officer was running down to the gates waving them through, and a moment later Dorio was riding into the palace grounds.

# Chapter Eleven

All Dorio could see through the drizzle and billows of smoke pouring out from the burning theatre were misty figures running indiscriminately in all directions; legionnaires, Praetorians, senators, Vigiles, equestrians, servants and slaves. It was impossible to distinguish who was who unless they were close. The only sense of order came from a long row of dead bodies laid out regimentally on top of a flower bed. Although Dorio was unable to make out whether Vivius was among them. There wasn't the opportunity to find out either, because he was obliged to follow the Decurion leading his unit towards the stables.

Once they were around the corner and away from the chaos, Dorio was surprised to find it incredibly quiet. Except for the gentle snort of welcome from Caligula's horses in the stables, and the occasional clop of their hooves, the courtyard was deserted. Even the stable hands were missing.

The Decurion ordered his unit to dismount in a low voice. Dorio, realising he had reached the point where it was impossible for him to turn back, reluctantly followed suit and followed the cavalry into the relative warmth of the stables.

The young cavalry man whose horse he'd been riding took his reins. 'Good luck, sir,' he whispered.

Dorio's fellow Decurion's face was grim. 'I've no idea what we'll find inside the palace, but if I were you I would start looking for your senator outside, among the dead and wounded,' he advised in a low voice.

'I will. Thank you. Thanks for your help.'

One by one the cavalry unit whispered their good wishes leaving Dorio almost believing he was involved in some noble mission for Rome again instead of wasting his time hunting for a brother-in-law who irritated the heck out of him.

As the last cavalrymen disappeared around the corner of the

courtyard, Dorio was acutely aware of the unnerving silence in the stables. He rubbed his chin as the question, 'What now?' forced him to accept that only he could take responsibility for that decision. Should he check on the dead first as the Decurion had suggested? That was probably the most sensible solution, but it was also the most dangerous, he decided. If it was discovered he had no authority to be here he could easily end up amongst the prisoners.

On the other hand, he reasoned. It would be a mammoth task rambling around the palace on the mere off-chance he'd bump into Vivius. He continued rubbing his chin. Perhaps the best solution would be to find a servant or stable hand who could tell him what was going on inside the palace.

Deciding that was as good a plan as any he made his way cautiously through the stables. He noticed there was horse feed in all the troughs and fresh water in the buckets, but there was no sign of the stable hands who'd put them there. Deserted or in hiding, he reckoned. On reaching the last stall he was about to turn back when the sight of a familiar horse stopped him abruptly in his tracks.

'Hello there, Warrior,' he whispered entering the stall. He rubbed the animal's long silky neck and Warrior responded by nuzzling his hand for food the way he always did when Dorio visited the olive grove. 'So, if you're here, your master must be here, eh? He wouldn't leave you, that's for sure.' He ran his hands over Warrior's back, his rump and legs. 'You feel dry and you're warm, so I guess you've been here a while, haven't you?' He peered through the stable door into the gloomy courtyard, his attention drawn to a door with bins of rotting vegetation outside. It wasn't hard to conclude that it led to the kitchens.

'What do you think?' he murmured. 'I could find a chef or servants who can tell me what's going on. Plus, kitchens have knives. I'd feel happier armed.'

Warrior snorted.

'Right, kitchen entrance it is then.' He stroked the animal's nose. 'Don't worry, I'll be back. No doubt feeling like a prize chump when I find your master's safe, and all I'll have had for my trouble is another lecture.'

Checking that the courtyard was still empty, Dorio edged out of the stables, ran swiftly across the wet ground, pressed his ear against the kitchen door and listened. Silence. The latch clicked as he pressed it. Sliding inside he closed the door quietly behind him.

It was the heat from the open fires that hit him first, followed by the smell of stew from the cauldrons on the hearth. But then came that same unsettling silence he had found in the stables. From his experience kitchens were noisy places alive with the rhythmic chopping of the chef's knife slicing vegetables, the bellowing of orders, and clattering of dishes. But despite a pile of unprepared vegetables, this kitchen was deserted.

He searched around for a weapon. There were countless sharp kitchen knives but he knew he was going to look pretty ridiculous if he came up against a professional soldier armed with a sword, and all he could produce was a vegetable knife. However, as that was all he could find he picked one up.

That was when he heard the shuffling. He stood perfectly still. It sounded as though it had come from the direction of what he took to be the larder. Treading softly across the kitchen floor he cautiously lifted the latch. Flinging the door open he raised his vegetable knife.

There were sharp intakes of breath from inside, but an exhale of breath from Dorio. He lowered his knife when he saw the handful of terrified kitchen staff huddled behind a carcass of beef hanging from the ceiling. The carcass swung sluggishly to one side and a fat, bald-headed chef brandishing an enormous carving knife, five times the size of Dorio's, stepped forward.

Dorio stepped back. 'Whoa! Hold it!'

Seeing that all he had to worry about was a one-armed

Decurion, the chef visibly relaxed.

'Where is everyone?' Dorio asked.

Dropping his carving knife to his side the chef gave a helpless shrug. 'Don't ask me, Decurion. Folk have been running around the palace like lunatics since it happened.'

'What did happen?'

'The Emperor Caligula was assassinated, sir. We heard the Praetorians are killing all his supporters, but there's reprisals from Germanic Guards. They're still on the loose and holding out against those involved in the assassination and ... I'm not sure who's fighting who to be honest. We even heard senators shouting that this was an opportunity to restore the Republic. It's chaos out there.' He jerked his thumb towards his staff. 'We decided to stay put till someone restores order. Besides, where would we go? My guess is there'll be riots in the city once word gets out that Caligula's dead.'

That thought hadn't occurred to Dorio. 'I'm looking for someone, a senator.'

The chef whistled through his lips. 'Good luck with that, Decurion. The palace is full of them. Those that weren't here for the games have begun arriving to help the Praetorian Guards restore order.' He pointed to one of the four doors in the kitchen. 'If you're serious about your search I suggest you start through there. Turn right and it'll lead you to the main corridor, but be careful. The Praetorians are still routing out Caligula's supporters from amongst the palace visitors. Many of them went into hiding when the fighting started.'

'Thank you.' Dorio was tempted to ask the chef if he would be willing to swap his enormous carving knife for his small vegetable knife, but deciding it might sound childish he reiterated his thanks, and stepped out of the kitchen.

As the door closed behind him he rubbed his forehead. Think Dorio! Think! Where would Vivius be? What would his first reaction be after the emperor had been assassinated? He certainly wouldn't be in hiding, nor would he be fighting indiscriminately. Knowing Vivius he'd … Yes, he'd probably be in the centre of operations trying to restore order. So, he pondered. Where did that conclusion get him?

'Hoy! You! Decurion! What are you doing?'

Dorio swung around. A Praetorian Guard was storming towards him from the main corridor, his sword unsheathed. Dorio held his breath. Hiding his vegetable knife behind his back he gave a forced laugh. 'Ah! Am I pleased to see you? I'm totally lost. I've been ordered in with my unit but I've no idea where I'm supposed to get my orders. Any suggestions?'

The guard studied him suspiciously. 'Why would they want the cavalry?'

Dorio managed to look blank. 'I've no idea. Like you, I simply obey orders.'

Lowering his sword, the Praetorian gave an exasperated sigh, as though a lost Decurion was of little consequence on the scale of all that had happened that afternoon. 'Try the library, top of the stairs and turn towards the paintings on the walls. I think that's where they've started to centralise operations. But be careful, we haven't rounded up all of Caligula's supporters yet.'

As soon as the Praetorian was out of sight, Dorio made his way into the main corridor. There was more activity here. Medics with stretchers were running backwards and forwards with the dead and wounded. They were accompanied by either legionaries or Praetorians for safety as clashing swords and the shouts of battle were still taking place somewhere in the palace. Officers were bellowing orders, who to Dorio wasn't sure as soldiers, clerks and guests were running in all directions but no one was listening.

Marching towards the staircase, trying to look as though he was on a mission of vast importance, it occurred to him that he had another problem. 'Damn you Vivius.' he muttered taking the stairs two at a time. 'You better be here otherwise I'll never get out of this place alive.'

He found a wounded Praetorian, his chest covered in blood, slumped against the wall at the top of the stairs. He made a vague attempt to raise his hand for help as Dorio approached.

'Hold on. I'll get a medic to you,' Dorio whispered.

Realising the Praetorian had little option but to 'hold on', Dorio took the corridor with its walls covered in paintings and began opening doors. He soon discovered that each room had its own story to tell. Unfinished meals and spilt drinks told of the flight of Caligula's guests. Others showed the unattended dead or wounded. While scattered papyrus rolls and upturned desks in the offices told virtually the same story about the clerks. It was when Dorio found the library that he realised the Praetorian downstairs was wrong. If the library had been the intended centre of operations, it certainly hadn't materialised yet. There was blood on the walls, discarded helmets and swords, a smashed bust of the emperor and a chequered board game with its pieces scattered over the floor. Amongst the wreckage were two senators lying in pools of their own blood. Dorio knew immediately that neither of them was Vivius as both of them were bald and fat. Nevertheless, he bent down and checked them for signs of life, while at the same time keeping a wary eye on the room in case their assailants were close by. Picking up a discarded short sword from one of the victims he stuck his vegetable knife into his belt and for a brief moment, wallowed in the satisfaction of feeling a fully armed Decurion again.

Making his way back to the hallway he stood pondering over his next step. Other than the sound of running feet in the distance as medics tended to the dead and wounded, the fighting had abated. Glancing along the hallway he was relieved to see the wounded Praetorian at the top of the stairs had been taken away. He hadn't been looking forward to trying to find medics and having to explain what he was doing here. Sword poised, he made his way down another corridor.

That was when it dawned on him that he was doing exactly what he said he wouldn't do, which was wander around the palace indiscriminately. He was about to stop and rethink his loosely set up strategy when he was alarmed to hear boots running up the stairs. Without stopping to consider whether their approach was friendly or hostile, he scuttled through the nearest door. A quick survey told him his refuge was an office. A heavy cloak draped over a wooden screen in front of the window, and broken wax tablets on the desk gave the impression that this occupant, like others, had left in haste.

Softly closing the door behind him, he pressed his ear to the crack, and with his hand resting lightly on the hilt of his sword, concentrated on whether the boots were heading in his direction. Perhaps, he mused, he might have been rather hasty in scuttling to safety. What he should have done was find out if they were Praetorians. If they were, they were bound to know where the senators were gathering. He chewed the inside of his cheek. On the other hand, they might attack first and ask questions later, or they could be Germanic Guards.

He wavered, unsure what to do. And that was when he felt the sharp point of a weapon dig into his back. He froze. No one spoke. Dorio raised his hand holding the sword. 'My name's Decurion Dorio Suranus.' He spoke softly so that his voice wouldn't carry into the corridor. 'All I'm doing is looking for my brother-in-law, Senator Vivius Marcianus.' He was about to turn his head to face his captor but the warning pressure on his back told him to stay perfectly still. He could feel the sweat building up on his forehead as the slamming of doors along the corridor told him it wouldn't be long before the searchers reached this office.

'Look,' he said keeping his voice low. 'I'm going to lay down my sword.' He moved unhurriedly as he lowered his weapon to the floor. Straightening up he murmured, 'I have no idea who you are, so I've no quarrel with you, but I've even less desire to be caught.'

The sword remained digging in his back.

'Raise y ...y ...your hands above your h ... h ... head.'

Dorio raised his hand again. The sword abruptly left the small of his back and flicked the side of his cloak that covered the stump of his other arm. There was a brief pause.

'Th ... this w ... way! Quickly!' His captor's sword prodded him behind the screen but the sword remained firmly in the small of his back.

A moment later the footsteps stopped outside. Dorio gritted his teeth as the pressure on his back intensified. The door burst open and through the wooden carvings on the screen he saw the unmistakable red flash of a Praetorian uniform.

A shout carried through from the corridor. 'It's a waste of time searching these rooms if you ask me. He'll either be in the grounds or he'll have headed for the city.'

Dorio breathed in sharply. *They were looking for him?* No, surely not. They couldn't be. No one knew he was here.

'You think so?' The reply was only feet away. But the Praetorian must have decided his comrade was right. A moment later the door slammed, and heavy boots faded into the distance.

Puffing up his cheeks, Dorio blew gently through his lips. The sword moved deliberately up to the side of his neck forcing him to catch his breath again.

'Caligula's dead, do you know that?' he ventured.

His comment was met with silence.

Deciding his captor would have killed him by now if he'd intended to, he decided to chance turning so that he could see who he was dealing with. This time no attempt was made to stop him.

It was the terrified expression on his captor's face that left Dorio in no doubt that this man was more scared of his prisoner than his prisoner was of him. Not a fighter that's for sure, Dorio decided. His forehead was high giving him the appearance of a man of intelligence, and his features, although not handsome, aristocratic. He didn't look like one of Caligula's rich eccentric acquaintances, yet he was too well dressed to be a member of staff. But what fascinated Dorio was the dribble of saliva running down his chin, and the twitching eye.

He indicated Dorio's missing arm. 'Where did you g ... get that?'

'Palestine, fighting the Jewish freedom fighters.'

'I see. Was your brother-in-law a ... at the palace for the games?'

'Yes.'

'What was his name a ... again?'

'Senator Vivius Marcianus.'

'Ah! Wasn't he the senator Caligula sent to J ... J ... Jerusalem?'

'You know about that?' Dorio made no attempt to hide his surprise. 'Yes ... He was sent to find out why the Governor of Syria had delayed installing the emperor's statues in the temple.' It was a gut feeling that made him add, 'My brother-in-law didn't like the idea of upsetting the religious culture of the Jews. Not good Roman policy, he reckoned.'

'Ah!'

The sword was abruptly withdrawn. Dorio rubbed the imprint on his throat.

His captor narrowed his eyes. 'Do you know w ... w ... who the Praetorians were looking for?'

'As long as it wasn't me I don't particularly care. I'm no politician. I've told you, all I'm interested in is finding my brother-in-law.'

His captor's face twitched as he backed away. Dorio noticed he limped.

'Then you better go, but be careful. The Germanic bodyguards have t ... t ... taken Caligula's death personally. Anyone they consider even remotely r ... responsible for his assassination they're putting to the sword.' He allowed a short pause before adding, 'I would be grateful if you didn't tell anyone I'm here.'

Making his way around the screen, Dorio picked up his sword. 'Don't worry. I have no intention of telling anyone you're here. Whoever you are, you can stay in hiding for as long as you like. I would say this is as good a place as any.'

The man visibly relaxed. 'I hope I didn't hurt you.'

Dorio smiled ruefully as he rubbed his throat. 'No, alarmed me, that's all.'

The aristocratic face gave a wan smile. 'S .. sorry about that. G .. g ... good luck in finding your senator, Decurion.'

Dorio inched the door open and peered outside. 'And good luck to you, my friend,' he whispered before stepping into the corridor.

He stood for a moment, listening to the murmur of voices in the distance before deciding he ought to continue his search of the palace.

Ten minutes later, he found himself in what he would have described as being an elegant hallway if it hadn't been for the discarded helmets, bloody swords and dead Germanic Guards. But it wasn't the bodies that distracted him. It was a child's rag doll. Tiptoeing as quietly across the marble floor as his boots would allow, he picked it up, curious as to why a child's doll should be here, in the palace. But then he saw the colourful childish murals of animals and realised he was outside a nursery. He stepped inside. A brief survey of his surroundings revealed broken toys, upturned chairs and ... his nostrils flared in revulsion as his eye lighted on what remained of a little girl in a pale blue dress. Her body was torn and sprawled across the carpet, but her brains and her soft brown curls were still clinging to the wall.

Dorio was used to violence and bloodshed. He'd come across sights like this many times, but that had been in battle with another country, a different race, a culture not his own. There'd been a reason for the fighting, and in his reasoning the children of that race were as much a casualty of war as those doing the fighting. But this was a *Roman* child. Why in the name of all the gods would anyone want to kill a *Roman* child? Dropping the rag doll in disgust he made his way into the adjoining room. Judging from the broken furniture, rucked carpets and smashed ornaments, the fighting had been worse in here. A dead Praetorian lay face down under the window with a Germanic Guard sprawled on top of him. A woman lay in a pool of her own blood behind the couch. Dorio paused, determining from the elegance of her dress and prosperity of her quarters that in all probability this was the Empress Caesonia. So, he concluded, the child must be her daughter, and whoever had assassinated Caligula had wanted to finish off his line of succession.

He gave a snort of disgust at the revolting battlefield, and was about to continue his search, when he was startled to see a jewelled dagger sticking out of the back of the Germanic Guard. Vivius's dagger! Dorio had always admired it. With its distinctive ruby inset in the handle he would have recognised it anywhere. Vivius would never abandon it, not his heirloom. Never! Kneeling down, Dorio was about to pull it out of the dead guard's body when he heard a footstep at the doorway. He spun round.

'What ... what are you ... doing?'

A wounded senator was leaning heavily against the doorway, his sword raised, blood drenching the shoulder of his toga.

'I'm looking for Senator Vivius Marcianus.'

The senator blinked rapidly as if he had misheard. 'Why?'

'He's my brother-in-law.' Dorio examined the figure in front of him carefully before giving a sigh of relief. 'Senator Felix Seneca. Remember me? Decurion Dorio Suranus. You helped us when we returned from Jerusalem with evidence against Pontius Pilate.'

The gaze wavered to Dorio's missing arm. 'Yes. I remember you ... Decurion ...?'

'Dorio Suranus. Vivius was here for the games, sir. His horse is in the stables, and that ...' he pointed to the dagger in the back of the Germanic Guard. 'Is his.' Turning back to the Germanic Guard he pulled the dagger out of the dead man's back, wiped the blood on the Germanic's uniform and handed it to Felix. 'See? It has the ruby inset and the family initials engraved on the blade.'

Felix examined the dagger. 'Yes. It belongs to ... to ... Ah!' He gritted his teeth as he fell back against the wall. 'Damned Germanic did this. Ah!' He slid to the ground.

Dorio glanced around the room, and seeing a stole draped over the edge of the couch he snatched it up, knelt down beside Felix and pressed it up against his shoulder.

Felix grasped his hand. 'Listen.' He licked his lips. 'Vivius is in ... in Mamertine Prison. He was accused of trying to stop the ... the assassination.'

'*What!*'

'They say he killed the Praetorian officer who ... who assassinated Caligula, and he threatened two others here, in the empress's quarters. He's been accused of siding with the Germanic Guards and Caligula's senators.'

Dorio frowned at the wounded senator as he raised Vivius's dagger. 'If Vivius was supporting the *Germanic* Guards, how come his dagger is in the back of one of them? That doesn't make sense.'

'None of it does. What was Vivius doing here, in the empress's quarters anyway?' Felix closed his eyes briefly as if trying to summon up enough strength to continue.

Dorio gave himself a moment to let the information sink in before asking, 'Who made these accusations? How reliable are they?'

'The accusation from the Praetorians, extremely reliable I would say.' Felix gave a harsh but weak laugh. 'But the others? One of them is from Pontius Pilate, would you believe? He claims to have been there when Caligula was assassinated. According to him, Vivius tried to bring Cassius Chaerea down in an attempt to protect the emperor.' He winced but then continued, 'We know Pilate's reasoning behind his claims. Revenge. But the other claim was made by a Senator Titus Venator. He says he was only yards away when Caligula was assassinated and he backs Pilate's accusations up. He also accuses Vivius of killing Cassius Chaerea.'

Dorio sat back on his haunches. 'Who's Senator Titus Venator?'

'No idea. But now is not the time to try ... try working it out.'

'What do you mean?'

There was a long pause. Dorio could see that talking was weakening Felix.

'The Praetorian Guards are rounding up anyone ...' Felix coughed, a harsh rasping cough. '... rounding up and burning the homes of anyone ... anyone they consider to have been supporting the emperor. If the Praetorians are suggesting Vivius was ... was ...'

A chill ran down Dorio's spine. 'You think Aurelia and the children could be in danger?'

Felix coughed again. 'Could be, if word gets out that Vivius is in Mamertine Prison. He was wounded in his fight against the Praetorians.'

'Vivius is wounded?'

Felix winced with pain. 'He is. And I wouldn't put it past Pontius Pilate to make sure word gets out to the right people that Vivius was a Caligula supporter. There's no order in Rome, nor will there be until the new emperor is announced and that ... that could be hours, even days away.'

Dorio swallowed hard. 'Look, Senator. I have to get you to the medics. And if I'm to get Aurelia and her family to safety you have to help me get out of here.'

Felix opened his eyes and frowned at him. 'How did you get

in?'

'Never mind, too long a story. Do you think you can stay conscious long enough to get me out?'

Taking a deep breath, Felix straightened his body against the wall. 'I can.' He raised his hand for assistance.

Wrapping his arm around Felix, Dorio hauled him to his feet.

'There's one other thing,' Felix panted as they made their way sluggishly down the corridor. 'Publius Petronius, the Governor of Syria.'

'What about him?'

'I need a rider dispatched with all haste to tell him of Caligula's death.'

'We can deal with that later, Senator. The most important ...'

'No!' Felix stopped in his tracks. 'We deal with this now, Decurion. Caligula sent a rider this morning ordering Petronius and his family end their lives immediately. Get me to the medics then get me an army officer. The death of this good and honourable man must be prevented at all costs.'

# Chapter Twelve

Guessing he was at a safe enough distance away from the city not to be stopped, Dorio reined in Vivius's horse, raised himself up in the saddle, and having ridden uphill for the last ten minutes peered over the old city wall. A red glow covered Palatine Hill. Blazing villas with flames soaring high into the early evening sky, told him that the reprisals and arrests for Caligula's supporters were underway. He swivelled around. Other than a few local men standing by the city gate watching the fires, he was relieved to see the main road leaving the city was free of troops. That could only mean one thing; if Pilate had persuaded the Praetorians to target Vivius's family they hadn't left yet – unless they were ahead of him.

Knowing he had over an hour's hard riding ahead of him, he settled back in the saddle, and digging his heels into Warrior's flank urged the animal on to the track heading into the hills. The decision as to whether he had been right in taking this route niggled on at the back of his mind. Admittedly, it was fractionally shorter than taking the main road, but he knew from bitter experience how treacherous this route could be in winter. The steady drizzle which had persisted all day would have soaked the already waterlogged fields making galloping not only difficult, but dangerous, especially with darkness descending. There'd be water-filled potholes and ditches, the terrain was rough, and if he was to reach the olive grove before dark he would have to force Warrior into a pace that was far from safe for either horse or rider. Still, he resolved, as long as there was enough light left to gallop at speed he would have to take the risk.

It had been tracking down the medics, then an Army Officer for Felix that had taken the time, he brooded. The officer had stood over the prostrate Felix, hands on hips.

'The army is already out in force,' he'd curtly told him. 'We're seeing to the dead and wounded, making arrests, dealing with pockets of violence in the city, *and* supporting the Vigiles. They're being stretched to the limit fighting fires. I honestly haven't the manpower to send riders to the Syrian Governor. Our first priority must be to regain control of Rome.'

It was watching a weakening Felix trying to argue his case that had prompted Dorio into searching for the cavalry unit he had come in with. Relieved to find them awaiting orders at the stables, he had persuaded the Decurion to speak to Felix and the Army Officer.

The officer ran his fingers through his hair in annoyance. 'Fine! Two of your best riders can go, but only two,' he relented. 'I need the rest of you here, and tell them to avoid the city centre at all costs.'

Having decided that was advice it might be wise to take for himself, Dorio had left Felix in the hands of the medics and taken the route around the old city wall.

He could feel Warrior panting with the exerted effort of galloping uphill, his muscles rippling, and his steamy breath merging into the mist and drizzle, his hooves splashing heedlessly through puddles as though the animal sensed the urgency of his mission.

Dorio only checked his speed when the path disappeared altogether and the terrain got rougher. Bringing the horse into a steady trot, Dorio ran his finger around the neck of his cloak and was amazed to find it drenched. He'd been totally oblivious of the rain trickling down his helmet and, finding a gap, soaking his inner garments.

He kept an eye on the main road, praying to the gods he wouldn't catch a glimpse of regimental lights, but other than the odd glimmer from a farmhouse the hillside was in darkness. He wondered briefly if he should call for help from his servants when he passed his own estate, but he just as briefly dismissed the idea. No, his first priority must be to get Aurelia and the boys to safety, he decided. *Safety!* He sucked in sharply through his teeth. Where in the name of Jupiter could he take them for safety? He hadn't given that a thought. Still, there was at least another four miles to go before he got to the olive grove so he had plenty of time to work that out. His first priority was to pick up the track again so that he could set Warrior off at a gallop.

Sure enough, the heavy rain enabled the road to pick itself out like a ribbon through the scrub, and with barely a nudge to Warrior they were on it and galloping at full speed. He only reined in the horse again when the track meandered on to the main road heading north from Rome. That was when he swivelled around in the saddle and was alarmed to see a snake of torches meandering up the hill. Of course, it could be locals he reasoned subduing the sudden rise of panic. Folk returning to their homes after the games, but there seemed to be too many lights for that. Besides, whoever they were would have a good half hour's walk before they reached the olive grove, *if* that's where they were heading. Digging his heels into Warrior's flank he set off at a gallop on the final haul of his journey.

Aurelia was waiting anxiously for him at the door when he arrived, or rather not for him, but for Vivius. Dorio knew she would have spotted the smoke rising from the city and would be alarmed. A single lamp dimly lit up her solitary figure showing the birth of her baby was close. When she saw it was him, and that he was riding Warrior she hurried towards him, one trembling hand across her mouth, the other clutching her swollen belly.

'What's happened?' Her voice was strained.

Dorio leapt off the horse. Indi emerged from the house to lead Warrior through to the stables but Dorio restrained him. 'No, we're not finished with him.' He reached out and grasped his sister's arms. 'Don't worry. Vivius is wounded, but he's alive,' he reassured her. He gave her a second to catch her breath. 'Aurelia, I have to get you and the boys to safety.'

'What? Why?'

'There's no time to explain.'

'Then I won't go. I won't go until I know what's happened to Vivius.'

Phaedo hurried out of the house, his eyebrows raised, and Dorio was relieved to see that as usual the Greek olive grove manager was calm. He needed that right now.

'Vivius is in Mamertine prison,' Dorio explained. 'He's accused of being a traitor ...'

Aurelia gave an unwomanly snort. 'Nonsense! Vivius is no traitor.'

'We know that but I'm not so sure about the people who put him there. That's why you have to get out of here. It's a precaution, that's all.'

He saw her fear. He hadn't wanted to frighten her, not in her condition.

'What happened?' Aurelia's voice trembled.

Dorio blew air gently through his pursed lips. 'There's no time to explain, Aurelia.' He saw her chin jut out, and he gave an exasperated sigh. He knew from a lifetime of experience that his sister was not going to move unless she had good reason. 'Caligula has been assassinated. Vivius is accused of killing his assassin, and attacking the Praetorian Guards. There, that's it. The details I'll get into later. Obviously, the accusations against him are false, I know that, you know that, even Felix knows ...'

'Felix? What's Felix got to do with this?'

Not wanting to be drawn into further discussion, Dorio ignored the question. 'Meanwhile Rome is in chaos, there's indiscriminate killings, arrests, fighting and ... and there are lights heading in this direction. It could be nothing,' he added hastily. 'But to be on the safe side, I need to get you and the boys out of here ...'

Aurelia had one hand on her hip, the other on her forehead as if she was trying to make sense of Dorio's story. 'But why would

Vivius attack Praetorian ...' she began but recognising he could spend the next hour trying to explain, and that the servants were hovering anxiously in the background listening, he decided to make good use of them.

Addressing the young Greek tutor who was standing with his arm wrapped protectively around his frightened charges, he said, 'I'm pleased you're still here.'

'I saw the smoke in the city,' he said by means of explanation. 'And when the master didn't return I guessed there was a problem so I stayed.'

Dorio gave him a nod of approval. 'Good man. You know where I live?'

'Yes Decurion.'

'Then I want you run to my estate. Tell the servants,' he bit his lip. 'Tell them to come here quickly. Tell them I don't want them to fight. I simply want them here in case the olive grove and house are set alight.'

Aurelia gasped. 'Set fire to ...'

'Yes sir.' The tutor paused. 'Can I ask where you're taking the boys sir?'

Dorio paused a beat before saying, 'Rome.' Because even as he had been talking he had figured out the ideal place to hide Aurelia and her children.

Aurelia grabbed his arm. 'But you told me Rome was in chaos? Why can't we stay with you?'

'Because I'm a member of this family and my visit to the palace may have raised questions.'

'You've been to the palace?' Aurelia was incredulous. 'You saw Vivius?'

'No!' Turning back to the Greek tutor he said, 'Go now! Go!'

'Yes sir.' With a reassuring pat on the shoulders of both his charges, the young man set off at the trot to the Suranus estate.

Dorio watched him go, cursing the fact that he could have done with the two slaves he'd had to sell to pay off his debts.

It was then he saw Vivius's servants were all looking to him, waiting for him to say or do something. He wiped the back of his hand across his mouth, trying to work out his next move and was surprised how easily it came to him.

'Indi, I want you to harness the horse and cart for your mistress. And make it the small cart. I'll need to manoeuvre through the night-time traffic in the city.'

Indi grunted his acknowledgement before hurrying in the direction of the stables.

Turning to Ruth he said, 'Ruth, pack clothes for your mistress and the boys, enough for three or four days. Hurry, there's no time to waste.'

'Yes sir.' Ruth bobbed her head before hurrying into the villa.

'Phaedo.'

'Yes sir.'

'Phaedo, you're the only one I can trust to handle the affairs of both estates.'

Phaedo held up his chin. 'Yes sir.'

'Hide any valuables ...'

Aurelia interrupted. 'Oh Dorio, there's no need ...'

Dorio ignored her. 'Hide anything the master considers valuable. Hide them in the lower part of the olive grove, but when those lights get close, you and the servants hide.' He pointed to the snake of lanterns now visible through the darkness.

'What? Oh no Master Dorio sir, we can fight we can ...'

'No you can't. I honestly have no idea who we're fighting. If it's the Praetorian Guards you don't stand a chance. That's an order Phaedo, is that clear? What you can do is stem the fire if they set light to the property – but only after they've left. And keep an eye on my stables. My horses ...' Dorio bit his lip. 'Can you manage?'

'Yes Master Dorio, and don't you worry about your horses, sir.'

Dorio took a deep breath as it dawned on him he'd been

issuing orders in a manner that he hadn't done since his days as an active Decurion in the Roman Army, and it actually felt good. Narrowing his eyes, he was relieved to see the young tutor had reached the Suranus estate. Dorio had no qualms his servants would take orders from Phaedo, they did that at harvest each year.

He watched Indi making final adjustments to the horse's harness, and Phaedo load the hastily assembled bags of clothes into the small cart. But as Ruth attempted to heave her mistress into the cart with them, Dorio experienced an unexpected wave of affection towards his sister. She was obviously shaken by the news, she was bulky and awkward climbing aboard with Rufus at her side, but she was attempting to stay calm for the sake of her children. She reached out her hand to draw Maximus into the cart with her but Dorio pulled him away and with his one good arm swung the boy easily on to Warrior.

Aurelia gave a cry of alarm. 'No Dorio, he can't ride Warrior. Vivius doesn't allow it. The horse is too big and strong, and Max is only a boy.'

'And tonight, he's a man, Aurelia.' He patted Maximus's leg. 'Can you manager her, Max?' he asked softly.

The boy's expression was one of alarm. 'I'm not supposed to ride her, Uncle Dorio. Father doesn't allow it.'

'But tonight, I'm allowing you to, Maximus. I know Warrior. He'll object to being tied behind a cart and I may need him when I'm in Rome. I have to drive the horse and cart.'

Maximus lifted his chin. 'Then you can trust me, Uncle Dorio. And if you need help getting my father out of prison, then you can count on me.'

Dorio flinched. *Getting Vivius out of prison? He hadn't given that a thought.*

\* \* \*

She had sensed there would be trouble from the moment she had woken up. She had rolled awkwardly in the bed, her belly heavy and cumbersome with the unborn baby. The movement had woken Vivius. She had known it would, he was such a light sleeper, but there was a limit to how long she could lie in the one position.

'Do you have to go?' she had pleaded. 'I have a bad feeling about today.' But he had simply laughed at what he called her irrational pregnancy fears, and spent breakfast listening to the boys chattering on their favourite subject, which was the battles Warrior had fought, imaginary and real. But now, curled up in the cart, one arm around her frightened youngest son she found strange comfort in realising her fears had not been irrational at all, but real. She caught a glimpse of Maximus's small skinny legs splayed across Warrior's enormous back.

'Help us dear Father God, help us. Help us dear Father God, help us.'

She had no idea why she was repeating the prayer Ruth had been murmuring as she had helped her on to the cart, except that she had found the gentle repetition comforting. She had experienced that same comfort on numerous occasions when she had overheard her Jewish maid praying to her God, and for some reason she felt better about turning to this God in prayer tonight rather than to Venus or Minerva, her favourite gods.

It was strange, she brooded, but since early this morning she had likened her fears to an approaching storm. She had sensed it gathering momentum the moment she had spotted the smoke rising from the city. And now the storm was here. It was on them. But oddly enough murmuring Ruth's prayer was like … like sinking below the waves; not drowning, but being drawn away from the storm, deep into the quiet depths where Ruth's God lived. It was a place of peace and safety in the midst of a chaotic world.

She winced as the cart jolted over a rut in the road and an

unexpected pain shot through her groin. 'What if ...' She bit her lip. Don't look at the problems,' she told herself. 'Go down deep and hold on to Ruth's God.'

Instinct told her that's what she had to do, but it wasn't easy. Her mother's heart was crying out for her eldest son. The rain was soaking through Maximus's cloak, his small hands were struggling to guide this huge animal around the potholes. He was trying to be brave, for her sake, but she could tell he was scared. What if the horse stumbled? What if Maximus fell off? And what about dear Rufus? She could feel his little body shivering with cold and fear. What if they were attacked by ... who? Who would want to harm them? How could Dorio protect them? What if ... what if ... what if ...?

'Protect us Father God, keep us safe. Protect us Father God, keep us safe.'

She gave a cry of pain as the cart landed in a pothole, jerking her whole body into the air. Dorio was going far too fast, dangerously fast. It was then it dawned on her that they had left the main road into Rome and were cutting across country, towards the old city wall.

'Rufus, sit on the floor in the corner my love and hold on tightly.'

Rufus scrambled into the corner, his worried face never leaving hers. She tried giving him a reassuring smile but her fingers were already squeezing the side of the cart as another pain, stronger this time, enveloped her body. She waited until it had subsided before cautiously moving her legs. She knew instinctively what she would find. Her legs were wet, she was ... She sucked in sharply through her teeth as the cart jerked again, more fiercely this time.

Dorio swivelled around in his seat. 'Sorry, didn't see that one. Are you okay?'

'Yes, we're okay, aren't we Rufus?' She tried to keep her voice light, giving the boy's hair a reassuring ruffle, but that wasn't easy when she knew what had happened. Her waters had broken. She breathed in fiercely through her nostrils. Oh dear God, not now, not now! Reaching over Rufus, she opened the bag Ruth had packed. Wise woman. There was not only a change of clothing for them but gowns, a sheet and a blanket for the unborn baby. Ruth had seen her cringe earlier that afternoon and suspected her time was imminent.

'It's probably a false alarm.' Aurelia had reassured her with a smile. 'I had that with Maximus and Rufus. Or it could be the meat we had for dinner. It was a little indigestible.'

She touched Dorio's back. 'How long before we reach Rome?'

Dorio shrugged. 'Difficult to say. At this pace and depending on what we encounter in the city, less than an hour.' He half swivelled around. 'You're all right, aren't you?'

'I ... Aahh!' She clenching her teeth as another powerful contraction overpowered her.

'Mama?' A fretful Rufus scrambled into a kneeling position and clasped her face between his podgy hands. 'Are you sick, mama?'

She didn't answer, she couldn't. All she could do was wait for the contraction to ease. She was aware Dorio was bringing the horse and cart to a standstill, and Maximus was drawing alongside the cart. Dorio swung his legs over the seat into the cart.

'It's discomfort, right? It was the wheel landing in the pothole, right?' He watched the muscles in her face contort. 'You can't give birth, not out here, Aurelia. You can't!'

'Like I have a choice,' she breathed through gritted teeth, and then, blessed relief, the contraction was over. She breathed deeply, wallowing in the minutes she would have before the next one.

'How long have we got?' Dorio looked almost as frightened as her children.

'A while, but I don't think we'll make it to Rome.'

He stood up, frantically scanning the countryside for shelter. It was raining, it was foggy, and it was dark. 'We're not far from the outskirts of the city,' he informed her. 'There are derelict stables along the old city wall. It's rough but … Can you hang on?'

'It's not a case of hanging on, Dorio,' she snapped. 'Babies come when they want to. I have no say in the matter.' And then she felt guilty for snapping.

'Of course,' he muttered. 'Don't worry. It'll be fine.' Swinging his legs over the seat he urged the horse forward. 'Keep close behind the cart, Max,' he called. 'And hold on tightly. The road gets smoother in a while.'

She noticed there was no answer from the brave little soldier on Warrior, he was too busy concentrating on his uncle's instructions. She ran her tongue around her dry mouth. This was no false alarm as she'd had with Maximus and Rufus. Rightly or wrongly this baby had decided to arrive in the midst of one of the worst nightmares of her life. Why would God – any god – allow this to happen – *now*? Surely, He could have prevented it until they had reached shelter and safety? Was it worth praying? Was it? Perhaps Vivius was right, prayer to any god was a waste of time. She lay down in the cart, aware that Rufus was watching her, his eyes wide and fearful.

The dull ache deep in her abdomen gave an indication that it wouldn't be long before she would be pushing this baby out. This one was in a hurry. Maybe she should have brought Ruth with her? Maybe she should have taken her chances and stayed in her own home? No one would hurt a child, would they?

The cart lurched as Dorio drove the animal full speed down the hill. She clung on to the side. She heard Dorio shout something to Maximus. What, she couldn't make out. Terrified, she watched her eldest boy clinging on to Warrior as the horse galloped after them. She closed her eyes. She couldn't bear to watch. The boys would have to take their own chances for the next ... however long it took. Her motherly instincts were beginning to rise in fierce protection for the baby she was about to bring into the world.

'Hold on Aurelia!'

'Hold on? Hold on? Stupid ...! How can I hang on? When a baby wants to come ... Aahh!' She had to push! She had to.

The cart was leaving the track. It was lurching over a rutted field. Now there were trees overhead, bushes. She could barely feel the rain on her face. Rufus was gripping the side of the cart, his wide, frightened expression as he watched her in pain was heartbreaking.

'Aahh!' She clenched her fists.

The cart skidded to a standstill. Dorio had driven it into ... where? It didn't matter. They were under shelter. She could feel they were out of the drizzle. They were in the dry. Thank God, they were in the dry, and they were safe, all of them.

The horses were panting, snorting, breathless. She could smell their sweat, feel the steam from their bodies. She had her eyes shut. When she opened them, she saw it was still dark but she could make out three stone walls and a roof.

'Rufus, jump out of the cart boy. Here, hold the reins of the cart horse, keep her calm while your mother delivers your new baby. Max, off your father's horse, quickly now. I want you to help Rufus keep the animal steady.'

She felt the cart shake but it was only Dorio, he had climbed aboard and was kneeling beside her. 'Aahh!' She was pushing with this contraction, pushing ... pushing ...

'Wait! Wait! Don't push, Aurelia. Now's not the time to push.'

Her head jerked up angrily, 'And how would you know, Dorio? You've never given birth!' She hadn't meant to scream at him.

'No but I've delivered horses.'

'And does it look like I'm giving birth to a horse ...? Aahh! Aahh!'

'Lie back. That's it, you're doing brilliantly.'

'Shut up! Just shut ...!'

Again, the pain eased.

She lay back on her crumpled cloak, exhausted. She could hear the horses breathing heavily, still panting from their race across the fields. There was a smell of hay and an overpowering smell of dung. It was dark and it was quiet, but it was dry; thank God it was dry. Dorio was at her side. How could he see what he was doing? Was he going to deliver this baby? Not Dorio; he only had one arm. She sensed another contraction coming and tried to control her breathing.

'Don't focus on the pain, Aurelia. Think of something else, anything.'

Aurelia knew the only thing on her mind was Vivius, and her boys but it was too painful to think about them. The baby. That was all she could think about now, delivering this child.

'Push at the next contraction, Aurelia and er ... try not to make a noise.'

'What! What do you mean try not to make a noise? How am I supposed to ...?' She grabbed Dorio's shoulder, her fingers digging into the flesh around his neck. This was it! One gigantic push and ...

'Grruuu!'

'Shh!'

'Grruuu!' She had the impression that her whole body was about to explode, as with every ounce of her being she pushed her baby into the frightening world she now lived in. Its tiny body slithered between her legs, warm, wet and incredibly precious. She could hear its quick breathing, its whimper, feel the movement of its tiny limbs. It was alive! With a sigh of relief, she lay back exhausted. She knew what she had to do next but so it appeared did Dorio. And even in the midst of this fearful excitement, it struck her she had never trusted her brother as completely as she did at that moment.

She lifted her head. Dorio was wrapping the tiny figure in the sheet and then the blanket.

'It's a girl, Aurelia,' he whispered. 'You have a daughter.'

It was so dark she was barely able to see the bundle he handed her, but resting her cheek on her daughter's warm wet face she felt her breath, and was aware of her tiny limbs moving under the blanket. 'Thank God. Oh, thank you God!' she whispered.

Dorio threw one of the blankets Rufus had been sitting on over her and the cart wobbled as he jumped down.

'Come on boys,' he said quietly. 'Up on to the cart and meet your little sister.'

And she realised it would have been the most precious moment of her life if Vivius had been there to share it with them.

# Chapter Thirteen

Dorio was alarmed to see how far the rule of law had broken down as he drove through the dark, wet and battle-weary streets of Rome. Overworked Vigiles were struggling between maintaining order and dowsing fires, which thankfully hadn't spread with any great ferocity due to the rain drenching the buildings all day. The Roman Army were also out in force. He assumed they were there to round up supporters of Caligula, but they passed more than one unit supporting the Vigiles in controlling gangs of youths fired up with excitement and drink.

Driving a horse and cart through the narrow streets at night was never easy, but Dorio found having to manoeuvre the cart around broken shutters, upturned carts and smashed flagons not only added to the difficulty but it was time consuming. He kept glancing behind to see how Maximus was doing but Warrior had been trained to deal with battle scenes and was neatly avoiding both marauding youths and the debris they left. Only once were they stopped and that was by an army blockade. Who they were looking for Dorio had no idea, but thankfully a small family unit was of no interest to them so they were waved on.

If the back streets were empty, and if they were wide enough for the cart, Dorio took them. It made the journey longer but safer. Nevertheless, he was relieved when the first few shops of Quirinal Hill came into sight. Crossing the empty market square at speed in case of troublemakers, he arrived at the other side, entered the narrow street, reined in the horse, leapt down from the cart and hammered on the door.

Standing there alone in the dark and empty street, the sheer madness of what he was doing unexpectedly hit home. He took a step back, rubbed his bristled chin and for the first time asked himself what in the name of all the gods was he doing calling on a Jew for help? *A Jew*? He groaned inwardly, wondering what madness had driven him to Abram and Judith's door. What had he been thinking? He hated Jews. How could he have possibly imagined he could impose on a Jew, and one he barely knew, in the middle of the night? This Jew in particular was hardly likely to welcome a Roman with open arms, especially if Sarah had told them he was responsible for Hektor's imprisonment, and certainly not while the Romans were persecuting his relatives in Palestine.

A light flickered on the wet cobbles. He raised his head. A candle flared in one of the upstairs rooms and he realised it was too late to walk away now anyway. Besides, where would he go? He waited uneasily, listening to the pattering of footsteps down the wooden stairs. A moment later the door edged open and Abram, a striped shawl over his nightgown, a candle dangerously close to his long grey beard, peered apprehensively through the crack.

'Dorio Suranus?' The door opened wider, his puzzled gaze wandering over Dorio's shoulder to the drenched and weary woman clutching her baby and the small boy in the cart, to the wet and scared Maximus, straddled on the back of an enormous horse.

'I'm sorry to land on you like this Abram but we ...' Dorio swung his hand towards Aurelia and the boys. 'We ...' he guessed his expression must have been showing the desperation of his situation because Abram didn't hesitate but beckoned them inside with open arms.

'Come in, come in, all of you.'

'This is Vivius's family. We had nowhere else to go and ... and my sister delivered her baby in the cart on our way here ...'

There was a cry of alarm from Abram's wife, Judith, who must have been listening in the background. Heedlessly pushing her husband to one side she hurried over to the cart in her bare feet, her hands in the air. 'You delivered your baby in the cart? Oh you poor dear, look at you. You're soaking wet. Come in!

Come in! And boys, come in, come in.'

With Judith's help, Aurelia alighted awkwardly from the cart clinging on to her daughter. Her hostess muttering, 'My poor dear, delivering a baby in a cart, and in this weather? Oh my poor girl!' as she led her into the house.

Sarah materialized in the doorway. By the light of the solitary candle Dorio saw the shawl only partially covered her nightclothes, her hair was tousled and she was shivering, but to him she couldn't have looked more beautiful. Her eyelashes flickered towards him, embarrassed that he should catch her like this. But then, giving him a brief smile, she gave her full attention to Maximus and Rufus.

Stepping into the wet street in her bare feet she reached out her hand to Rufus in the cart. 'Come on, jump down. I bet you boys are cold and hungry after your adventure.' Her voice was calming, reassuring and Dorio was grateful for that. Rufus clung to her as he jumped down from the cart. She was about to help Maximus down when the boy swung his leg over Warrior's back and jumped down of his own accord. He threw her the type of smug expression that reminded Dorio of Vivius.

Unperturbed, Sarah gestured to the open door. 'Come inside and warm yourselves. You can tell me all about your adventure over milk and biscuits.'

As soon as his charges were inside, Dorio turned apologetically to his host. 'Abram, I'm so embarrassed about arriving on your doorstep like this but I … I … needed a safe place to go and …'

Abram waved the apology away. 'You are welcome here, Dorio. Please accept our hospitality for as long as you need it. But before you tell me what's happened, we should get the horses dried off and stabled and the cart off the road.'

Dorio wiped the rain off his face. 'Of course. Yes of course.' He'd forgotten about his transport. The last thing he wanted was to draw attention to himself by having the Vigiles knocking on Abram's door the following morning charging him with having a cart on the narrow streets of Rome through the day. Although, no doubt the Vigiles would have more important matters to deal with than one small cart breaking the traffic laws, he reasoned.

He watched Abram pulling on his sandals before grabbing Warrior's reins and following Abram, the mare and the cart through a narrow arch at the side of the tailor's shop. At the other side he found a small square courtyard with a sizeable stable leaning against the side of the house. It housed one small donkey.

'We'd heard rumours of the emperor's assassination,' Abram said throwing him a heavy cloth to dry Warrior down. 'But tell me, has something happened to Senator Marcianus?' He began unhitching the mare and backing her into the stable next to the donkey.

'It has,' Dorio answered fiercely rubbing the animal's back, and while they worked he proceeded to give the Jew an update of what had taken place.

'How badly is he wounded?' Abram asked shaking feed into the horses' trough.

'No idea.' Dorio threw the towel over the side of the stall. 'I've been too pre-occupied with getting my sister and the children to safety to think of Vivius.'

Abram nodded his understanding. 'So, I would imagine when you visit the prison you'll need to take a physician with you, yes?'

Dorio hesitated as visiting the prison hadn't occurred to him. 'Yes, I suppose I will.'

Abram cast an expert eye around the stable. 'There, that's the animals settled. Now, no more talk until my wife has prepared food for you, and of course for the senator. He'll need to be fed.'

Dorio realised that that hadn't occurred to him either, and it was rather comforting having someone else, albeit a Jew, thinking of his next step. Following his host into his shop and through the neatly stacked bales of material and ready-made clothes, he was led into an inner room which he was surprised to find comfortably furnished and warmed by an iron brazier and flickering oil lamps.

Maximus and Rufus were slumped over the table in their mud splattered tunics, their eyelids drooping, milky rims around their mouths. As Dorio sank down on the couch near the brazier an unexpected wave of exhaustion washed over him.

Sarah smiled at him briefly and pointed to a door under the wooden staircase. 'Judith is settling your sister and the baby in there. It's a store-room but there's a bed there for unexpected guests.'

'Thank you.' Pulling off his helmet he was embarrassed to see that his clothes were already beginning to steam with the heat from the brazier.

Wrapping her arms around Maximus and Rufus, Sarah lightly addressed the boys. 'I've made beds for you two upstairs. Best get in them before your Uncle Dorio pinches them. From the looks of him I don't think he's going to stay awake, do you?'

Dorio gave her a wan smile at her attempt to bring a touch of normality to what must have been a frightening experience for his nephews. He watched them drag themselves up the staircase, and only when they had disappeared out of sight did he allowed his eyelids to droop. His final thought before the welcome blanket of sleep descended was to wonder what he was going to do about Vivius.

* * *

As Dorio splashed his way through the wet streets of Rome he had to force his tired mind to stay focussed. An hour's sleep, that's all Abram had given him. An hour before gently shaking him awake with a dish of soup, warm bread and an idea.

'I was pondering while you were sleeping. Dorio.' He had spoken quietly so as not to wake the sleeping household. 'I wondered if you should visit the senator now, tonight. If there's rioting in the city the Vigiles and the army will be fully occupied keeping order, and presumably the Praetorians and senators will be locked away deciding who's to be Caligula's successor. So, with no real authority in Rome you'll stand a better chance of the prison guards letting you in. And don't forget to take a physician with you. Do you know one?'

Even through his tiredness, Dorio had recognised the soundness of Abram's thinking. All he had to do now, he brooded taking a side street to avoid a gang of youths, was summon up the energy to do it.

It was less than half an hour's brisk walk to where Lucanus the Greek physician lived. But in the dark and rain, and with his clothes still damp, and with thugs roaming the streets and pockets of fighting still going on, it was an unpleasant walk. So, he was relieved when he reached Lucanus's insula (apartment block) without incident. He peered up at the window of the third floor. It was in darkness.

Like many of the inhabitants of Rome who had no claim to wealth and were poorly paid, Lucanus lived in an old and badly built insula with crooked beams, broken shutters and surroundings that were far from elegant. The ground floor was a baker's shop, which meant that no matter how late he went to bed he would be woken early by the heat from the ovens and the clattering of bakers preparing bread.

Making his way up to the third floor by the outside staircase, Dorio reached Lucanus's apartment and pressed his ear to the door. It was quiet inside, so he guessed the physician was either working at the hospital, or sleeping. He knocked. There was silence, followed by a groan, followed by footsteps padding across the floor. The door squeaked as it opened, and Dorio found himself confronting a frowning physician.

'Do you know what time it is?' he grumbled when he saw who it was. His hair was tousled, his face flushed with sleep and his shift crumpled. 'You're not drunk, are you?'

'No, I'm not drunk. Yes, I know what time it is, and if you invite me in out of the rain I'll tell you why I'm here while you get ready.'

Lucanus reluctantly stood back to let him in. 'I'm worn out Dorio. I've had a hard day at the hospital with more deaths and injuries than you can imagine. You've heard about the assassination I suppose?' He glared at Dorio as the previous comment caught up with him. 'What do you mean, "While I get ready"?'

Dorio surveyed the sparsely furnished room and wondered, not for the first time, how anyone could possibly live in one room. All it consisted of was a table, two chairs, a bed, rows of shelves containing neatly piled personal belongings, of which there were few, and a cupboard with a bowl on top. Making his way over to the bed he sank down. It was still warm from where its owner had left it so he stretched out.

'We're going to Mamertine Prison.'

'Why?'

'To see to Vivius. He's wounded.'

'Vivius is in jail?' Lucanus puffed up his cheeks and whistled softly through his puckered lips. 'Tell me what happened while I get ready.'

In an amazingly short time Lucanus had washed, pulled on a clean tunic and donned his cloak, his expression growing more serious with the telling of the tale. When Dorio had finished, Lucanus grabbed his medical bag, and they were about to walk out of the door when Dorio yanked the blanket off his bed.

'Whoa!' Lucanus grabbed it back. 'What are you doing? I only have the one blanket.'

'So, Vivius will buy you two new blankets when he's released. Now let's go.'

Heading directly to the prison wasn't as easy as Dorio had imagined. Pockets of drunken troublemakers were still lurking on the streets, but that's all they were, drunken troublemakers who had probably forgotten why they were roaming the streets in the first place. Knowing from bitter experience where brawling could lead, Dorio took detours wherever possible.

'So, how do we get in?' Lucanus asked as they approached the prison doors.

'Ah! Good question.'

Lucanus looked at him sharply. 'Don't tell me you haven't got a letter of entry?'

Dorio patted his tunic where the clinking of coins revealed he was carrying a considerable amount of money. 'Not a letter no. But I did pick up a few influential names at the palace. I'll try using them, and if that doesn't work the guards might be susceptible to a bribe.'

'A bribe? Where did *you* get money for a bribe?'

'Another good question.'

'Well?'

'I took it out of Aurelia's bags while she was sleeping.'

'You stole it!'

'Not exactly.' Dorio faltered. 'I could hardly wake her after all she's been through. Besides, she would have given it me if she knew it was for Vivius.' The stony silence beside him was indication enough that the physician was not happy with the situation.

At their knock, a guard's tired face appeared at the hatch of the prison door.

'What do you want?' he asked irritably.

Dorio's smile was pleasant but inwardly he smirked with satisfaction. So, Abram's assumptions had been correct. The guards were exhausted after a long hard shift dealing with streams of new prisoners, so if he were to throw around the name of Senator Felix Seneca like a threat, then offer a ridiculous amount of money to be allowed to see a prisoner, that should be a good enough reason for them to open their doors. Besides, having a physician telling them the prisoner was wounded and it would be on their heads if he died, especially as he was a senator, was bound to secure their entry. It did.

With grumbles that visiting shouldn't be allowed at these ungodly hours of the night, a surly guard with a helmet parked precariously over an excessive amount of hair, lit two lanterns and handing one to Dorio, led them down a dimly lit passage. At the end of the passage he stopped at a thick cell door and peered through a narrow slit. Making an unnecessary show of rattling keys he flung the door open and gestured for Dorio and Lucanus to step inside.

'You've a few minutes, that's all,' the guard snarled and a portion of the light disappeared as he slammed the door behind them.

Lifting his lantern Dorio peered through the darkness. 'Vivius?'

The figure sprawled in the corner moved cautiously. 'Who … who is it?'

Moving swiftly across the cell, Lucanus knelt down at his patient's side and opened his medical bag. 'Dorio, bring that light over here so I can see what I'm doing,' he ordered. 'We haven't time to waste.'

Dorio grimaced at the stench of urine and bodily odours but as he moved forward with the lantern he was horrified to see the condition of his brother-in-law. It could have been that the lantern was dim but Vivius's face was ashen, his eyes sunken in his head and there was blood on his head, his chest and his side. Dorio made no comment but watched Lucanus extract a knife from his medical bag. Cutting through Vivius's garment he exposed a gaping and bloody wound in his side. The physician's expression never faltered. 'You've lost a lot of blood,' was his only comment.

'Aurelia? The boys?' Vivius's voice was so faint Dorio could barely hear him.

'They're safe; they're in hiding,' Dorio informed him.

The sigh of relief was long and deep. After a while he said, 'Water! I need ...'

Dorio glanced apprehensively at Lucanus. 'Can we sit him up?'

'Yes, but carefully. I don't want to start that wound bleeding again.'

Vivius gritted his teeth as they took an arm each and hauled him into a sitting position against the wall. Then Dorio handed him the water skin and as he drank Dorio inspected the foul conditions of the cell. 'How in the name of all the gods did you end up in a place like this?'

Vivius wiped away the water dribbling down his chin. 'I ... I've been trying to put the pieces together myself.' He took another drink before adding, 'You know the emperor's dead, don't ... don't you?'

'I know. What happened?'

'It's ... it's a blur ... but I was there. I saw it. I remember Praetorian Officer Cassius Chaerea drawing ... drawing his sword against the emperor but ...' He clenched his teeth as Lucanus bathed his wound and Dorio could see he was in acute pain. It was a while before he was able to continue. 'I intervened. I brought a Germanic Guard down giving Cassius time to do what he had come to do.'

'Can Cassius Chaerea confirm this?'

'He could if he were still alive, but he was ... Aahh!' He clenched his teeth as Lucanus pulled the torn pieces of flesh together. Eventually he said, 'The last thing I ... I remember was falling over his body in the empress's quarters.'

'What were you doing in the empress's quarters?'

'I think ... I was trying to find Cassius or ... someone to send to ...' He grasped Dorio's arm as another memory jogged into place. 'Petronius, the Governor of Syria. I have to get riders to him without delay. Caligula has ordered his suicide ...'

'It's done. I had riders dispatched to him late in the afternoon.'

Vivius looked startled. '*You* had …?'

'Just get on with the story, Vivius. We're running out of time. Tell me about your attack on the Praetorian Guards.'

'How …?'

'Tell me.'

An unexpected coughing fit prevented him from saying anything for a while. When he had spat out the phlegm he said, 'You should have seen what they did to the empress and her child.'

'I did. I was at the palace.'

Vivius blinked rapidly. 'You were … what were you doing at the … palace?'

Dorio handed him the bag of bread, cheese and honey cakes. 'Here, eat this. It's from Abram and Judith. Go on with your story.'

Vivius examined the contents of the bag curiously before saying, 'Aurelia and the boys. Where are they?'

'Rome.'

Vivius narrowed his eyes. Dorio recognised the warning signs. He braced himself.

'Rome?' Although his voice was weak, for a wounded man it still had a considerable strength. 'Are you mad? Rome is the last place you should have brought my family!' He breathed in fiercely as Lucanus pressed on his wound.

'Aurelia and the boys are with Abram and Judith because no one will dream of looking for a wealthy senator's family with a poor Jewish tailor,' Dorio said coldly. 'No one knows the connection except us.'

Dorio ignored the warning frown from Lucanus not to upset his patient. 'Talking of families,' the physician said, 'I should congratulate you senator. Thanks to Dorio, your wife was safely delivered of a daughter.'

Vivius's mood changed unexpectedly to one of sheer bewilderment. 'A … a daughter?' he whispered. 'I have a daughter?'

'You have indeed,' Lucanus said.

'I have a daughter?'

Dorio couldn't recall ever having seen his brother-in-law with an expression of sheer incredulity before. Pleasure momentarily overtook his pain. He lifted the water skin to his lips and drank like a man celebrating the good news with a flagon of wine instead of water. He only stopped drinking to be reassured he'd heard correctly. 'But they're safe, all of them?'

'Yes. They're perfectly safe, all of them,' Lucanus answered.

Dorio waited for the usual barrage of instructions but none came. He gave Vivius time to soak in his good news before saying, 'Vivius, if we're to get you out of here I have to ask you a few questions.'

A dribble of water ran down Vivius's chin and he looked at Dorio warily. 'Go on.' He glowered at Lucanus as the physician wrapped bandages tightly around his midriff. 'That's too tight.'

'It has to be tight senator, trust me. Dorio throw this water down the hole in the corner and refill the bowl from the water skin, will you?'

Rising to his feet Dorio picked up the bloodied water bowl. 'Pontius Pilate is claiming you tried to foil the assassination plot, Vivius.' Now he was accustomed to the darkness Dorio could see a drain in the corner. He poured the water down it. 'I think we can prove his ulterior motive is one of revenge, but there's a Senator Titus Venator who backs his story up. Both of them are accusing you of killing Praetorian Chaerea. So, who is Senator Titus Venator, and why would he have anything against you? I asked Felix but he had no idea.' Retrieving the water skin from Vivius he refilled the bowl.

'Neither do I.' Vivius regarded him suspiciously. 'How come you know all this?'

Ignoring the question, Dorio handed him back the water skin. 'So far we only have one piece of evidence in our favour.

Withdrawing Vivius's dagger from his belt, he held it up. 'This!'

'My dagger. How did you ...?'

'I found it in the back of a Germanic bodyguard in the empress's quarters. Felix Seneca was there and will testify to that. Having been discovered in the back of a *Germanic* Guard proves you weren't fighting the Praetorians. But this one piece of evidence is not enough. We need to disprove these accusations of you being a supporter of Caligula. Could Senator Titus Venator hold a grudge against you, do you think?'

Vivius shook his head. 'I'm bound to have made enemies over the years.'

'Keep still, senator. I need to examine that wound on your head.' Lucanus wiped at the matted blood on his scull with a wet cloth. 'Actually,' he said examining the wound carefully. 'You might have more evidence than you think.'

'I might? How?'

'I wouldn't want to raise your hopes, but the name Praetorian Officer Cassius Chaerea does sound vaguely familiar. I'm fairly sure he was brought into the army hospital late this afternoon. Apparently he was found under the body of a Germanic Guard. He was barely alive when they brought him in.' He tilted his head thoughtfully. 'I think I'll have to put a bandage on that head wound.'

'He's alive?' Seeing the physician was concentrating on Vivius's head wound rather than on this vital piece of information, Dorio was forced to pull his hands away from his patient to get his attention. 'So, we could speak to this Praetorian when we leave here, yes?'

Lucanus shrugged him off. 'Definitely not!' he said focussing his attention back on his patient again. 'Besides, he was unconscious when I left the hospital.' He spread a lint cloth over the gash on Vivius's head and proceeded to wrap a bandage around it.

'But he could regain consciousness, couldn't he?'

'He could, but I can't take you into an army hospital Dorio, if that's what you're thinking. There senator, that's about all I can do for you at the moment, I'm afraid. How are you feeling?'

'Better for knowing my family are safe.'

Reaching into his medical bag Lucanus withdrew a small phial. 'Here, drink this.'

Vivius peered warily inside the phial. 'What is it?'

'You wouldn't be any the wiser if I told you but it'll help ease the pain.'

'No, I don't want ...'

Dorio waved his arm impatiently. 'Drink the damned stuff will you, Vivius! Some of us have had one hell of a night and have got more important things to do, like getting you out of here, than mess about like this.'

Vivius glowered at him, but lifted the phial to his mouth and drank. His face soured as he handed it back to Lucanus. 'I was thinking ...' he began but stopped when Dorio stood up.

'I bet you were, Vivius but if you're about to land me with a list of instructions, forget it,' he snapped.

Vivius slumped back against the wall. 'All I was going to say,' he added wearily, 'is that when I went to see Caligula, I noticed Pontius Pilate engrossed in conversation with a senator who looked vaguely familiar.' He knit his brow. 'I can't remember where I've seen him before but it was the same man who had me arrested on the charges of attacking the Praetorians. I don't know his name but it could have been this Senator Titus Venator.'

'That's helpful. Thank you,' Dorio said stiffly and as he heard the approaching clatter of boots indicating their sour-faced guard was returning added, 'I'll tell Aurelia you'll live then, shall I?'

Vivius gave a wan smile. 'Do that.' But Dorio noticed that as they left the cell he still couldn't bring himself to say, 'Thank you.' That would be too much to ask from a man like Senator Vivius Marcianus.

# Chapter Fourteen

'Absolutely not! The sentries will never let you in,' Lucanus said crossly. As he stepped out of the gloomy prison and into the daylight he screwed up his face.

'They will if they think I'm wounded and you're taking me to hospital.' Dorio glanced up, surprised to see that while they'd been visiting Vivius the rain had stopped and a faint orange glow was struggling to break through the mist to proclaim another day to a silent city. Suspecting it wouldn't stay silent for long, Dorio set off at a brisk pace towards the military hospital. Lucanus followed reluctantly and for a while they walked in silence.

'They'll crucify me if they discover I helped you,' Lucanus complained. 'Do you know the sacrifices I had to make to get this position?'

Dorio pursed his lips, determined not to feel guilty. Yes, he knew the sacrifices Lucanus had made, and the long hours he had worked in the Temple of Aesculapius researching the diseases of the common citizens of Rome, the slaves, the old and those unable to pay. But he had learned all he could from the experienced physicians who had practised medicine on the island on the River Tiber. The work had been long and arduous, and Lucanus had been so poorly paid he barely had enough to eat some days, but Dorio had rarely heard him complain and had secretly admired him for his dedication.

'And do you realise the honour in being asked to continue my research work in the military hospital?'

Dorio snorted through his nose. 'Honour? Last I heard you were grumbling that the Health Service were sending you too many poor patients, and because they got their treatment free you hardly had enough to eat some days. Anyway, what about the patients who pay you with food or clothing, and what about your rich patients who have to pay?'

'My life,' Lucanus pointedly added, 'would be made considerably easier if some of my rich patients didn't take advantage of our friendship, call me out whenever they get drunk, and then forget to pay me, wouldn't it Dorio?'

Dorio glanced at him sideways, wishing he'd never started this line of conversation. 'I will pay you within the month. You have my word on it. Now, about getting into the hospital?'

Lucanus was obviously not going to let the subject rest. 'I don't dare contemplate what my superiors will say if they discover I've abused their trust and smuggled you in to question a patient. A move like this could ruin me.'

'Look,' Dorio said using his most persuasive tone of voice. 'I'm a Decurion in uniform, aren't I? When we reach the military camp we'll tell them … hum. I got us into Mamertine Prison, didn't I? Don't worry, I'll think of something.'

'When, Dorio? When? We're nearly there.'

As they drew closer to the military camp Dorio examined the guards apprehensively. As an active Decurion he had trained here before being sent on active service, so he knew how difficult it would be to gain entry. He scrambled around in his overtired brain for a solution, and was startled to find Abram's advice on entering Mamertine Prison sounded equally as plausible for the military camp.

'My guess is the sentries will be exhausted. They'll have been on duty all night, and they'll be dizzy with the comings and goings of the dead and wounded.' He slowed down to give himself time to explain. 'So, all you have to do is assist a wounded Decurion into the camp. And if anyone asks, you picked me up on the road on the way to work.

'And where's the blood and the wound to confirm that story? And what happens if we're caught questioning this Praetorian Guard?' Lucanus demanded.

'Stop worrying; trust me. I'll make it up as we go along.'

Despite hating making a show of his amputated arm he threw his cloak over his shoulder, developed a limp, twisted his face into an expression he hoped resembled pain, and leaning heavily on Lucanus hobbled towards the gates. He could feel the physician's body tensing, and could smell his sweat of fear as the sentries watched their approach.

'And yet another one.' Lucanus greeted the sentries with over-acted cheerfulness.

Dorio cringed, but fortunately, one of the sentries, recognising the physician, waved them through, his gaze dropping briefly to Dorio's stump.

'See, easy,' Dorio murmured as they hobbled through the gate.

'We haven't reached the hospital yet. Keep limping.'

Dorio found that other than an early morning delivery of food made by a wagon with a squeaking wheel, the barracks were remarkably quiet. He guessed the army was still at the palace or keeping order in Rome. The hospital was a completely different matter. Getting inside was easy enough but he found the corridors buzzing with activity. Exhausted physicians were still working feverishly with the influx of wounded soldiers, Praetorians and senators from the previous day. The only bleary-eyed physician who did look up as they passed was standing over a sink washing surgical instruments, which at first glance Dorio took to be tools of war rather than instruments of healing.

Lucanus led him along a corridor overflowing with makeshift mattresses for the wounded soldiers. At the end of the corridor lay an exhausted physician sprawled out on the floor asleep. Lucanus placed his finger on his lips, although why he should do so Dorio had no idea, as neither of them intended waking him to say they were making an illegal entry.

Lucanus opened a door, and hurried him inside. An officers' ward, Dorio could tell from his own experience in an army hospital. It had six beds regimentally lined up either side of the room with ample space between them.

Lucanus pointed to a bed in the far corner. 'I think that's Praetorian Officer Cassius Chaerea,' he whispered closing the door quietly behind them.

'You *think*? We've gone to all this trouble and you only *think* you have the right man?' Dorio hissed.

Lucanus examined the name on the bed. 'Yes, it's him.'

Dorio examined the inert figure in the bed. Praetorian Officer Cassius Chaerea, Caligula's assassin, was either sleeping or still unconscious. The top of his head was swathed in bandages as was his arm, but his girlish face was so deathly white Dorio wouldn't have been surprised if Lucanus had declared him dead.

'What do you intend to do?' Lucanus whispered. 'Wake him?'

'Well I didn't come all this way just to look at him,' Dorio whispered back. He examined the patient in the next bed. His chest was moving rhythmically up and down, whereas Cassius Chaerea lay perfectly still. Bending down to make sure he wasn't dead, Dorio was relieved to feel the faintest breath on his cheek. Hesitantly he touched the patient's arm. 'Officer Chaerea,' he whispered.

Cassius's eyes flashed open as though he had been resting rather than sleeping. Startled, Dorio jerked back. He cleared his throat. 'My name is Decurion Dorio Suranus,' he said quietly. 'I'm the brother-in-law of Senator Vivius Marcianus. Do you feel up to answering a few questions, sir?'

Cassius licked his white lips. 'No.' His voice was faint.

Dorio tried to muster up the same empathic responses he'd heard the physicians use on their patients. 'I wouldn't be disturbing you if it wasn't important, sir.'

Cassius's pain-lined face examined the two men at his bedside. 'What do you want?'

'Senator Vivius Marcianus is in Mamertine Prison charged with being a supporter of Caligula. They say he attacked you in an attempt to prevent the assassination of Caligula.'

Cassius blinked as if trying to digest the information. 'Who charges him?'

'A Senator Titus Venator and Pontius Pilate, former Governor of Judea. They claim they were present when Caligula was assassinated. My brother-in-law was arrested because of their statements.'

There was a long pause before Cassius whispered, 'Then they're lying.'

Dorio leant forward eagerly to make sure he'd heard correctly. 'So, you dispute their claim?'

Cassius furrowed his brow in concentration. 'I've met Pontius Pilate but I don't recall the other one, the senator.' His eyes glazed over. 'I remember ... the corridor ... Caligula ... drawing my sword and ... a Germanic bodyguard storming towards me.' Cassius tightened his lips giving indication that he was in considerable pain. It was a while before he continued, and Dorio was conscious of Lucanus hovering behind him, glancing nervously towards the door. Cassius ran his tongue around the inside of his mouth. 'Senator Marcianus ... he dived in between me and the Germanic Guard. He cleared the way for me to reach Cal ... Caligula. But ... why anyone would accuse Sen ... Senator Marcianus of ...'

'I think Praetorian Chaerea has had enough,' Lucanus whispered.

Cassius raised the hand without the bandage. 'No, wait!' It took him longer to regain his strength this time and when he did his voice was weaker. 'Senator Marcianus was also in the empress's quarters.' There was a long pause. 'He tried to prevent a Germanic Guard putting his sword through me. After that ... I can't ... I think I lost consciousness.'

'Would you testify to what you've told me?'

'Yes of ... of ...' Cassius winced.

'Dorio! That's enough! That's definitely enough!'

But Dorio had already stepped back. Even he could see that

the soft-faced Praetorian Officer had had enough. 'A speedy recovery to you, sir,' he whispered. 'And thank you.'

Lucanus closed the ward door quietly behind him as they left. 'Now all I have to do is get you out of here,' he said grimly. 'So, don't forget to walk with a limp as you pass the sentries. We do an excellent job of healing in this hospital, but having a patient come in with a limp it would look highly suspicious if he walked out ten minutes later instantly cured.' He indicated they should turn left as they came to the end of the hospital building and head towards the armoury. 'It also occurred to me that if we're to present Officer Chaerea's evidence to a higher authority like the courts, then we need credible witnesses.'

'You're saying we're not credible?'

'No. But the courts are hardly likely to take notice of the senator's Decurion brother-in-law, and a mere physician. Not when accusations come from a higher-class senator and the former Governor of Judea, are they?'

'So, what are you suggesting?'

'Senior officers make regular visits to the hospital to check on their men. If I could get one of them to witness Praetorian Chaerea's story, I might even be able to get a written and signed statement. What do you think?'

Dorio gave the physician a sideways look of admiration as he limped towards the entrance. The idea was so simple he wondered why he hadn't thought of it himself. 'What do I think? I think I made an excellent choice in bringing you along.'

Lucanus gave him a wry grin.

'So, what are you going to do now?' he asked acknowledging the sentry as they left the military camp.

Dorio waited until he was out of sight of the sentries before answering. He came to a standstill in the middle of the market square and flexed his legs. Walking with a limp for any considerable distance wasn't as easy as he'd imagined. He peered up at what remained of the orange glow of sunrise. The best part of it had been replaced by a thin grey cloud which hung threateningly over the city, undecided whether its citizens should take another day of drenching. Undeterred, market traders were setting out their stalls and businessmen and shopkeepers were hurrying to their place of work, doggedly going about the business of clearing up the previous night's debris. Nothing was going to threaten their way of life – neither bad weather nor a dead emperor.

'If you want my opinion, I think you should return to the tailor's shop,' Lucanus ventured. 'You look dreadful. You need food and you need sleep. There's nothing we can do for Vivius, not for the next few hours, and I dare say the senator's family will be anxiously awaiting an update. When I get what we need from Praetorian Chaerea, I'll bring it to the tailor's shop. Didn't you say his premises were off the market place on Quirinal Hill?'

Dorio nodded absently. 'Makes a change trying to get someone out of prison instead of landing them in it,' he admitted soberly.

'I gather you're talking about Hektor?'

'Yes.'

'Then put yourself out of your misery and ask Sarah what's happened to him.'

'I might.' Dorio yawned. All of a sudden, he felt tired, hungry and in need of a bath.

* * *

Dorio figured it was around mid-morning when the last dregs of sleep drifted away. Forcing himself into a state of wakefulness he remembered how refreshing he used to find these short naps when he was on active service. He yawned, stretched his body down the bed, and placing his hand behind his head examined the tiny upstairs bedroom. Sarah's room, he judged from the dresses in the box and the hairbrush on the table in the corner.

He lay for a while listening to the movements below, the hum of voices in the tailor's shop, Rufus's infectious giggle followed by a murmur, and then a door slammed and silence. Dorio smiled to himself. It wasn't hard to guess they'd taken his noisy nephew outside to be amused in case Rufus woke him. Then the baby cried. It sounded like the meow of a hungry kitten, but Dorio found himself warming to the cry. That, he told himself with a burst of pride, was the little girl *he* had brought into the world. *He'd* been the first one to hold that tiny life. She was special, he already felt he had a bond with her. Aurelia must have picked her up to feed her because the hungry cry faded abruptly.

Aurelia! He hadn't been surprised to find her waiting for him when he'd arrived back at the tailor's shop in the early hours of the morning. He hadn't gone into all the details of his night as he knew there'd be time enough for that later, and he hoped he hadn't made too light of Vivius's wounds either, but common sense told him there was no sense in worrying her unnecessarily.

A horse snorted in the courtyard below. Dorio peered out of the partially closed shutters. The mist was low, hovering over the River Tiber the way it always did in the winter months, and there was that infernal smell from the river itself – or ...?

He sat up, dropped his chin to his chest, breathed in deeply then screwed up his face.

'Well done, Dorio, well done,' he muttered. 'You're sleeping in Sarah's bed smelling like a sewer.' Flinging off his blanket he stood up, briefly rinsed the sleep off his face from the tiny bowl of water standing by the hairbrush, then ran his fingers through his curls.

When he arrived downstairs, he found Abram sitting at the kitchen table alone, his hands folded neatly over his striped robe. The Jew regarded him steadily. 'Good day to you, sir. You slept deeply I trust?' He gestured to the seat opposite.

'I did.' Dorio sat down, unexpectedly finding himself hungry from the smell of warm bread, biscuits, sausages and honey cakes spread in front of him. Judith had obviously been up early baking for her unexpected influx of guests. He wondered briefly how Abram had afforded to pay for the feeding of four extra mouths and two extra horses and felt a sudden pang of guilt for harbouring such bitterness towards Jews. 'Where is everyone?' he asked.

'Sarah has taken the boys out to explore the market place, Judith is in the shop, although I doubt we'll be doing any business today, and your sister is feeding the baby in the temporary bedroom we've made for them. Please, eat all you can, Dorio. You must be hungry.'

Dorio broke a chunk off the warm loaf of bread.

Abram slid a rolled parchment across the table to him. 'A Greek physician by the name of Lucanus called an hour ago. I gather this is what you have been waiting for?'

'Ah! It is!' Grabbing the parchment, he rolled it open. 'It's a statement made by Praetorian Officer Cassius Chaerea and signed by his commanding officer,' he explained brushing away the crumbs. He briefly scanned the contents. 'Let me see … Cassius gives an account of the events leading up to the assassination and … he states that Vivius brought down a Germanic bodyguard giving him the space to assassinate the Emperor Caligula.' There was a long pause as Dorio continued to read. 'Then Officer Chaerea goes on to say that when he was in the empress's quarters, Vivius threw his dagger into a Germanic Guard in an attempt to save him. Excellent!' With a sigh of relief, Dorio rolled the parchment up and set it down at the end of the table.

'It is. And tell me, how was the senator when you visited him?'

Dorio dropped his mouth at the corners. 'Not so good.' He reached for a sausage. 'He'd lost a lot of blood so we'll need to get him out of prison as soon as we can.'

'How do you intend to do that?'

'No idea, Abram, but I'll have to think of something.' He

snorted through his nose and without thinking added, 'If it was up to me I'd probably leave him where he is, but I can hardly leave my sister without her husband, and the children without their father can I?' He only realised his tongue had run away with him again when he saw Abram raise a questioning eyebrow. He bit into the sausage and shrugged. 'Vivius and I irritate each other,' he admitted by way of explanation. 'I tolerate him because of Aurelia, and he does the same to me.'

'And yet you go to all this trouble for him?'

'As I said, not for him, for my sister and my nephews – and my niece,' he added.

'Hmm. Interesting.' Abram leant his elbows on the table. 'So, I gather you have two pieces of evidence to clear the senator's name. Firstly, you have the signed testimony of Cassius Chaerea, and secondly the testimony of Senator Felix Seneca, who witnessed Vivius's dagger in the back of a *Germanic* Guard. Proof of where the senator's loyalties lie.' He watched Dorio spreading honey liberally over the warm bread. 'Is that enough, do you think?'

'I guess so. What else do I need?'

'What would seal the case,' Abram continued. 'Would be to discredit those false accusations completely.'

'Huh-huh! Good point. But as a mere semi-retired Decurion I can hardly ask an influential and high-class senator of Rome, or a former Governor of Judea as to why they made false accusations against my brother-in-law, can I? I have neither the authority nor the standing in society, and I certainly don't mix in the same elite circles as them.' He paused a beat when he saw Abram's amused expression.

'What?'

'For a man of little standing you didn't seem to have a problem entering a heavily guarded palace, did you?'

'That was different.'

'Or conning your way into the notorious Mamertine prison.'

'I was …'

'Or bluffing your way into the heart of a Roman military camp. Your physician friend told me.'

'I was lucky.'

Abram shook his head. 'No. You were fearless and you used your wits.'

Unused to compliments, Dorio concentrated on helping himself to the wheat biscuits. 'The sooner order is restored to Rome and a new emperor chosen the better chance Vivius stands,' he said by way of changing the subject.

'So, you wait for a new emperor to put the city in order, is that your plan?' Abram didn't wait for an answer but continued, 'The word on the street is that the Senate and Praetorian Guards are still fighting amongst themselves as to who will be Caligula's successor, so it could take a while.' He paused. 'Except that Vivius might not have a while.'

'Meaning he might die of his wounds?'

'Either that or, being a political prisoner, he may be executed without due process of a trial, especially if there's a breakdown in law and order. You may not have time to get your information to the correct authorities, whoever the new authorities are.'

'True,' Dorio murmured. He hadn't thought of that.

Abram stroked his beard in long rhythmic ponderous movements. 'Why would these men make false accusations against Vivius?'

'As far as Governor Pontius Pilate is concerned, that's easy. Revenge. Some years ago, Vivius was given an assignment by the Emperor Tiberius to compile a detailed report on Pilate's dealings with the Jews. His report contained evidence of embezzlement, anti-Semitism, undue harsh treatment of the Jews, and proof that Pontius Pilate was following policies laid down by the commander of the Praetorian Guards at the time, Sejanus; not the Emperor Tiberius's policies. The Emperor Tiberius found Vivius's report damming enough to recall Pilate back to Rome in disgrace.'

Abram regarded him with interest. 'Ah! Revenge. The old enemy. What about Senator Titus Venator?'

Dorio concentrated on making a pyramid of crumbs on his plate. 'All I know about him is his name. Not even Felix knows who he is and Vivius can't remember having met him so ...'

He trailed off as the door to the storeroom opened and his sister, looking surprisingly slim in her grey dress considering she had only given birth to a baby a few hours ago, stood on the threshold biting her lip.

'This er ... Senator Titus Venator,' she began.

'Don't tell me you've heard of him?'

To his astonishment his sister nodded. 'He called at the olive grove when you and Vivius were away. I didn't tell Vivius because he was distracted when he got back from Jerusalem. Besides, it didn't seem important at the time.'

'You've meet him? He called at the villa? What did he want?'

'He asked questions.' Aurelia slid on to the chair at the top of the table. 'I can't remember the whole of our conversation but I do remember him asking about the olive grove, and if Vivius would be back in time for some meeting with a Praetorian Officer ...' she rolled her gaze towards the ceiling.

'Was it Pretorian Officer Cassius Chaerea?'

'It could have been. I can't remember. He asked where they were holding the meeting.'

'What meeting? What did you tell him?'

'What did I tell him?' she repeated with a cynical smile. 'What do you think, Dorio? Nothing, because I know nothing. I never know what's going on because no one tells me anything.' She glared pointedly at him. 'Besides, there was something about him I didn't like.'

'What?'

'I'm not sure. He made me ... uneasy.'

'So,' Abram folded his long fingers together as if in prayer.

'Senator Titus Venator was showing an interest in Senator Marcianus before the assassination. If he was asking about a meeting with Praetorian Officer Chaerea, then he may have suspected that Vivius was involved in the planning of Caligula's assassination?' As he pondered aloud he tapped his thumbs together. 'Would he have been?'

'I doubt it. Not his style.' He helped himself to another wheat biscuit. Not that he was hungry, his appetite had been satisfied but he found nibbling usually helped him when he was pondering. This time, however, he sat with a blank mind until the biscuit was finished. 'Why? What are you thinking, Abram?'

'I'm thinking ...' Abram said deliberately. 'I'm thinking that we can discredit Pontius Pilate easily enough by showing his accusation up as being one act of revenge. But Senator Titus Venator's motives?' Abram tapped his lower lip with his forefinger. 'If we can discover his motives then we will have a powerfully strong case to put before the court.'

Dorio didn't miss the word 'we', and was surprised how reassured he felt by that. He slumped back in his chair. 'In theory that sounds fine, but an investigation will take time and time is not on our side. Besides, how can I find out who he is when I don't know what he looks like, where he lives or what he does?'

Aurelia touched his arm. 'But I do. I know what he looks like.'

'So? Where does that get us?' Ignoring her, Dorio addressed Abram. 'I think my only option is to take what proof I have to Senator Felix Seneca. He'll know what to do.' He pushed the parchment into his tunic. 'I'll go to the Senate House this morning. If Felix is anything like Vivius, wounded or not, that's where he'll be. He won't want to miss out on the debate for a new emperor.'

Aurelia squeezed his arm. 'I'm coming with you.'

'Don't be ridiculous. Besides, why would you?'

'Because if Felix is badly wounded and hasn't made it to the Senate House he'll be at home. You have no idea where he lives.

I do, and unlike you Dorio, I have mixed in the right circles. If Felix sends us to a magistrate I shall probably know him and be able to get prompt action.'

'And have you forgotten you gave birth to a baby only hours ago?'

'I'll take her with me.'

'What! Walk all the way to ... You can't possibly ...' With a sigh he dropped his head in his hand. Having had a lifetime of seeing that expression on his sister's face, he knew arguing was useless.

'I shall get ready,' Aurelia rose from her chair. 'Perhaps Sarah will come with me, that is if ...' she paused, uncertain.

'Yes, yes, my dear lady. Leave your boys with us.' An impish smile passed his lips. 'I might even teach them how to sew like tailors.'

She touched his shoulder. 'Thank you Abram.'

There was silence between the two men after she had closed the storeroom door behind her, but after talking for so long, Dorio found it to be a comfortable silence. That was what prompted him to ask a question that had bothered him since his return from Jerusalem. He cleared his throat. 'I'm glad of this opportunity to speak to you Abram. I wanted to er ... apologise.'

The Jew regarded him curiously. 'What for?'

'It was my fault ... Hektor and Iola ...' he licked his lips.

'Ah! Yes. Sarah told me. But it ended satisfactorily, didn't it?'

Dorio looked at him, puzzled. 'What do you mean?'

'When Hektor was released.'

'Released?'

'I gather Senator Marcianus spoke to the authorities before he left Jerusalem.'

Dorio's words were measured. 'Vivius ... did ... What?'

Sensing he was on dangerous ground, Abram hesitated before speaking. 'I may be mistaken, but I was led to understand the senator got Hektor released on the grounds that he wasn't preaching on what the Nazarene taught, simply telling the story of how he met him. A technicality in the law perhaps, but enough to get him released. You weren't aware of this?'

Dorio's lips were pressed too tightly together to answer.

# Chapter Fifteen

The Forum was Dorio's favourite location, primarily because it was the beating heart of the city, always bustling with life, public, political, social and legal. The Senate House was the heart's political centre, and while the assembly of senators would gather inside to debate new legislations, public monies and other matters of state, Dorio would be outside doing business with horse traders under the grandeur of the lofty temples or the splendour of the triumphal arches, or meeting friends around the cooling fountains, drinking in the inns or enjoying a social gathering at the nearby baths. That was why, when he arrived at the Forum with Aurelia, Sarah and the baby, he was relieved to see the debris from the previous night had been cleared away. He would hate to have seen a blemish on his favourite haunt.

'Are you tired?' he asked. Aurelia was leaning heavily on his arm.

'That's the fourth time you've asked, Dorio. Stop fussing,' she snapped. There was silence at his side before she said, 'Sorry,' and then soberly added, 'We will get him out, won't we, Dodo?'

He grinned at her childhood name for him. 'Of course,' he said injecting a note of confidence that he was far from feeling. 'All we have to do is find Felix.' The parchment cracked as he patted his tunic. 'I reckon we've enough proof here to have Vivius released within hours.'

'You think so?'

'Of course. Trust me.'

She gave him a withering look before giving a cry of dismay and pointing to the Senate House rising high into the skyline. 'Oh no! Look at all the people. We'll never get to Felix through that crowd.'

Dorio examined the massive gathering apprehensively before jerking his head towards the fountain which stood behind the crowds. 'We'll wait over there. It's further from the Senate steps but it'll be safer for you, Sarah and the baby.'

Realising this could be a long wait, he found a space on the fountain steps for them while he wandered around the perimeter of the crowd straining his ears for the latest news. Not that he had any preference as to who the next emperor would be, one was as bad as the other as far as he was concerned. In fact, Dorio reckoned he could name over a dozen generals in the army who would make better Caesars than the last two. But he found it interesting listening to anxious businessmen discussing whether the next emperor was likely to raise taxes, and lingering near stall holders and shoppers deliberating whether the next emperor would affect business. Even men less enthusiastic on the outcome, like himself, didn't want to miss out on this momentous occasion, but waited eagerly for the huge double doors of the Senate House to burst open and the senators to emerge for their midday break.

Dorio found himself envying not only their break but their forthcoming visit to the public baths, and wished he'd had time for a warm soak himself. He was in no doubt that his actions over the last twenty-four hours had left him with an unpleasant mixture of smells, although no one had been rude enough to say so.

He surveyed the heavy grey clouds apprehensively as he made his way back to the women. 'Shouldn't be long now. As soon as I spot Felix I'll bring him over here. He'll know what to do with Chaerea's statement.'

His lower lip jutted out. And then there'll be more running around, he brooded with an unexpected surge of resentment. Why, in the name of all that was holy, should he put himself out for a brother-in-law who hadn't even the decency to let him know that Hektor was safe? Vivius knew how upset he had been over the incident. Why didn't he say he had cleared the Greek of all charges before leaving Jerusalem? It would have saved months of worry. Dorio's lower lip hardened with anger over the notion that Vivius had taken it upon himself to act as a god to teach him a lesson.

'What's wrong?' Aurelia asked, as if wondering at his angry expression, but he was saved from having to give an explanation by the heavy double doors of the Senate House swinging open and an assembly of weary looking senators emerging, their pristine togas not looking quite so pristine after a night of intensive discussions.

The citizens of Rome surged forward.

'Have you reached a decision yet?'

'How close are you to an agreement?'

'Who killed Caligula?'

'Has anyone been arrested for his death?'

'Is Claudius our next emperor?'

'Is it true the Praetorians have Claudius locked away for safety?'

Dorio listened to the barrage of questions being hurled in the senators' direction, but it was obvious from their sombre expressions that they still weren't in agreement. He glanced anxiously at his sister. Being on the steps of the fountain, she had a good view of the Senate doors, nevertheless she was on her toes scrutinizing each senator as he made his way down the steps and into the Forum. Shaking his head at Sarah to indicate the futility of finding Felix among the hundreds of white togas edged with purple, he was about to suggest he should leave them and move forward when a chance encounter took place. It could have been coincidence; such things do happen, he reasoned later. It could have been the luck of the gods, an omen. He knew the majority of Romans swore by the divine intervention of the gods. They firmly believed unexplainable events occurred when you'd reached the end of your own human recourses, but Dorio had never been one to ponder deeply on such matters, nor to experience them. However, when this chance encounter took place his initial response was one of pure astonishment.

'That's him!' Aurelia's arm shot out in the direction of the Senate steps.

'Felix? Where?'

'No, not Felix. Senator Titus Venator,' she said excitedly. 'See? He's standing halfway down the steps. The tall, thin one, dark hair, sniffing as if he has a cold.'

Dorio observed the moving figures. It was difficult to pick out any one particular senator, they all looked alike. But eventually his eye fell on the man of Aurelia's description. He was standing on the Senate steps, surveying the citizens of Rome as if he was looking for someone.

'You're sure?'

'Positive.'

Dorio rubbed the bristles on his chin, although wishing he'd had time for a shave was the last thing on his mind. On the spur of the moment he pulled Cassius Chaerea's signed statement out of his tunic and handed it to his sister. 'If you don't see Felix in the next few minutes I want you and Sarah to go to his house with these.'

'Why?' She examined his face anxiously. 'What are you going to do?'

'Follow Titus Venator. This is too good an opportunity to miss.' He looked pleadingly at Sarah. 'I'm sorry to land this on you Sarah but ...?'

Her smile was one of encouragement. 'Go, Dorio. Do what you have to do.'

Aurelia grabbed his arm. 'No, Dorio. No! It's too dangerous. You can't ...'

He grinned down at her. 'Now who's fussing?' Patting his sister's hand, he moved quickly through the crowd towards Senator Titus Venator.

* * *

Vivius dragged his eyes open. They felt heavy, as though the lids were weighed down with rocks, but once open they fell on the pale grey light filtering through the narrow slit high in the wall. So, it was daytime. Although what time of day he couldn't say. He lay perfectly still, taking small pleasure in the fact that for the moment he was reasonably comfortable. The stabbing pain around his lungs had eased and if it hadn't been for that foul potion Lucanus had made him drink he'd be feeling reasonably normal.

'Ease the pain,' the physician had assured him. Vivius gave a grunt of annoyance. It might have eased the pain but it had left him with a serious bout of diarrhoea. Damned physician! He should have been around when his patient had been forced to crawl over to the drain in the corner to relieve himself. The pain had been excruciating then, the stench overwhelming. Strange, he mused. He barely noticed the smell now.

He allowed his mind to drift.

So, he had a daughter, eh? A little girl, and she and his family were safe, that's what Dorio had said. Vivius smiled to himself as he tried to imagine his daughter. But then his sense of pleasure dimmed as the image of another little girl emerged, one whose small body had been cruelly smashed against a wall. He squeezed his eyes shut, fighting against his imagination showing pictures of that happening to his own daughter if his family were caught. When he had control of this thoughts again he deliberately moved them elsewhere.

So, Caligula had been assassinated, but had the Senate agreed to support the Praetorian Guards in their push to make Claudius emperor? He could easily imagine the fraught tempers, the shouting and arguments in the assembly of senators. There'd be the covert comments, the small cliques, even bribes to … And that's where he should be, in the Senate, adding his weight to the opinions, not lying here a victim of the whole sorry process. He closed his mind to that line of reflection as well.

Opening his eyes he moved for the first time, cautiously pulling his blanket up to his chin. The problem with lying still, he decided, was he was apt to feel the cold. He wouldn't last long in this dampness and in his condition unless someone acted promptly to get him out. Even now he had a sense that it wouldn't be long before delirium set in. Breathing in fiercely he berated himself for not instructing Dorio to inform Felix where he was. But he found to his cost that breathing in fiercely only had the effect of setting off the pain around his lungs again.

So, he contemplated as the pain eased, unless Felix was alive and knew what was going on, his survival looked like it would depend on Dorio.

Dorio! He dropped his hand over his eyes in despair. Surely that drunken layabout wasn't the only one trying to get him out? If that was true he was likely to be in here for the duration. Even if Dorio was sober he wouldn't have the first idea who to contact, and in the present political climate he could easily contact the wrong people. No doubt about it, the Decurion was well out of his depth when it came to politics; which was probably why he was at this moment in the nearest inn getting drunk. Useless! Absolutely useless! The only positive thing that Decurion had ever done in his life was ... was ...

*'Dorio delivered your wife of a daughter during their escape to the city.'*

As Lucanus's voice drifted through his recollections he found it draining his mounting frustrations like a plug being pulled out of a water bottle. He lay perfectly still as another scenario unfolded in his head. Dorio escaping with Aurelia and the boys from the olive grove in the dark – the long drive to safety – being forced to deliver a baby en route and ...

As Dorio's role in the safe delivery of his family took on a life of its own, Vivius found guilt winding its way in as he recalled how sharply he had criticised his brother-in-law for bringing Aurelia and the boys to Rome. Whereas now, having had time to think about it, Rome was probably the safest place to be. No one would think of looking for them in the centre of the city, and certainly not in the shop of a poor Jewish tailor.

A fly buzzed with an annoying persistence around his nose.

*His dagger?* Vivius stirred uneasily as he remembered Dorio waving his dagger in front of him. How in the name of Jupiter had Dorio retrieved his dagger? Pulling a crusty piece of skin off his lip with his teeth, Vivius pondered over their earlier conversation. Dorio had insinuated he'd got into the palace, hadn't he? *How in the name of Jupiter had Dorio got into the palace?* Vivius found his mind was beginning to spin with questions to which he had no answers.

Shuffling himself into a position where he could rest on one elbow, he removed the cloth covering the food. Food! Dorio had had the foresight to bring him food – and a blanket? At least he'd done something right, he thought and as he began eating the bread, cheese and honey cakes he contemplated uneasily what was going to happen next.

\* \* \*

As Dorio pushed his way through the crowds around the steps of the Senate House he noticed Senator Titus Venator was beginning to descend. Using the huddles of sightseers as shields, he hung back until the senator had reached street level and was elbowing his way through the demanding citizens wanting answers from fraught senators. Once clear of them he strode purposefully north of Capitoline Hill, and in the general direction of the river. Dorio followed at a distance.

Reasoning told him the senator could be going anywhere; an inn for a meal, the baths, home for a sleep, but ignoring reason, he continued listening to his gut feeling which argued that following Senator Titus Venator might at least give some indication of where he lived, who he was or even his contacts.

So he continued trailing him through the maze of narrow streets ignoring the question of what he intended to do when Venator reached his destination. That, he decided, was a problem he would face when it arrived.

The main problem, which he found swirled continually around his head like an eddy, was whether he'd been wise in leaving Aurelia, Sarah and the baby outside the Senate in an unpredictable crowd, and then having the nerve to suggest they walk all the way to the home of Felix Seneca. He didn't need to be told that the answer to that was definitely 'no'. Not one of his better suggestions given that his sister had barely recovered from childbirth.

Accepting the fact that there was nothing he could do about that now, he focussed his attention on Senator Titus Venator. He realised they were now away from the shops, baths and markets and were approaching Campus Martius, near where the river curved. As there were fewer people around, Dorio lengthened the distance between them so he wouldn't be spotted and followed him through a maze of narrow alleys. He was about to follow him around a corner when he saw Venator had stopped by a row of dilapidated houses with tall walls covered in greenery. Brushing aside a trail of overgrown ivy, he disappeared through an archway.

Dorio marched smartly up to the archway and squinted up at the building. It was small, and far from being the type of elegant villa associated with a wealthy senator. He paused opposite the archway, pondering on his next move. If Venator was simply visiting a lady he wouldn't like to barge in and find the man in a compromising position, he mused. But on the other hand, Venator might have fallen on hard times and could actually live here.

A fat woman with a huge bosom and down at the heel sandals shuffled by giving him a sideways glance. Not wanting to arouse suspicion, he sauntered casually over to the archway and leant against the wall as though he was waiting for someone. She continued shuffling down the street but didn't look back. He was pleased he'd moved because from this position he could hear raised voices inside the house, although he couldn't actually hear what was being said.

Taking a quick look up and down the lane, he saw the woman had disappeared. Probably into one of the houses, he guessed, because other than a handful of children playing with a puppy, the lane was quiet. He debated whether he dare slip into the courtyard to see who Venator was arguing with. He didn't debate for long. Lifting the trail of ivy to one side he stepped inside. The courtyard was small, overgrown, and the partially open door gave the impression that one good push would have it off its hinges, but he could hear the voices clearly now.

'By all the gods Venator, Caligula's only been dead twenty-four hours. Give me a chance to think.' There was a long pause. 'If Claudius is voted in as Caesar, it won't do any harm to remind him of my previous record. That's your job. I was nothing if not tough on those Jews.'

'You're saying you want re-instating as Governor of Judea?'

*Pilate*? Dorio edged up to the partly closed shutters and peered through the crack. All he could make out was the back of a man. He was kicking the ash in the grate of an empty brazier as if to show his disgust at the lack of heat. There was an elderly bald-headed senator seated with his back to the window, but Dorio was unable to see his face, and the only other person in the room was Senator Titus Venator. He was pacing the floor, head down, hands behind his back. Occasionally Dorio lost sight of him through the limited crack in the shutter.

'Not particularly, but can you see any other way through this? If there's not going to be the blood bath we'd hoped for, we need someone in Judea who knows what they're doing. But I insist we get rid of Senator Marcianus first. I can't risk a repercussion of what happened last time. Can you do that?'

It was the bald-headed senator who answered. 'I don't see why not. I have the contacts. But we'll need to act swiftly, before order is fully restored and someone realises he's in Mamertine Prison.' He addressed the man still nudging the ashes in the brazier as if by some miracle he could set a blaze going again. 'Frankly, I'm astonished you want to return to Judea, Pilate, I understood you'd had enough of that place.'

The figure by the fire turned and Dorio breathed in sharply. No doubt about it, it was Pontius Pilate, former Governor of Judea.

'I had, and I don't relish the idea of returning to the area where I'm known as the Roman who crucified that Jew.'

'You must have crucified hundreds of Jews.'

'I did, but not one that rose from the dead again.'

'Ach! You don't believe that tale, do you?'

'He was seen. If it was only by one or two I could have discounted the story. Imaginative people these Jews, but to be seen by two or three hundred is another matter. Actually ...' There was a slight hesitation. 'Actually, I was riding through the city and I'm sure I ... ' Pilate rubbed his arms as if he was cold. 'It was ... him. I'm sure of it.'

'You saw him?'

Pilate's footsteps clattered across the wooden floor and there was a creak as though he had sat down on a chair or a sofa, but Dorio's crack in the shutters didn't cover that part of the room.

'I ... I did. I was convinced time would see the rumours dwindle, but no. His followers have been spreading across the Roman Empire like the plague.' Pilate's voice dropped. 'I still have nightmares about him, this Nazarene.' There was a clatter as if he'd kicked something. 'Damn it! All we needed was a few weeks, just long enough for Caligula to install his statues in Jerusalem's temple. A move like that would have caused a blood bath; that's all we needed to rid the world of this Jewish God and its Messiah once and for all, and force those damned Jews to recognise the authority of Rome. Caligula's death was most untimely.'

Titus Venator cut across the crack in the shutters momentarily blocking out Dorio's line of sight. 'No point dwelling on it. Caligula's dead. But I agree. He was the only one who saw a way of breaking through this one-God belief system that they've clung on to for hundreds of years. All those rules that *must* be obeyed; it's crippling, degrading, uncivilized. It's this God of theirs that stops them from acknowledging Rome as their authority.'

'To get back to the point in hand,' the bald-headed senator interrupted. 'If the Senate do vote for Claudius and we're able to persuade him to return you to Judea as governor, are you sure his policies will allow you the freedom to continue the work you were doing when you were governor?'

'No doubt about it. Claudius is friendly enough with King Agrippa, and the Jewish King is as anxious to annihilate this Messiah cult as we are. We may have a problem getting rid of Marullus, the present Governor of Judea, but I believe that's our only alternative now we no longer have Caligula.'

The bald-headed senator stretched his arm across the back of the couch. 'Obviously there are the finer details to work through but I see no reason why we can't continue with our initial plan. And if you're serious about being re-instated as Governor of Judea, Pilate, we need to work out a strategy. Our people are still in place so picking up the businesses of the Jews we get rid of shouldn't cause too many difficulties.' The crack in the shutters was unexpectedly blocked by the bald-headed senator standing up. 'Failing to get you re-instated though means we need to keep a close eye on likely candidates. Make sure we can er ... use them. Give that matter your consideration, eh gentlemen? We can't afford to get that wrong.' He gave a short laugh. 'Now, I must go. The Senate reconvenes in an hour and I need time at the baths. Venator, I will see you back at the Senate?'

'You will indeed.'

Dorio was about to dart across the courtyard to avoid the departing senator when he saw the man was making his exit through another door, so he stayed where he was.

There was silence after the bald-headed senator had left the room. Silence that is, except for Venator sniffing. 'Do you think he'll do it?'

'Get rid of Senator Marcianus? Absolutely. He's a useful contact to have. He lost as much as we did from Marcianus's report. In fact, it was a miracle he was never arrested. If he can persuade Claudius to re-instate me in Judea ...'

Dorio breathed in sharply as the point of a dagger dug into his neck. He raised his arm, his brain scrambling around for some reason for being here. Giving a short but shaky laugh he said, 'Oh dear. I think I've got the wrong house. My apologies.' He tried to make it sound as though he had innocently made a mistake, and was about to chance his luck in turning to leave when his captor added pressure with the dagger.

'Remove your weapon slowly.' The voice meant business.

Dorio cursed under his breath but nevertheless his sword clattered on to the cobbles.

'Inside.'

A sharp prod in the back propelled him towards the door. He glanced surreptitiously behind. It was the bald-headed senator who was picking up his sword. Dorio swore silently over his stupidity at not watching where the man had gone after leaving his companions. The two men looked up sharply as he stepped through the doorway.

'I discovered him loitering in the courtyard listening.'

Dorio gave his short laugh again, but even he recognised how unconvincing it sounded this time. 'As I was saying, I think I've come to the wrong ...' his voice trailed off.

Titus Venator was standing in front of a cold brazier. His dark black eyes glinted a warning. 'Listening you say? Then he better come inside.'

A further prod forced Dorio into the centre of a dingy room with half-closed shutters, and a worn wooden floor partially covered by a threadbare rug. Two shabby couches faced each other with a low heavily knotted table between them. Dusty icons of Roman gods filled a shelf the length of one wall. Dorio's impression, as far as he could make one with the point of a dagger in his neck, was that Pontius Pilate, in his high-quality clothing and heavy gold rings looked strangely out of place in these surroundings.

He shuffled uncomfortably as the former Governor of Judea scrutinized him through lowered lids. He recognised it. It was a look that was meant to unnerve. Vivius had used it on him many times and he hated it. Disarm your opponent, make him feel awkward, guilty, out of his depth. Lifting his head, he did his best to stare unwaveringly back.

'Who are you and what do you want?' Pilate asked with deliberate smoothness.

Dorio was acutely conscious of the fact that he was dealing with intelligent men, men more used to battling with words than the sword. Deciding he had passed the point of acting the naive Decurion who had entered the wrong house, he decided to opt for the truth, see where that would get him.

'My name is Decurion Dorio Suranus.' He addressed Venator first. 'I followed you from the Senate House. I've come to find out why you're making false accusations against my brother-in-law, Senator Vivius Marcianus.'

Titus Venator gave a cold smile. 'Ah! So that's who you are?' He wiped the edge of his nose with his forefinger. 'False accusations against your brother-in-law? I don't think so. Decurion. We were there, we saw Caligula's assassination. Did you?' He gestured to the couch opposite Pilate. 'Please take a seat.'

That was another tactic, Dorio realised. Seat your opponent lower than yourself, keep them at a disadvantage. 'Thank you, but I would prefer to stand.'

'Refreshments?'

'With a dagger at my neck? I don't think so, do you?'

Venator jerked his head at the bald-headed senator.

'Then I shall leave you to er ... deal with this matter gentlemen?' His captor's voice rose at the end making it a question rather than a statement. Dorio breathed a sigh of relief as the dagger was withdrawn from his neck. Without waiting for a reply, the senator gave a courteous nod to his colleagues before sliding silently out of the room. Dorio watched him rest his captured sword against the furthest wall.

'Then I hope you don't mind if I sit down,' Venator sank down on the couch with a sigh. 'This cold weather affects an old knee injury. You were saying, Decurion?'

Dorio rubbed his neck where the dagger had been prodding. 'I was saying ...' He paused, distracted by all the pleasantries. 'No, you were saying you saw the assassination.'

'We did.' Pilate threw his arm casually over the back of the couch. 'And we reported what we had seen to the Praetorian Guards. No one has come forward to dispute our allegations because,' his thin lips twitched. 'Because sadly, there's no one left alive to do so.'

Dorio took up a position between the two drab couches – it was slightly closer to his sword. 'That's not exactly correct.'

Pilate blinked twice, rapidly. 'Oh?'

Dorio squared his shoulders. 'There is another witness. Caligula's assassin, Praetorian Officer Cassius Chaerea.'

Pilate visibly relaxed and gave a half laugh. 'He's dead. Decurion.'

'Not as dead as you might imagine.'

The smirk on Pilate's face wavered. 'Who told you that?'

Deciding a slight exaggeration might be justified in the circumstances, Dorio answered, 'Early this morning Praetorian Officer Cassius Chaerea was sitting up in a hospital bed telling me, his physician and his commanding officer a completely different story from the one you're telling me.' He didn't miss the fleeting look that passed between the two men. Dropping his gaze, Pilate spread his hand and casually examined the heavy gold rings adorning his fingers.

'And further proof of false accusations against my brother-in-law is in your motives, sir,' Dorio inclined his head towards Pilate.

Pilate raised his head sharply. 'My motives?'

'Vivius Marcianus's report was one of the reasons you were recalled back to Rome nearly ten years ago. I would imagine that losing your position as Governor of Judea, your reputation, your standing in society, *and* your illegal money-making schemes would leave you with a strong motive for retaliation.' Dorio tried to keep his tone respectful. The last thing he wanted to do was force physical aggression. Their four hands against his one didn't strike him as particularly good odds. 'I dare say when the authorities are informed of your motives they will take a very different view of your allegations. Revenge, I think it's called.'

The silence that followed was heavy. Pilate continued examining his rings. Venator rose to his feet. Dorio inched closer to his sword.

'And er ... you Senator Venator. I assume you too lost financially when Senator Marcianus compiled his report?'

Venator didn't answer but making his way over to the clay lamps on the wall began lighting them. The wick on one of them flickered unhappily. He watched it struggling to come to life but only when it had flared and a yellowy glow had spread across the walls did he answer him. 'You think this is all about money, Decurion?'

'Isn't it?' Dorio wondered if he could keep the conversation going long enough for him to reach his sword.

'Not totally. It's also about culture and religion. Why shouldn't the Jews be free to worship Caligula as their god, or whoever they want for that matter? If the system of many gods works for the Romans, it'll work for the Jews.'

'From what I've seen, the Jews seem perfectly happy with their own God and their own culture. Why mess with it?'

Being in the shadows, Dorio couldn't see Venator's expression but he heard the scorn in his voice. 'And how would you know, Decurion? How many trips have you made to Palestine? Two, three, and you think you have all the answers?' Lighting a long taper from one of the wall lights he made his way over to the shelf of gods and lit a candle at the end. The flame flickered, casting a shadow of Venator's hawk-like features across the wall.

Pilate sat forward on the couch. 'Why mess with it, you ask? You call yourself a loyal Roman and you ask a question like that? We are tolerant of other religions as long as Roman authority is recognised, but these ... *Jews* ...' he spat the word out. '... will neither acknowledge our authority, bow to our emperors or our Roman gods while they're fixated on this God of theirs. This religion, and especially this claim of a Messiah, needs to be stamped out before it gets out of hand and poses a real threat to Rome.' He pointedly eyeballed his missing arm. 'You can't have any love for the Jews, Decurion, not after they left you with one arm?' He gave a slow smile when he saw Dorio's surprise. 'I have a good memory. You were Senator Marcianus's excuse for coming to Jerusalem all those years ago.' He glanced pointedly at Venator before relaxing back on the couch and saying, 'You could turn this situation to your advantage you know.'

Dorio felt the prickles standing up on the back of his neck. 'How?'

Pilate pursed his lips as though he was giving the question consideration but Dorio suspected he was intelligent enough to have already worked his proposal through. 'Supposing – just supposing – your brother-in-law were out of the way.' He raised a hand as Dorio opened his mouth to speak. 'Hear me out. Now, who would run that huge olive grove of his? You! His sons have years to go before they're at an age to claim their heritage and until then you could make yourself a fortune.'

A gust of wind flung open the shutters and swirled aggressively through the room. It blew out the candle and brought with it fallen leaves and the first drops of rain from the approaching storm.

'And what makes you think I would betray my brother-in-law?'

'Wouldn't you?' Pilate gave a thin-lipped smile. We suspected Vivius Marcianus of being involved in the assassination plot when we saw him with Praetorian Cassius Chaerea at the baths, so we've had men watching him for some time. Don't you feel humiliated by the way he bails you out of debt and orders you around? I'm sure you can raise up any number of grudges against him.'

Dorio made no comment.

'You could be useful to us.'

Dorio was uneasy at how long it took him to say, 'How?'

'This Jewish cult needs to be wiped out of Rome before it spreads any further.' Pilate tapped his lower lip with his forefinger. 'I would imagine the Nazarene's followers will trust the brother-in-law of Senator Vivius Marcianus, the Roman they helped escape from Jerusalem with their valuable information. With a bit of persuasion, they may even tell you where and who heads up their Meeting Houses.' There was an ominous pause before he pointedly added, 'You will be paid a considerable sum for your efforts, of course. Certainly enough to settle your debts and build up your stables again.'

Dorio licked his lips. All of a sudden his mouth felt dry, not through fear for himself, he realised with surprise, but fear for a kindly old Jew who had taken in him *and* his family regardless of cost or danger to himself. The Jew who had willingly shared his wisdom and insights to get an innocent Roman out of jail; a Jew who was a follower of this Nazarene. It was quickly followed by the image of a beautiful and spirited Jewess who was not afraid to talk about her faith in this Nazarene, and even when she was forced to leave her home and friends was willing to forgive the man who brought this upon her. These then were the followers of this Jesus of Nazareth, the Jew Pilate had crucified.

Tucking his thumb into his belt, Dorio pursed his lips and made a pretence of thinking about their offer. Striding purposefully across the room towards the window he stopped, then strode back again, ending up as close to his sword as he dared. He gave a lopsided grin. 'It's tempting. But I shall need to think about this.'

There was a bang as Titus Venator slammed the wooden shutter against the elements. The floor around the window was wet from the onset of rain and one of the clay lamps on the wall had blown out. He moved away from the window, his sandals leaving wet imprints across the floor.

Casually picking up his sword, but deliberately keeping the blade lowered, Dorio backed towards the door. Neither Pontius Pilate nor Titus Venator spoke, but they didn't make any attempt to stop him either. They simply watched him open the door, it shuddered on the floor. He stepped backwards into the courtyard, quickly closing the door behind him. Pushing aside the wet and overgrown ivy he stepped into the lane.

He grimaced as he was greeted by a squally wind from the north. It whipped at his cloak, blasting his face with icy sheets of rain and drenching him unmercifully. As he marched swiftly away from the house he turned frequently to make sure he hadn't been followed. At first, he couldn't believe his good luck when he saw that the only people around were citizens scurrying home to avoid the storm. He was beginning to think he had escaped without repercussions when he was alarmed to see three armed Middle-Eastern men, thugs rather than servants from the looks of them, had emerged out of nowhere and were keeping pace with him, If they were after him, the odds were not good; he decided picking up his pace. He doubted whether they'd start a fight, not while there were people around, but as the rain grew heavier, the streets began emptying and he grew uneasy. Deciding his best option was to head for the markets and shops, he hurried towards the next south facing street. If his sense of direction was correct, he told himself, this should be a shortcut into the city.

As soon as he rounded the corner he knew he'd made the wrong decision. The street was deserted. As it was too late to turn back he kept marching; the sound of his boots echoing on the cobbles made him feel uncannily isolated. So, what was his next move? Come on Dorio; think! He spotted an alley to his left. It too was deserted. On the other hand, he reasoned, being forced into fighting in a narrow alley could be to his advantage. It would stop his assailants from spreading out or getting behind him. He dodged into the alley. The clatter of footsteps behind confirmed his Middle-Eastern companions were not only following but had broken into a trot to catch up with him.

Dorio slowed down and made contact with his sword. When he judged the men were close enough he swung round and drew his sword in one easy movement. The three men were poised, ready for action, their clothes whipped by the wind, turban ends flapping, swords drawn, advancing. Dorio felt his body tensing. So, this was how Pilate and Venator intended to settle matters, was it? Obviously, he hadn't shown sufficient enthusiasm for their offer.

Dorio had always welcomed the cut and thrust of battle, but on this occasion he would have preferred better odds. Still, he told himself, and purely in an attempt to boost his morale, at least he was a trained soldier and, judging from his opponents' attire, they were nothing more than thugs. That should give him an advantage.

And then they came. The first one to attack crashed his short sword against Dorio's in a manner that suggested he was no swordsman but a one-armed Decurion couldn't be too difficult to bring down, could he? With a twist of his weapon Dorio had unarmed him, lunged forward and stabbed him in the thigh. His assailant stared at him in astonishment before slumping to the ground.

Attackers two and three advanced, warily this time. But the narrow alley forced them too close together to attack effectively. Dorio swung his sword at his second opponent. Seeing what had happened to his colleague, the man hung back. Dorio advanced. He shouldn't have done that, but he realised his mistake too late. Assailant three dived into the gap, smashing his sword on the side of Dorio's helmet.

Momentarily dazed, Dorio staggered back. He felt a trickle of warm blood run down his face. He kept his sword poised, ready for another attack, but restricted with one arm he was unable to wipe the blood away from his eyes. He was vaguely aware of a blurred figure leaping in front of him, but before he had a chance to react he received a heavy blow to his stomach. Doubling up and blinded by blood he swung his sword wildly and was astonished to hear a weapon clatter to the ground. He'd hit someone then? Taking a chance, he swiftly brushed his arm over his face so he could see. One of his assailants was on his knees, his hands clamped to his bloody leg.

There was still one left on his feet, so Dorio charged. Steel clashed against steel. In one swift movement the Middle-Eastern servant drew a dagger; Dorio kicked out. He might only have one arm but by Jupiter he had feet, didn't he? There was a splash as his victim landed in a puddle. Recovering quickly, the man lunged forward with sword and dagger. Dorio darted to the side, but not quickly enough. He gasped as a glancing blow of the blade sliced his left thigh, his unprotected side. He stumbled back against a door. What he didn't expect was for the door to swing open.

'In! In! Get in quick!'

Dorio felt himself being dragged into the house. A drop of boiling water splashed his leg. He bit back a cry; the recipient of the pan of boiling water didn't. There was a scream, a clatter of steel, and a bang as the door was slammed against the war zone. A bolt shot into place.

Then there was silence.

Dorio found himself sprawled across a wooden floor. He wiped the blood from his face and was astounded to find his rescuer was a stooped, white haired old man with bandy legs that gave the impression they'd been straddling a horse since the founding of the Roman Empire. He waddled over to the shuttered windows and peered through the cracks.

'Ay, they've gone.' He gave Dorio a toothless grin. 'It's a privilege to be of assistance to a fellow Decurion.' He pointed to his missing arm. 'Took courage facing thugs like that, especially you only having one arm. Lose it in battle, did you?'

'Judea.'

'Ay. Terrible business that. If you can stand up I'll help you to the couch. What'd they call you?'

'Decurion Dorio Suranus.'

'I'm Decurion Horatius Appius. Come on, up you get.'

The old man was so frail that Dorio felt if he rested his whole weight on the bony shoulders he'd crush him to powder, but somehow Horatio managed to drag him over to a torn and lumpy couch. Slumping down, Dorio vaguely registered that he was in a small, sparse but pleasant room warmed by clay lamps. Gently removing his helmet and his tunic, Horatio began to bathe his wounds.

'Aye, the torn flesh on your thigh's not too bad. I've seen worse on the battlefield but that face of yours isn't going to look too pretty. Your jaw isn't broken, neither is your nose and you've still got all your teeth but I reckon you'll have one damnable headache in the morning.'

Dorio sucked in sharply through gritted teeth as cold water

dribbled over the cut on his head. 'I gather you've done this before.'

'I have that,' Horatio began and it was the only encouragement he needed to launch into tales of the wars he'd fought in, the units he'd been attached to, the horses he'd handled and the emperors he had served under.

# Chapter Sixteen

The weather deteriorated rapidly from mid-afternoon keeping the tailor, his family and their guests tied to the tiny house. During the evening meal, Aurelia managed to keep up a cheerful chatter for the sake of the boys, but as soon as Abram had lit the lamps, and Sarah had put the boys to bed her worries deepened. At first they sat in silence listening to the boys settling down for the night, and then they tried going over what could have happened to Dorio. But it wasn't until the oil lamps were flickering low that discussions dried up altogether, and the tailor and his wife wandered upstairs to their bedrooms, not so much to sleep, but to wait anxiously for Dorio's return.

Aurelia made her way into her tiny guest room. Lying on her narrow bed she gently stroked her baby's silky soft hair. It felt fine and feathery. The reassuring contact sent her daughter's mouth rhythmically sucking in anticipation of her next feed.

'Don't worry little one. It'll be fine,' she whispered. She wasn't sure who she was trying to convince, her baby who couldn't understand a word she was saying, or herself, but simply hearing the words spoken aloud was comforting enough.

Running her fingers over the rough wooden box, the sides of which had been covered with cuttings of soft material from the tailor's shop, she gave a sigh. This wasn't what she had envisaged for the first few days of her daughter's life at all. She thought longingly of Phaedo's hand-carved cot standing in the nursery at home, the warm blankets piled high on the stool, and the neatly stitched baby clothes, which she had spent months sewing. She raised her head at the gentle knock on the door.

'Come in,' she said softly.

Sarah crept in with a steaming mug of liquid that smelled sweet. 'I know it's late but I saw the light of your candle and wondered if you'd like a honey drink,' she whispered perching on the edge of the bed. 'It's supposed to be good for when you're feeding a baby.' She gave an embarrassed laugh. 'Not that I know of course.' Her smile faded as she handed her guest the mug. 'Have you had any ideas of how we're going to get those parchments to Senator Felix Seneca?'

Aurelia wrapped her fingers around the hot cup. 'I don't think there's anything we can do till morning. I must admit that when his servant said he'd been called to the palace my heart sank. We need him, we really do.' Her brow furrowed in annoyance. 'I do wish Dorio hadn't gone barging off like that. I hope he hasn't got himself into trouble. He has a tendency to act before he thinks.'

'Yes, I had noticed that about him,' Sarah said warmly.

Aurelia gave the girl a sideways glance. 'Did you see a lot of him in Jerusalem?'

'Dorio? I ... we did. He came to the Meeting House.'

'The Meeting House?'

'It's where followers of the Nazarene meet.'

'Ah yes. Vivius told me about this Jesus of Nazareth.' Aurelia sipped her honey drink. 'I worship the Roman gods. Venus is my favourite or Minerva, the goddess of wisdom. But my servant, Ruth is a Jew and worships your God.' She licked her sweetened lips thoughtfully. 'Strange, but during our escape to Rome in the cart, I caught myself praying to this Jewish God of yours. It was Ruth's prayer that did it. She was loading my luggage at the time. Her prayer sounded so ... reassuring I suppose. Yet I actually know nothing about Him. Do you have an idol of Him?'

With a smile Sarah shook her head, curled her legs under her, and for a while they talked about the Jewish God and His Messiah Son. But even though Aurelia knew that under different circumstances she would have been fascinated by the story, this evening she was only half listening. Her mind had a habit of wandering off, either to her wounded husband in Mamertine Prison or to the worrying late arrival of her brother.

It was Sarah who gave the long sigh and said, 'Where can he

be; Dorio I mean?'

That was when it struck Aurelia that the girl was as worried as she was.

They dozed fitfully for a while, seeking refuge in their shared concern for Dorio. It was the heavy hammering on the door that stirred them. They stared at each other in alarm before Sarah leapt off the bed and rushed into the living quarters, Aurelia was close behind her. They stumbled into Abram and Judith tiptoeing down the stairs in bare feet.

Abram flung open the front door and a wet and dishevelled Dorio staggered into the shop. His uniform was torn, his cheek bruised, eye swollen; there was a wet and bloody bandage around his head and another around his thigh.

Aurelia clasped her hands to her face. 'Oh no! What's happened to you, Dorio?'

'Nothing.' His jaw barely moved and when he spoke it was with difficulty because of the deep cut on his lip.

'Don't be ridiculous! How can it be nothing? Look at the state of you.'

'Yes, well.' He shrugged her off with a, 'Don't fuss, Aurelia.' Hobbling over to the long couch he flung himself across it but made no objection when Sarah raised him up again to peel off his wet cloak.

Gently removing his helmet, she asked, 'What happened?'

He grunted as she pulled off his boots. 'Nothing for any of you to worry about.'

Aurelia ran her fingers through her hair in frustration. 'Not to worry about? Don't be ridiculous! We've been frantic with worry. Where've you been all this time?'

Dorio threw her a tantalising grin but then winced with pain over the movement on his lip. His touched it gingerly with his tongue before turning to Abram who was standing at the back of the room watching his niece unbuckle a sword smeared with blood. 'Let's say I've been following your advice, Abram. I challenged Pilate and Venator. Trouble is, this is what I got for my efforts.'

'Oh Dorio, you shouldn't have ...'

'Then I headed back via Mamertine Prison, left food for Vivius, and told the guard he better treat his prisoner with care as his release was imminent.'

Aurelia was visibly startled. 'What?'

Judith carried in a bowl of hot water and a cloth, laid it at the foot of the couch and proceeded to unwrap the wet and bloody bandage around his thigh.

'It is if you got that parchment to Felix.' It was the crestfallen faces, not the hot cloth Sarah had placed on his swollen cheekbone that made him groan. 'You didn't?'

'We didn't,' Aurelia said. 'We were told he'd been called to the palace urgently.' She gave a 'tut' of annoyance. 'It didn't seem to matter to those in higher authority that he'd been wounded and advised by his physician not to go. He went anyway. So ...' She blinked rapidly. 'So, does that mean Vivius won't be ...'

Dorio lifted his hand. 'Aurelia, I've barely slept for two days, I've been beaten up, my head is pounding and I'm too exhausted to make rational decisions. Do you mind if we discuss our options in the morning?' He paused a beat before adding, 'But don't worry, I still think we're a step closer to getting Vivius out.'

'You do?' Aurelia wrung her hands. 'I don't know what makes you think that when we've failed to contact Felix, but ...'

Dorio inclined his ear. 'Is that the baby I hear whimpering?'

Aurelia stopped mid-flow. It was then she noticed that Judith had stepped back and Dorio was obviously relishing having Sarah to himself to bathe his wounds and fuss over his comforts. Shaking her head in exasperation she took the hint because by then the baby had started to whimper and the last thing she wanted to do was to wake the boys. Besides, Abram and Judith, seeing Dorio was in good hands, were also mumbling their goodnights.

Leaving the door slightly ajar, she sat on the edge of her bed cradling the baby in her arms. Her daughter made sucking motions with her mouth; she was a hungry little creature. Aurelia stroked the tiny head as she unbuttoned her dress. 'You're going to be a wonderful surprise for your father little one,' she whispered.

Her little girl opened her mouth wide as if to answer, but it was only her response to feeding time.

\* \* \*

Boots echoed along the stone corridor, a key rattled in the lock and the cell door complained with a long loud creak as it swung open. To Vivius's astonishment it was the jailor carrying a plate of food which he laid down courteously beside his prisoner. Normally the food was shoved in through the gap at the bottom of the door and Vivius was forced to crawl along the floor to get it.

'Was that cheering I heard outside?' he ventured.

The jailor stepped back. 'It was, sir. Rumour is that the Senate have approved Claudius as the next emperor. But I couldn't rightly say what truth there is in that, sir.'

Sir? The jailor called him sir? Vivius stared down at the unexpected feast of chicken, fruit and bread.

The jailor must have seen his puzzlement. 'A Decurion brought it in last night. He said you might be hungry,' he explained.

'So, they've approved Claudius as emperor, have they?'

'I heard them mention him by name, but I don't rightly know for certain.'

There was silence as Vivius struggled into a sitting position.

'I can bring you warm water for your wound if you like,' the jailor offered. He made it sound like a favour, as though he was in the habit of kindly gestures.

Wary of the unexpected generosity, Vivius decided a stiff nod would suffice but the jailor's fingers played idly with the bolt on the cell door, leaving the impression there was more to say. 'The Decurion who called last night. He paid me to give you a message.'

Vivius raised an eyebrow as a question and then took a bite of bread.

'Aye, the Decurion says to tell you your physician will call shortly, and for you to keep your spirits up as he intends to have you out of here by the end of the day.'

Vivius choked, splattering crumbs across the floor. 'He said what?'

The jailer wiped his nose with the sleeve of his tunic. 'You want me to repeat it?'

Vivius shook his head. 'Was he drunk when he came?'

'Don't think so. He'd been badly beaten up but he wasn't drunk.' He paused before saying, 'I'll be getting that water then, eh?' The cell door slammed behind him.

Vivius stared at the locked door. Beaten up? And ... how in the name of all the gods did Dorio expect to get him out of here by the end of the day?

* * *

Dorio stroked Warrior's silky soft nose as they approached the palace gates. 'Okay boy, now work with me on this one,' he murmured. 'You're my way into this place.'

Warrior snorted. He was used to the army uniforms, the barking of orders and the life of the military, but almost as though he sensed he had a part to play in this new drama, he dropped his head in a docile manner and allowed Dorio to lead him up to the sentries.

An officer with a long brooding face moved forward as Dorio limped towards him and shook his head in disgust at his appearance. Dorio shuffled uncomfortably. Despite Sarah's best efforts with his uniform it was still bloodstained and patched and he had a dint in his helmet. There was one clean bandage around his head, another around his thigh, but this morning his face was not only grotesquely swollen but badly discoloured. And that was only his outward appearance. Discomfort had kept him awake for what was left of the night, so he was not only exhausted but his head was throbbing and the intense pain from his thigh was making it difficult to walk. Unable to stand fully to attention he gave his best salute anyway.

'Good morning, sir. I'm Decurion Dorio Suranus. I think this is the last of the emperor's horses.'

'What?'

'The Emperor Caligula's horses, they escaped on the day of his assassination. I was ordered to round them up.'

'And you expect to be admitted into the palace looking like that? I don't think so, Decurion.'

Dorio's heart sank. He cleared his throat. 'Forgive my uniform sir, but my men and I have spent the last two days quelling riots and running messages in an attempt to preserve the dignity of Rome.'

The officer glared at him suspiciously.

'Then my orders were to round up the palace horses that escaped during the upheaval. As you can see, I've done that. Now all I want to do is to get this poor creature back to his stable and myself back to the barracks – sir.'

Warrior began pawing the ground, drawing the officer's attention away from Dorio. Dorio could sense his change of attitude as he sauntered over to the animal. 'One thing I'll say for Caligula, he knew how to care for his horses,' he said stroking Warrior's neck. 'Yes, he's a fine horse.' Warrior nuzzled his hand as if expecting a tit-bit. Amused, the officer gave him a final pat and stepping back bellowed, 'Porcius!'

A gangly, fresh-faced recruit with frizzy hair protruding

from under his helmet arrived at his side at the trot and saluted.

'Accompany this Decurion to the stables with this horse then bring him back again.' With a slap to Warrior's rump the officer gave Dorio a curt nod of dismissal.

Dorio limped into the palace grounds. Hurdle one overcome; only another twenty or so and I might even achieve my objective, he thought with a touch of irony.

As they headed towards the stables he noticed a vast improvement in the palace grounds from the last time he was here. The clearing up operation was well underway. Charred wood from the burnt-out theatre was being dismantled by slaves, the animal attractions had been removed, Praetorian Guards were overseeing the removal of broken statues, a stack of discarded weapons lay on the grass, next to a pile of sheets where the dead and wounded had lain. The only obstacle he had now, Dorio decided, was how he was going to get into the palace, because as far as he could see all the entrances had doubled their sentries.

'Why the extra security?' he asked.

The young recruit straightened his helmet. 'Ah!' he informed him with an air of being knowledgeable over such issues. 'That'll be for the new emperor, Claudius.'

'He's here? In the palace?'

'He is. My officer says the Praetorians discovered him hiding and hailed him as emperor. The Senate didn't initially agree with their choice, and my officer says Claudius wasn't too keen on their choice either, so that's why leading Senators, dignitaries and other high officials are here, to persuade him. But my officer says Claudius is entitled to the position as he was related to the Emperor Tiberius. From what my officer heard this morning, agreement was reached by all parties late last night, hence the extra security.'

'Your officer seems well informed,' Dorio murmured with a touch of sarcasm.

'Yes sir, he is, sir.'

Dorio patted the parchment under his tunic. How, he wondered, was he expected to get Chaerea's signed statement to Felix if the palace was swarming with dignitaries, guards and sentries? Even if he did get inside, who was going to be interested in the release of one senator when the whole world stood poised, waiting for the official naming of the next Emperor of the Roman Empire?

He was still pondering over this dilemma as they ambled up to the stable courtyard. He glanced in the direction of the kitchens and concluded that his best bet for gaining entry was probably the same as last time. Now all he had to do was find a way of getting rid of Porcius. With a winning smile he addressed the recruit. 'Thanks Porcius. I can find my way from here.'

Porcius acquired the same doubtful expression as his commanding officer. 'I don't know about that, sir. My orders were to take you to the stables and bring you back again.'

'And are you going to wait around while I rub this poor animal down and feed him?'

'Can't you leave that to the stable hands, sir?'

Dorio cursed under his breath at the way this recruit had an answer to everything – like his officer. But he discovered there was little he could do when two stable hands emerged from the stables. Left with no other option he handed Warrior over to them. One of the stable hands gave the horse a puzzled frown as he took his reins, but to Dorio's relief he refrained from questioning the arrival of a strange horse and led him into the stables without comment.

Dorio hovered in the courtyard, conscious that Porcius was getting impatient. 'I'm er … I'm now supposed to report to a Senator Felix Seneca,' Dorio explained deciding Felix was his best option. 'My orders are to inform him when all the horses have been brought back.'

Porcius gave him another of those doubtful looks. 'Why

would a senator be interested in that? What about your own commanding officer? Isn't that his job?'

Deciding Porcius was becoming a darned nuisance he racked his brains for another excuse to get rid of him. He didn't need to. It was the unexpected arrival of two immaculate Praetorian Guards that had the desired effect on Porcius. Snapping to attention the recruit saluted as if his very life depended on it.

'Sir, this Decurion has brought back the last of the missing horses.'

One of the Praetorians gave Dorio a look resembling one he would give to a mangy cur. 'What missing horses?'

'The ones that escaped during the fighting,' Dorio explained and in a tone which he hoped suggested he was surprised the Praetorians hadn't been informed. 'Then my orders were to report directly to Senator Felix Seneca.'

'And why would he be interested in the return of horses?'

Dorio gave an exaggerated sigh. 'Don't ask me. No one seems to have any idea what's happening. I'm simply obeying orders but I keep getting them countermanded. All I can say is, the senator was quite adamant that I report to him.'

The Praetorians eyeballed each other in such a manner that Dorio got the impression that orders and the countermanding of orders had been commonplace since the assassination.

The Praetorian who had initially spoken scratched his head. 'I suppose you better come with me then, Decurion. You, legionary, back to your post.'

'Yes sir.' Porcius gave another smart salute before returning to his commanding officer at the trot; no doubt to report the latest outcome and keep his officer informed.

As the Praetorian Guards marched either side of him from the stable courtyard to the main entrance, Dorio consoled himself with the thought that he might be feeling like a something that had been dragged out of the sewers compared to his pristine uniformed escorts, but at least he'd achieved his objective – he had found a way into the palace. He gave himself an imaginary pat on the back as he stepped into the entrance hall through the wide double doors.

'Wait here, Decurion. I'll see if I can find Senator Seneca,' one of the Praetorians ordered. He moved away; his companion stayed.

Dorio studied the activities in the entrance hall carefully. He noticed sentries had been placed at various points down the main corridor. A complete waste of time in his opinion as clerks were scurrying between offices clutching rolls of parchments, puffed up senators strode from room to room loudly venting their opinions in the hope they could make their mark on this new regime, and the clatter of Praetorian Officers' boots echoed noisily on the stone floor in an attempt to prove that they were the ones who instigated this change-over. It would be impossible for the sentries to keep track of all the comings and goings. He also made a mental note of the fact that the cavalry was regularly marching in and out of the palace clutching wax tablets or parchments. Presumably its orders were to spread word of the new emperor to outlying areas and the colonies.

It was then he spotted a familiar cloak, Vivius's cloak. It was hanging across a chair in the corner of the entrance hall. Deciding it would be a good cover for his shabby uniform, he was about to retrieve it when it occurred to him that no one would believe an expensive cloak like that would belong to a Decurion, and his mission was difficult enough without adding theft to his list of recent activities.

A shout from outside distracted him. His Praetorian escort raised his arm in reply then gave a huff of exasperation. Eyeing Dorio uneasily he said, 'I'm wanted. You, stay here!'

'I will. No problem.' Dorio made sure he gave the Praetorian a friendly smile alongside his reassuring nod, although, 'Staying here!' was not on his agenda. Not that he had an agenda, he reflected, but if he had it wouldn't be 'staying here'.

He waited until his escort was out of sight before pulling the parchment out of his tunic. 'And down goes another obstacle,' he murmured, marching purposefully down the corridor. He tried not to limp and so draw attention to himself, but attempted to give the impression he was a man on a mission and hoped no one would guess the effort it was taking him to brave out this illusion. His head was pounding with a ferociousness that was making him nauseous. But at least, he consoled himself, he was less conspicuous than on his last visit to the palace. This time there were soldiers, guards and clerks scuttling or marching around the palace as if there was a sense of purpose in it all. All he had to do was look as though he was one of them. His only concern now was that it wouldn't take his escorts long to realise he was missing.

He aimed for the carved double doors at the end of the corridor as he guessed from his previous observations that this was where the activities stemmed from. Getting there was easy enough but the sight of the two hefty Praetorians on sentry duty either side of the door left him decidedly uneasy. Straightening his shoulders, he approached them with a confidence he was far from feeling. He waved his parchments in the air.

'Urgent message for Senator Felix Seneca,' he informed them marching straight past. To his amazement they virtually ignored him, which only confirmed his theory that with the cavalry coming and going since early morning, one more delivery was hardly worth bothering with.

The room he entered had a highly carved ceiling, marble busts, ornaments and colourful murals depicting naked men and women. Dorio whistled softly through his lips, not at the murals but at the status of the gathering. It looked as though every high official in the Roman Empire had arrived for this momentous occasion. Senior Praetorians, Army Commanders, Equestrians, Procurators, Senators and the Consul. They stood around in small groups filling the room with a babble of noise. Everyone appearing to have something of importance to say, but no one appearing interested enough to listen.

Dorio scanned the room for senators, but it was difficult to pick Felix out of so many white togas edged in purple. He rubbed his chin apprehensively, knowing his escorts couldn't be far behind, his only hope of getting out of here in one piece would be Felix.

He moved cautiously to another part of the room but then stepped smartly back behind a column. He held his breath, for standing in the corner of the room in deep discussion with a group of senators was Senator Titus Venator.

Dorio puzzled momentarily as to what he was doing here, as he hadn't thought Venator had the high office or the standing in the Senate of Vivius or Felix. But then deciding he had more urgent matters to deal with than Senator Titus Venator, he scanned the room again for Felix, urgently this time.

His attention was drawn to him purely by the awkwardness of his posture. Felix! Despite having his back to him, Dorio recognised him immediately. Clearly, he hadn't recovered from his wound but probably stubborn minded, like Vivius, it hadn't prevented him from his duty at the palace. He appeared to be involved in a heated argument with a group of senators, and judging from the stabbing of fingers in the air there was considerable disagreement over some issue.

Dorio hesitated, willing Felix to turn in his direction so he wouldn't be forced to walk the full length of the room and reveal himself to Titus Venator. He glanced towards the double doors knowing the Praetorian Guards could arrive at any moment, and concluded that whatever he did, had to be done instantly. Felix continued to have his back to him.

Taking a firm grip on his aching body, Dorio straightened himself up and limped self-consciously through the influential gathering until he stood behind Felix. He coughed discreetly.

To his relief, Felix swung around. Visibly startled to see

him he raised a forefinger as indication that he wait. Laying an apologetic hand on the arm of a senator with severe white eyebrows, and a paunch that stretched his toga to the limit, he said, 'My apologies for interrupting you, senator but I need to speak to this Decurion urgently. He's been investigating a matter of vital importance for me.' Turning to Dorio he frowned his displeasure. 'How in the name of Jupiter did you get in here?' he hissed.

'Don't ask,' Dorio said in a low voice. He held up the parchment. 'This is Officer Chaerea's statement, sir. As you will see it's been signed by his commanding officer. It clears Vivius of the accusations made against him, as will your statement of finding Vivius's dagger in the back of a Germanic Guard.' His gaze momentarily flickered towards the door. People were coming and going but there was still no sign of his escort. 'I've also discovered what Pontius Pilate and Senator Titus Venator are up to but I'll fill you in on that later.' He paused as Felix read through Chaerea's statement. 'Do you think we have sufficient evidence to have Vivius released, sir?' Dorio had been keeping his voice low but clearly not low enough.

The senator with the severe white eyebrows had obviously overheard at least part of their conversation. He spun around. 'Did I hear you mention the name of Officer Chaerea, Decurion?' he thundered. 'That was Caligula's assassin, wasn't it? What in the name of Jupiter have you been investigating?' His eyes narrowed as they landed upon Felix. 'And for whom?'

Felix gestured discretion by a gentle pressure on the senator's sleeve. 'It's a private matter,' he murmured.

'Private? Private? Forgive me for being blunt Senator Seneca but I get alarmed when I hear such talk. With Caligula barely cold in his grave and Claudius not yet established on the throne, we cannot be too careful. These covert gatherings must be brought to an end. We need openness, clarity.'

Dorio was uncomfortably aware that the senator's booming

voice was drawing attention to them.

An Army Commander sauntered over. 'What's all this about Officer Chaerea?'

The senator with the severe white eyebrows waved a pointing finger in Dorio's direction. 'Seems this er ... Decurion fellow has evidence relating to Officer Chaerea and the assassination.'

The Army Commander frowned. 'Evidence? What evidence? And what's a mere Decurion doing investigating the assassination?'

The severe white eyebrows quivered at Dorio. 'Do you have information we don't know about, Decurion?'

Dorio glanced uneasily at Felix who was doing his best to make light of the matter, and deflect attention away from them. He might have succeeded had not Dorio seen his Praetorian escorts storm in through the double doors. Alarmed by their drawn swords he watched them stop, their extra height giving them the ability to sweep over the heads of the dignitaries with ease. Realising he wouldn't be hard to miss in his patched and bloodstained uniform, dinted helmet and bandaged head he impulsively addressed the senator with the severe white eyebrows.

Raising his voice, he said, 'Yes sir, as a matter of fact I do have information that needs to be brought to your attention.' Ignoring the warning frown from Felix he continued, 'My brother-in-law, Senator Vivius Marcianus, was falsely accused of being involved in the plot to assassinate the Emperor Caligula and thrown into Mamertine Prison. He's been labelled a traitor for going against the Praetorians.' A brief glance over at the double doors confirmed his escorts were still craning their necks. 'But he's innocent of all charges and I have proof. That's what I was bringing ...'

'What's this got to do with our new emperor?' the white browed senator barked.

'Can't this wait?' another snapped.

'If your brother-in-law is in Mamertine Prison then there must be a good reason.'

'Who is this Decurion?'

'Look at the state of him. Who let him in here?'

'Mamertine Prison? Who is in Mamertine Prison?'

Dorio noticed, with a quiver of alarm, that his Praetorian escorts, drawn by the raised voices, were now looking in their direction. He held his breath. But then one particular voice close by caught his attention, not because it was loud, but because it was familiar.

'M ... M ... Mamertine P ... Prison? So, you found your b ... brother-in-l ... law in Mamertine P ... P ... Prison?'

Dorio had no chance to respond. There was a shout, followed by heavy boots clattering across the marble floor and a flash of red uniforms. Startled cries echoed around the room. There wasn't time for him to draw his sword. Besides, common sense told him it would be useless as the Praetorians were vastly superior to him in swordsmanship.

He braced himself, telling himself not to panic otherwise he would only make things worse, and then they were on him. One escort grabbed his arm, twisted it behind his back and drove him to his knees. He cried out as his knees hit the marble floor and his thigh wound opened up. Then he gritted his teeth as his head was slammed to the ground and a sword pressed warningly into the back of his neck. Somewhere amongst the shouts, orders and the raised voices he heard Felix shouting, 'Stop! Stop!'

He didn't dare move. All he could see from his limited viewpoint was blood from his throbbing head wound spreading across the marble floor, and a gathering of sandals and boots around him as curiosity drew the cream of the Roman Empire in their direction. He deliberately kept his breathing steady, forcing himself not to panic, realising his only hope now lay in Felix.

A boot stamped close to his ear. 'Apologies Caesar. This Decurion gained unlawful entry into the palace. We feared for your safety.'

Dorio cringed. Caesar? *Caesar!* By all the gods, surely … surely, they didn't think he'd come here to assassinate the new Caesar? They wouldn't think that, would they? Panicked by the assumptions he shouted, 'I'm not here to threaten anyone! All I want is justice! Aahh!' The blade dug warningly into the back of his neck.

There were murmurs and mumblings around him and then he heard Felix's voice. He couldn't hear what was being said but his tone sounded urgent. He clenched his teeth, as being forced into a crouching position he could feel the wound on his thigh pumping out blood like a tap. The wait seemed interminable but then, blessed relief, the blade on his neck was withdrawn. He decided to remain perfectly still. No sense in tempting an over-zealous guard to use him as target practice in an attempt to get noticed by the new emperor. He watched the sandals and boots in his line of vision shuffle back leaving him in the centre of a wide and empty circle. Only two pairs of sandals and one pair of boots remained.

'S … s … stand up, D … Decurion. Stand up.'

Dorio struggled to his feet, conscious that his thigh was now bleeding profusely, running down his leg and on to his boots. The dignitaries were standing well back. The Praetorian Sentry was close by, but Dorio was relieved to see his sword lowered. The nod Felix gave was barely noticeable but it was reassuring. Beside Felix stood the man with the dribbling mouth and twitch, the stuttering man who had held him at sword point on the day of the assassination. He was regarding him curiously but not in an unfriendly manner.

'D … did you hear him? This Decurion is crying out for j … j … justice gentlemen.'

The mumbles around the room fell into silence.

'And he's a soldier, a Decurion. Is this how we t … t … treat our army after they show Rome their … l … loyalty in battle and return to us w ... with limbs missing?'

Dorio felt his mouth drying up as it dawned on him who was speaking.

Disregarding his bleeding thigh, he stumbled forward and fell on one knee. 'Forgive me, Caesar,' he stuttered. 'I had no idea who you were when we met in the palace two days ago.'

'Come Decurion. I wasn't emperor two days ago.'

The rumble of curiosity, which Dorio discovered is a tone higher than one of disgruntlement, gave him cause for encouragement. A hand slid under his elbow, and he couldn't make out whether he felt dizzy with loosing so much blood or because he was actually being assisted to his feet by the Emperor of Rome.

'C ... can I suggest you get back to the business in hand g ... gentlemen.' Claudius gave the influential officials of Rome a wave of dismissal. Reluctantly they melted back into their own intimate groups, with the exception of Felix and a Praetorian Prefect. 'Now.' Claudius addressed Dorio. 'You have the b ... bravery, or should I call it the effrontery to break into my palace, twice I may add, in the search for justice for your brother-in-law.' Claudius gathered up his toga and wrapped it over his arm. 'Justice is what Rome needs to make it strong again, and courage, the type of courage I have witnessed in you, Decurion.' He deliberated for a moment before saying, 'You must be extremely devoted to this brother-in-law of yours?'

*Devoted to Vivius?* Dorio would have burst out laughing if he hadn't deemed it unwise in the present company. He wavered, dropped his head and focussed on his boots.

Claudius's mouth quivered with amusement at the obvious implications. 'And yet you demand justice for him? This sounds like a story I'd like to hear, but not while you're bleeding all over my floor.' He waved his hand in an attempt to gain attention and was immediately swamped with hovering aides waiting for an order that would bring them to the attention of the new emperor. 'Will someone send for a physician?'

As Claudius gestured him towards the window, away from the main body of dignitaries, Dorio caught a glimpse of Titus Venator hurrying through the double doors. He wondered momentarily if he should have him stopped, but realising he was in no position to do that he had no other option but to let him go.

Felix took his elbow and assisted him over to a long wooden semi-circular seat padded with cushions, and pointing to a picturesque view across the gardens. The Consul, two senators, a Praetorian Officer and an Army Commander were ordered to join them. They stood at ease in a semi-circle, waiting. Claudius sat down beside him.

'So, Decurion,' he said. 'Am I correct in assuming the senator's imprisonment has to do with the assassination of Caligula?'

'Yes Excellency.'

'So, tell me, t ... tell me.'

Felix handed over the blood-stained parchment to the Praetorian Prefect as Dorio began telling his story. An elderly physician, his bag overflowing with bandages and ointments, began tending his wounds. Only once did Dorio wince, and that was when the physician pulled the existing blood-stained bandage from his thigh.

'You say you spoke to Officer Chaerea, Caligula's assassin in the Army Hospital,' Claudius interrupted. May I ask how you got into a Military Camp? Where were the guards?'

Sweat broke out on Dorio's forehead and he knew it wasn't with the hot cloth the doctor was using on his wound. 'I er ...' His mind raced. The last thing he wanted to do was get Lucanus into trouble.

Seeing his embarrassment, Claudius shook his head. 'Probably the same way you got into my palace,' he said dryly. Turning to the Army Commander, he gave him a purposeful look. 'I think one of our first tasks is to review our security,' he stated wryly. 'Go on,' he added turning back to Dorio.

Dorio was relieved that there were parts of the story where Felix could intervene, like being there when Vivius's dagger was discovered in the back of a Germanic Bodyguard. Felix was a fluent and persuasive speaker, so by the time he had finished Dorio was convinced no one could be in any doubt of Vivius's loyalty to Rome.

The Praetorian Prefect handed Cassius's statement to Claudius and with an embarrassed clearing of the throat cut into the conversation. 'Regarding Cassius Chaerea, and those directly involved in the assassination, Caesar. I'm afraid to say my Praetorians went beyond the terms of their orders. As far as I understand it, they came to the conclusion it would be prudent to wipe out the entire imperial family. I've no doubt Senator Marcianus tried to prevent the assassination of the empress and her daughter. As for the accusations made by my Praetorians who claimed Vivius Marcianus threatened them ...' He cleared his throat again. 'What with the games being on, the crowds, the extra guests, there was er ... complete confusion in the palace that day, complete confusion.'

Dorio watched Claudius carefully. His gaze had wandered into the garden. Dorio had no doubt Claudius knew of the confusion. He'd been there, hiding in the office, avoiding the inevitable. Claudius focussed his attention to the blood-stained statement Dorio had produced. Silence lingered as he read it.

'So, in this confusion it looks like Senator Marcianus's accusers were mistaken, doesn't it? Who were they again?'

'Pontius Pilate and Senator Titus Venator, Excellency.'

'Hmm.' Claudius handed the parchment back to the Praetorian Prefect. 'There can be no d ... denying this statement from Cassius Chaerea. Witnessed by his Commanding Officer, I see.'

'Yes, sire,' Dorio said.

'B ... But that doesn't explain how you have all these er ... injuries, D ... Decurion. You didn't have them last time we met.

What have you been doing, other than breaking into my palace, bribing your way into the Mamertine Prison and conning your way into a Military Hospital?'

There was an amused snigger from one of the senators.

Dorio touched his bruised face gingerly, conscious of the fact that the only part of his story he had omitted was Pilate's and Venator's plans to destroy the Jewish religion and its Nazarene's cult. He was about launch into what he'd learned when he found himself stopping to think of the consequences. If Claudius was anti-Semitic, he reasoned, and at this point in his career as emperor there was no knowing that, then any comments concerning the Jews would only antagonise him and that, Dorio decided, was the last thing he wanted to do. He flashed an unspoken appeal for help to Felix.

Felix, recognising that Dorio was out of his depth, intervened. 'I'm afraid there have been gangs of youths causing chaos in Rome, Caesar, and with all the running around the Decurion has been doing for Senator Vivius Marcianus, I believe he got caught up in the violence.'

'Mm.' Claudius tapped his finger suspiciously over his lower lip.

Dorio wiped the sweat off his forehead. 'Forgive me Excellency but ... but ... as Felix Seneca says, it's been a ... rough few days. I was set upon by thugs and ... and ...' He realised that now he'd finished telling his story his head was pounding with a fierceness that resembled a cavalry charge in battle. '... and then my sister ... I had to deliver her baby on our way to Rome and ... and ...' Aware that delivering a baby had absolutely nothing to do with the issue at hand, and that he was beginning to ramble he slumped in his seat.

'So, Decurion.' Claudius stood up. 'Perhaps my first task as Emperor of Rome should be to see that Senator Vivius Marcianus gets a fair hearing.' Turning to the Praetorian Prefect he thrust out the blood-stained parchment. 'And he's had that. Having read Chaerea's statement the matter seems clear enough to me. Can you see to the senator's release immediately?'

The Praetorian Prefect saluted. 'Yes, Excellency.'

Dorio rose shakily to his feet. He tried to ignore the way the floor tilted and the people around him tilted with it.

Claudius's mouth drooped into that strangely twisted but pleasant smile of his. 'I like you, Decurion. I like your tenacity.' His voice dropped and when he spoke again it was to lean forward so that his comment was for Dorio's ear only. 'I more than most men, understand what it takes to overcome physical difficulties. You have done a good job. You have played a useful part in restoring one of Rome's loyal senators to his rightful place.'

Dorio simply stared at him. Useful? Who? *Him?*

# Chapter Seventeen

As the initial dregs of sleep washed away, Aurelia had found herself with the strangest feeling of ... what? She hadn't been able to identify it exactly, other than there was a sense of hope, expectation, that hadn't been there before. She had rolled over in the narrow bed, yawned and dragged her eyes open. And that was when the worries had flooded in. Vivius! Was he still alive? How would they get him out of the Mamertine? Where had Dorio gone so early in the morning, and why had he taken Warrior with him? Where was Felix? What had happened to her home? Had it been burnt down? Were her servants safe? Phaedo, Indi, and Ruth, dear Ruth with her strange Jewish God, was she safe? Yet Aurelia found that not even her fretting had been able to dampen that glimmer of hope. It had lingered all morning, between helping Judith and Sarah with the chores to feeding the baby. She had clung on to it, trying not to let worry take the upper hand. So, when midday arrived and an excitable Maximus shouted, 'He's coming! Uncle Dorio's coming and ... and ... Wow!' Aurelia felt justified in being able to let out a long sigh of relief that at least one of the men in her life was safe.

Hurrying to the front door she stopped abruptly when she saw Dorio approaching the tailor's shop on Warrior, accompanied by two huge, immaculate Praetorian Guards on huge, immaculate horses. Maximus's and Rufus's jaws dropped open as their idols dismounted.

Aurelia clasped her hands together in concern. 'What's happened, Dorio? Don't tell me you've been arrested?'

'No, I haven't been arrested,' Dorio snapped. 'Why do you always have to assume I'm in trouble?' He dismounted before adding. 'Don't answer that one, and no questions, not now Aurelia. All I want you to do is get the children ready. We're going home.'

She gave a short gasp. 'We're going home? What about Vivius?'

'Including Vivius, or at least he will be included when we get him out of Mamertine Prison. I'll hitch up the horse and cart.'

She glanced uneasily at the Praetorian Guards. 'You're taking a horse and cart through Rome – during the day,' she ventured. 'Is it … allowed?'

'Our escort assures me it is.'

'What do you mean, our escort? How …?'

'Please, Aurelia. Pack, will you?'

She opened her mouth to argue, but sensing his mood decided better of it, and without another word hurried upstairs to pack their belongings. But she noticed from the upstairs window that while Dorio and Abram hitched up the horse and cart, the Jew was hearing his story in greater detail.

The farewells were hastily made, the Praetorian Guards made sure of that. They deposited their baggage, Rufus, Aurelia and the baby in the cart in that order and in quick succession. Then, at Dorio's request, one of the Praetorian Guards tossed Maximus on to the back of Warrior. Maximus flushed with pride, not only because he was on his father's horse again. But because this time he would have a Praetorian Guard riding beside him through the streets of Rome.

When they reached Mamertine Prison their escort dismounted, were gained entry immediately and emerged some time later supporting a white and unshaven Vivius in his filthy, torn and bloody toga, and bandaged but still bloody head. Aurelia's hand flew to her mouth when she saw the state of her husband. Thrusting her baby daughter into Rufus's arms, she leapt off the cart.

'Oh my dearest,' she choked.

Shrugging off the supporting Praetorian Guards, Vivius reached out to her. How she had the strength to support his weight she'd never know, but she did, and he clung to her, burying his face into her neck. She could smell the stench of prison on him, feel him shaking with weakness, but then taking a deep breath he grasped her by the shoulders, and the love in his eyes said all there was to say – for the moment.

He reached out to his boys. Rufus was crying, the tears streaming down his cheeks and falling on the baby's blanket. 'F ... father! Father!' was all he could stammer. He didn't dare move, not with this precious bundle in his arms. Maximus on Warrior was struggling to be brave in front of the Praetorian Guards, but Aurelia could see his lower lip was quivering. Vivius staggered to the cart to hug his youngest son and take the first look at his daughter, but his legs gave way from under him.

The Praetorians moved swiftly forward with the intention of lifting him on to the cart but he waved them away.

'No! No! I'll ride. That animal's far too big for my son, and once I'm mounted I'll be fine.'

Dorio didn't even bother swivelling around from the front seat of the cart. 'Whatever he says, he's not riding. If he falls off that horse I'll never get him back on again. Put him in the cart.'

'I'm not ...' Vivius began indignantly but one of the Praetorians intervened.

'The Decurion's correct, Senator,' he said apologetically. 'After all the Decurion's been through, and with him only having one arm, he'd not have the energy to get you back on your horse if you fell off.'

Vivius glowered at the Praetorian for countermanding his order, but to Aurelia's amazement, allowed them to lift him gently into the cart without an argument.

It took a while for them to get through the crowded streets, but when they reached the main road leading into the hills the Praetorians pulled up either side of the cart. 'Will you be able to manage from here on, Decurion?' one of them asked. 'We will accompany you further if you want.'

'No, I shall be fine from here,' Dorio answered and Aurelia

had to hide a smile when she saw Vivius narrow his eyes in puzzlement as he tried to work out why Praetorian Guards would be deferring to a mere Decurion when there was a high-ranking senator present.

This next leg of the journey would be slow, she knew that. The cart was heavily laden so the horse was forced to lower his head, straining his muscles as the gradiant became steeper, or the cart wheels stuck in the mud from the constant rain. The animal sweated despite the cold wind, the rhythmic steam from his breath coming loudly and with the occasional snort.

Aurelia noticed the late afternoon sunshine had done nothing to dry out the saturated ground. Rivulets still trickled between the horse's legs but he was careful where he put his hooves. Aurelia pulled the hood of her cloak over her head as the higher they climbed the cooler the icy wind blowing down from the hills.

She smiled at Vivius stretched out under a blanket. He smiled wearily back. She could tell that despite his discomfort he was relieved it was all over. Rufus was kneeling beside him, shivering. Vivius drew him under his blanket before anxiously turning to Maximus. His eldest son's legs were splayed across Warrior's back, his hands and legs pink with cold.

'I can handle him father, don't worry.' Maximus spoke with the same air of confidence as his father. 'I even galloped across the hills in the dark and in the rain when we were escaping the vigilantes. Didn't I Uncle Dorio?'

Catching her husband's alarmed expression Aurelia hastily pointed ahead. 'Look, we're nearly there boys.' Then she reached over to touch Vivius on the shoulder. Her baby daughter disturbed by the movement whimpered under her cloak. 'Are you comfortable my love?'

Vivius gave a grunt. 'I am but I'll be relieved when I get Maximus off my horse,' he said testily. It was an effort to roll on to his side but he did, with a groan. Resting on one elbow he frowned at their driver. 'What on earth possessed you to let Max ride my horse, Dorio? Warrior's far too big for him.'

'Uh-huh!' Was the only response.

Conscious that Dorio had barely spoken a word on the journey home she said, 'I don't know how you managed it, Dorio but … we're grateful, aren't we Vivius? You've done a wonderful job.'

Dorio gave a weary nod. 'That's what the emperor said.'

'What?' She stared at him in astonishment. 'The emperor said you'd done a wonderful job? When did you meet the emperor?'

'This morning.'

She glanced at Vivius but he looked equally as puzzled and shrugged his shoulders. Besides, at this point in the journey the steep gradient fell away and they were able to have their first glimpse of the tips of the olive trees.

'Home,' she whispered to the bundle in her arms. 'You're nearly home. Look Vivius, there's a light burning in the kitchen. Cook must be preparing the evening meal.'

'At least the vigilantes didn't touch the olive grove, father.' Maximus called.

Again, that look of alarm from Vivius. Aurelia flashed her senator a smile. 'Dorio got us away before they arrived,' she explained. She shaded her eyes from the watery sunlight to watch Phaedo who, having seen them coming up the hill, had raced into the house to announce their imminent arrival. A moment later Ruth and Indi arrived at the door. 'See?' she said. 'Our family is safe; our servants are safe and our home and olive grove are safe …'

Vivius's face soured. 'But this isn't the way I planned to introduce our daughter to her home.'

Aurelia laughed softly and was pleased to see how it made her family smile. 'Oh Vivius, don't be silly. She's not a week old yet. It's not going to make any difference to her where she lives. As long as we're here to love her and feed her she'll be happy.' And then she waved in excitement as their servants ran down the road to welcome them home.

\* \* \*

Dorio drove slowly towards the Marcianus villa and their excited servants, wondering if his servants would be as pleased to see him. Probably not, he concluded. He'd treated them appallingly of late. In fact, he'd been treating everyone he knew appallingly. He breathed in fiercely through his nostrils. All that had to change, it had to if he wanted Sarah to ... And he could do it. He could. After all, the Emperor Claudius reckoned he had tenacity, didn't he? He had showered him with praise, told him he'd done a good job in restoring one of Rome's loyal senators to his rightful place. He'd said that he, Dorio, was useful and ... Yes! If the Emperor of the Roman Empire could overcome his physical difficulties, then ...

As for his friends? ... Dorio pulled his mouth down at the corners. The present lot were nothing more than drunkards, thugs and womanizers, he decided. They had stuck with him because he was fun to be with and he'd had money but they'd never talked in depth about anything serious, not like he and Abram, or even he and Sarah had talked. He gave a wry smile when he thought of the old Jew. But then his smile faded.

What was that remark Pilate had made? Something about hoping Claudius would become Caesar as he had no love for the Jews? Would Abram, Judith and Sarah be safe here, in Rome, now that Claudius was emperor? Would the man who had befriended him soon become their enemy?

He brought the horse and cart to a standstill outside Vivius's villa and dismissed his underlying concerns. Whether Claudius would be an enemy to the Jews he would simply have to wait and see. That was for another day he decided handing Phaedo the reins. He embarked from the cart stiffly and stifling a grunt of pain. 'I need to borrow your horse to get home, Vivius.'

He watched his sister's mouth open and shut like a goldfish. 'Home? You're not going home, Dorio! No, I insist you stay with us, at least overnight.'

He gave her a wan smile, finding comfort in her concern. 'I'll be fine.'

'No, you won't. You need someone to look after you. Tell him, Vivius, tell him to stay.'

'Dorio knows he can stay if he wants to,' Vivius muttered struggling to get off the cart.

'Thank you for your gracious offer, Vivius,' Dorio said dryly. 'But all I need from you is your horse.'

'Yes, of course, take him. I doubt I shall be riding for a while.'

Aurelia wrinkled her brow. 'You need to be nursed, Dorio. You need rest. You need company. After all you've done for us …'

'Whoa!' Dorio raised his hand to stem the overflow of concern. Although he loved his sister dearly he knew it wasn't her concern he needed. 'I'm going to get nursed and … all that,' he said, and then to hide his embarrassment looked up at Maximus who, despite being home was reluctant to dismount from his father's horse. 'Okay, my cavalry officer, down you come and may I be the first to congratulate you on being a valuable member of the army assigned to deliver babies and release fathers from jail.'

'I was?'

'Of course you were. I couldn't have managed without you boy. I'm grateful. Now, down you get and follow your brother into the house.'

With a considerable amount of cooing and wooing, Ruth took the baby to allow Aurelia to alight from the cart. Aurelia straightened her dress once her feet were on the ground. Dorio could feel her examining him suspiciously.

'Oh, by the way.' He fumbled in his tunic pocket and brought out two bloodstained coins. 'I raided your bag. I needed to bribe the guard, buy food for Vivius, and buy Lucanus a new blanket and ... Anyway, I'm afraid that's all that's left.'

She examined the coins in the palm of his hand and her mouth twitched at the corners. 'You stole my money?'

'Sort of.' He dropped them into her outstretched hand.

'Uh-Huh! And now you tell me you're going to be nursed? Am I allowed to ask who is to be doing the nursing?'

He concentrated on adjusting the reins of Vivius's horse. 'Abram suggested Sarah and Judith should ... er see to me.'

'See to you?'

'They're coming to stay for a ... while.'

'A while?'

'Or so.' Dorio indicated to Indi that he needed help getting on the horse and a moment later he sat astride Warrior and was looking down on them. 'Don't make a scene, Aurelia.'

'I'm not making a scene, Dorio. I'm not saying a word. In fact, I'm delighted Sarah's staying with you. She's a lovely girl. You realise she's Jewish, don't you?'

'Of course,' he said stiffly. 'And what's wrong with that?'

Aurelia made her way around the cart. 'Nothing, absolutely nothing.' She watched Phaedo and Indi wrap Vivius's arms around their shoulders to help him up the path towards their villa. She followed them. 'But do me a favour will you?' she called back.

He steered the horse towards the Suranus stables. 'What?'

'Take a bath! You're never going to win the lady over smelling like that!'

* * *

He should have made some comment, anything. A word of thanks wouldn't have come amiss. After all, according to the Praetorian Guards who had come to get him out of the Mamertine Prison, it had been Dorio's persistence, his sheer nerve and utter disregard for his own safety that had got him out of jail. They'd laughed when they'd told him that, as though there was more to that story. Clearly they'd been impressed by the Decurion, and Vivius knew from experience how hard it was to impress Praetorians. Puzzled, he stopped halfway up the path. Phaedo, Indi and Aurelia were forced to stop with him. Turning around he shouted at the receding figure.

'I want my horse back by the end of the week.'

He wondered whether Dorio had heard him but then, without turning, he raised his arm as indication he had.

'And you might as well bring yourself and Sarah for a meal.' He coughed. Shouting in his condition wasn't doing him any good. 'You know of course that my only interest is getting my horse back,' he called. 'And I'll also be interested in hearing how you met the Emperor Claudius! You were serious about that, you met the emperor, right?'

This time Dorio did turn and Vivius was relieved to see that familiar cheeky grin.

'Right!' he shouted back. 'I met the emperor.' And with the expertise of a cavalryman he spurred Warrior into a gallop towards the Suranus stables and the Jewish woman waiting for him.

# Author's Note

The Caesars under which Senator Vivius Marcianus served:

*Augustus: Rome's first Emperor from 27 BCE–14 CE*

An intelligent politician who won popular support by giving generously to the poor and his soldiers. He strengthened the army, and ushered in a new age of peace and prosperity which enabled the Marcianus olive grove to become a thriving business. It was during his reign that Vivius was born, but while Vivius's father took an active part in following Augustus in extending Rome's borders, the motherless Vivius was left to be reared by a succession of cruel house-slaves.

*Tiberius: Emperor from 14 CE–37 CE: The adopted son of Augustus*

A brilliant general before he became emperor. It was under his command that Vivius campaigned, extending Rome's borders along the Rhine. Vivius rose quickly through the ranks and soon attained his ambition to become a Praetorian Guard, one of the emperor's elite personal bodyguards. With his increased wealth and intense studies, Vivius became a magistrate and senator. It was during the latter years of Tiberius's reign that the emperor asked him to investigate Pontius Pilate, Governor of Judea. (*The Senator's Assignment* reveals the difficulties of this task.)

*Caligula: Emperor from 37 CE–41 CE: A direct descendant of Augustus.*

## Also in this series

# The Senator's Assignment

### Joan E. Histon

ISBN: 978-1-78535-855-5 / 978-1-78535-856-2 (ebook).

Rome 30 AD
A Senator is plunged into the dark heart of the Roman Empire,
sent to investigate the corrupt practices of Pontius Pilate in
Jerusalem by Caesar Tiberius.

In this tense historical thriller can Senator Vivius Marcianus
outmanoeuvre charges of treason, devastating secrets
resurfaced from his own troubled past, and the political snake
pit of Rome to save himself and the woman he loves?

Deadly are the power games of Rome at the height of
the Empire.

"A pacey, intelligent plot will delight lovers of Roman history."
**Richard Tearle**

**TOP HAT**
**BOOKS**

## Top Hat Books

## Historical fiction that lives

We publish fiction that captures the contrasts, the achievements, the optimism and the radicalism of ordinary and extraordinary times across the world.

We're open to all time periods and we strive to go beyond the narrow, foggy slums of Victorian London. Where are the tales of the people of fifteenth century Australasia? The stories of eighth century India? The voices from Africa, Arabia, cities and forests, deserts and towns? Our books thrill, excite, delight and inspire.

The genres will be broad but clear. Whether we're publishing romance, thrillers, crime, or something else entirely, the unifying themes are timescale and enthusiasm. These books will be a celebration of the chaotic power of the human spirit in difficult times. The reader, when they finish, will snap the book closed with a satisfied smile.
If you have enjoyed this book, why not tell other readers by posting a review on your preferred book site.

Recent bestsellers from Tops Hat Books are:

### Grendel's Mother
The Saga of the Wyrd-Wife
Susan Signe Morrison
Grendel's mother, a queen from Beowulf, threatens the fragile
political stability on this windswept land.
Paperback: 978-1-78535-009-2 ebook: 978-1-78535-010-8

### Queen of Sparta
A Novel of Ancient Greece
T.S. Chaudhry
History has relegated her to the role of bystander, what if Gorgo,
Queen of Sparta, had played a central role in the Greek resistance
to the Persian invasion?
Paperback: 978-1-78279-750-0 ebook: 978-1-78279-749-4

### Mercenary
R.J. Connor
Richard Longsword is a mercenary, but this time it's not for
money, this time it's for revenge...
Paperback: 978-1-78279-236-9 ebook: 978-1-78279-198-0

### Black Tom
Terror on the Hudson
Ron Semple
A tale of sabotage, subterfuge and political shenanigans
in Jersey City in 1916; America is on the cusp of war and the fate of
the nation hinges on the decision of one young policeman.
Paperback: 978-1-78535-110-5 ebook: 978-1-78535-111-2

## Destiny Between Two Worlds
A Novel about Okinawa
Jacques L. Fuqua, Jr.
A fateful October 1944 morning offered no inkling that the lives of
thousands of Okinawans would be profoundly changed — forever.
Paperback: 978-1-78279-892-7 ebook: 978-1-78279-893-4

## Cowards
Trent Portigal
A family's life falls into turmoil when the parents' timid political
dissidence is discovered by their far more enterprising children.
Paperback: 978-1-78535-070-2 ebook: 978-1-78535-071-9

## Godwine Kingmaker
Part One of The Last Great Saxon Earls
Mercedes Rochelle
The life of Earl Godwine is one of the enduring enigmas of English
history. Who was this Godwine, first Earl of Wessex;
unscrupulous schemer or protector of the English? The answer
depends on whom you ask...
Paperback: 978-1-78279-801-9 ebook: 978-1-78279-800-2

## The Last Stork Summer
Mary Brigid Surber
Eva, a young Polish child, battles to survive the designation of
"racially worthless" under Hitler's Germanization Program.
Paperback: 978-1-78279-934-4 ebook: 978-1-78279-935-1 $4.99 £2.99

## Messiah Love
Music and Malice at a Time of Handel
Sheena Vernon
The tale of Harry Walsh's faltering steps on his journey to success
and happiness, performing in the playhouses of Georgian London.
Paperback: 978-1-78279-768-5 ebook: 978-1-78279-761-6

**A Terrible Unrest**
Philip Duke
A young immigrant family must confront the horrors of the
Colorado Coalfield War to live the American Dream.
Paperback: 978-1-78279-437-0 ebook: 978-1-78279-436-3

Readers of ebooks can buy or view any of these bestsellers by
clicking on the live link in the title. Most titles are published
in paperback and as an ebook. Paperbacks are available in
traditional bookshops. Both print and ebook formats are
available online.

Find more titles and sign up to our readers' newsletter at
http://www.johnhuntpublishing.com/fiction

Follow us on Facebook at https://www.facebook.com/JHPfiction
and Twitter at https://twitter.com/JHPFiction